Meagan's
MARINE

Halos & Horns: Book Three

LARGE PRINT EDITION

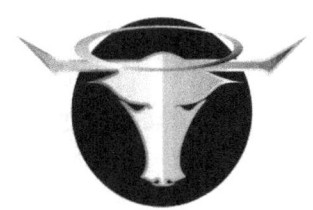

LORI LEGER

CAJUNFLAIR
PUBLISHING

ISBN-13: 978-1-940305-03-5

P.O. Box 641
Kinder, LA. 70648
www.CajunflairPublishing.com
http://www.facebook.com/CajunflairPublishing

Praise for Lori Leger's La Fleur de Love series…

"Lori Leger pens a novel with charming characters that you cannot help but relate to. The secondary characters are fun and feisty."… "If you are looking for an easy and charming read, then pick up SOME DAY SOMEBODY by Lori H. Leger."
(4/5 Stars) Romance Junkies reviewer

(On LAST FIRST KISS) "Lori Leger pens a romance that will break your heart and then leave your heart leaping for joy." "...a sweet romance that will warm your heart..."
(4/5 Stars) Romance Junkies reviewer

(On HART'S DESIRE) "This beautifully written, heart-wrenching short story has well-developed characters that reach out, grab the reader and draw them into their conflict…Exquisitely done.
(5/5 Stars & Crowned Heart) InD'tale Magazine Reviewer: *Carol Conley*

A truly heartwarming story, BROWN EYED GIRL…is a passionate, witty contemporary romance that kept me reading well up into the night…I highly recommend BROWN EYED GIRL and look forward to reading more of the stories in this delightful series. **(5 STARS) Romance Junkies Reviewer:** *Dottie*

"BROWN EYED GIRL is a sweet romantic story, with a scrumptious love triangle between Tiffany, Tanner, and Red! ... Lori Leger is a master at great romance, though, and the one between Tiffany and Red is a perfect example.
(4 ½ Stars/Crowned Heart) InD'tale Magazine reviewer: *Victoria Z. Burg*

(On HEAVEN IN YOUR EYES) "A thrilling read...After reading this story, I immediately purchased the rest of the books, and cannot wait to read them."
(5 Stars) Romance Junkies Reviewer

Praise for Lori Leger's Halos & Horns series…

"GREEN EYED TEMPTATION (Halos and Horns)" by Lori Leger is a modern romance with a lot of punch in it." "The author's style is conversational and easy, with a humorous touch." … "She creates sensual situations as skillfully as she builds tension and intrigue, and is a polished, accomplished author."
Readers' Favorite Reviewer: *Stephanie D.*

Seasons of Love

Praise for Seasons of Love series...

HEARTS, HEARTHS & HOLIDAYS: Is a wonderful compendium of romance reads to ring in the holidays. Romance is the order of the day, and Seasons of Love does not disappoint. **(5 Stars/Crowned Heart) InD'tale Magazine Reviewer:** *Victoria Z. Burg*

SPRING PROMISE: These very talented authors have written four stories that will entertain and delight any reader looking for love! Each one is unique and just long enough...take one away without spending the day!." **(4 Stars) InD'tale:** *Rose Mary Espinoza*

SWEET SUMMERTIME LOVE: "Still Loving Cat" by Lori Leger has two lifelong friends who finally acknowledge their mutual feelings. When Cat loses her memory of their non-platonic love in a car accident Zach won't give up on her." "Still Loving Cat" captivates die-hard romantics and fans of the friends-to-lovers theme. Readers will adore the sigh-worthy Zach, and his steadfast love for Cat." **(3 ½ Stars) InD'tale Reviewer:** *Danielle Hill*

DEDICATION

To MOM, I hope you're gardening to your heart's content, and watching Saints football on the biggest jumbotron in heaven, with surround sound! I surely do miss our game time discussions over the phone, among so many other things.

And to the Book Club ladies: Melissa Landry, Dolores Derouen, Lee Derouen, Joan Granger, Margaret Viator, Debbie Andrews, Renee Bertrand, Trish Leger, and Sherrill Sonnier. Thank you for your honest critiques and for forcing me to read books out of my 'box' every now and then.

Special thanks go out to the techs from Talecris Plasma Resources in Lake Charles, LA, for all your hard work and help in researching the subject matter. Plasma donations save lives, so always remember that you're all doing a good thing.

ACKNOWLEDGMENTS

To my wonderful husband, Michael. You will always
be my hero, and to our children and grandchildren…
from eighteen to a year…you are all adored!

Special thanks to Kim Killion of The Killion Group
for the fabulous cover design, yet again.
www.thekilliongroupinc.com

Joan Granger of Simple Memories Photography
In Welsh, LA for the fabulous photo of the author.
www.simplememories.org/index.htm

Once again, to the two tiny book stores with big
hearts
who carried my books long before anyone else did:

Sean and James Gayle of **Patti's Book Nook** in
My old hometown of Gueydan, La.
www.pattisbooknook.com
and
Christy Lepretre of **Java Joltz** in Jennings, LA

Other books by LORI LEGER

La Fleur de Love Series

Book One: *Some Day Somebody*
Book Two: *Last First Kiss*
Book Two and a Half: *Hart's Desire* (Novella)
Book Three: *Brown Eyed Girl*
Book Four: *Heaven in Your Eyes*

Halos & Horns Series

Book One: *Green Eyed Temptation*
Book Two: *Sarah Smile*
Book Three: *Meagan's Marine*

Seasons of Love Series

Book One: *Hearts, Hearths & Holidays*
Book Two: *Spring Promise*
Book Three: *Sweet Summer Romance*
Book Four: *Candlelight & Christmas*
(title subject to change)
Release Date November 2013

Table of Contents

CHAPTER 1
The Armpit of the Middle East

September 1st

"Well, I'll be damned!"

Master Sergeant Mitchell Hebert fell on his cot with a pensive sigh. The lean, muscular Marine lifted his arms over his head, and stretched to his full 6' length.

Sergeant Matthew "Tex" Broussard swaggered over to Mitch, leaned his massive frame against the makeshift desk made from wooden crates. "You're already in Afghanistan, the arm pit of the middle east. How much more damned could you be?" The east Texas drawl that prompted his nickname in boot camp twenty years earlier, still present and accounted for. "What's up, Cajun Heat?

"Looks like I'll have time for that barbeque at your place after all, Tex. My sister, Sarah, is getting married in two weeks. My soon to be brother-in-law emailed me to see if I could walk her down the aisle in my dress blues two Saturdays from now. He doesn't want her to know he contacted me, but wants me to show up just in time for the ceremony." Mitch grinned at his friend, his Marine brother he considered as close as blood.

Tex beamed at him, revealing his pearly whites. "That's great, man. She still doesn't know you're going home for good?"

"Nope. I want to surprise her. Sarah's wanted this for so long."

"She'll be surprised, all right," Tex snorted. "You're gonna give that poor girl a heart attack on her wedding day. So, what gives with the guy she's hitching? You think he'll be good to her?"

Mitch scratched at his two-day stubble. "I think this one's worthy of her, Tex."

"Well, if he ain't, I'm sure you'll be there to whip him into shape."

Mitch stretched out on the cot. "You got that right. I dropped the ball for years with that first son of a bitch she married. That ain't happening again."

"Man, you couldn't stop what you didn't know about. She kept all that from you."

"I know. She took beatings so I wouldn't be distracted over here." He muttered a low string of curses. "I owe her, man. She had to deal with my mom's cancer, then dad dying, and she did it all on her own. She was just a kid when I joined up, and she's had it rough."

Tex grunted in agreement before tossing a dirty sock at Mitch. "Well, if that dude's really a brain surgeon like you said he is, she won't have it rough anymore. Big brother will be around this time to make sure nobody's mistreating his little sis. I can understand how you feel, though. God help the poor bastard who *ever* lays a hand on my little sister, Haley."

"Damn straight." Mitch shuddered at the stinky sock and threw it back at Tex, who caught it before leaving the room. He settled back on his cot and thought about his sister and her impending nuptials to Dr. Tanner Collins.

For nearly a year, he'd beaten himself up about nearly losing her to an abusive husband. She'd tried hard to escape, had moved into a woman's shelter and began divorce proceedings. The controlling bastard had tracked her down, kidnapped her and her twin babies. After beating the hell out of Sarah, he'd left her and the girls locked up with no food for nearly a week while he went to work on a land rig. Her breast-feeding had sustained the infants, but had nearly killed their mother. Finally, someone had heard the cries and they'd been rescued.

Mitch clenched his fist, regretting his no good brother-in-law had met an untimely demise in the treacherous storm waters of the Gulf of Mexico. What a waste. He'd longed to give the bastard a painful reminder of what a man could and would do to protect his family.

He settled in for an unaccustomed nap, on what would be his last afternoon in Afghanistan. He owed it to his sister and nieces to be *there* for them. After twenty years as a Marine, maybe he owed it to himself as well.

His eyes drifted shut, and his thoughts shifted from his sister, to a pair of cobalt blue eyes framed by long, black lashes. A face materialized suddenly, one with a perky nose, slightly cleft chin, and high cheekbones, with hair as black as coal. He pictured the engaging smile of a certain bar maid in Lake Coburn, Louisiana—her straight, white teeth and pouty red lips—lips made for kissing, though he hadn't had the opportunity on their one and only date his last visit home. Not one that counted, anyway. He'd wanted to, but she held back, pulled herself away from him. It hadn't stopped him from fantasizing about her, holding her tight little body in his arms.

The initial image faded, turning instead to one of her, this time holding a little boy…the spitting image of his mama. His gut wrenched painfully. No way in hell was he ready for the commitment of a woman with a child.

He winced as Tex's drawl floated to him from outside the tent. Why, he asked himself, for the thousandth time, did Meagan have to speak with the same twang as a guy he saw and heard nearly every day since he'd been back here? Each time he heard it, he couldn't help but think of her.

Mitch folded his pillow over his head, issuing a silent plea that Tex would just once, shut the hell up. It didn't work, of course, as the twang filtered through the barely there pillow.

Meagan.

Not good. Not good at all.

CHAPTER 2
Weddings, Receptions, and Misconceptions

Meagan Hutton released her breath in a rush as she entered the room where the bride waited impatiently. "Oh, honey! Tanner is going to flip when he sees you."

Sarah faced the full-length mirror and ran both hands down her sides. "I can't believe it's me in this gorgeous dress." She looked up, catching the reflected gazes of her friends. "It still feels like a dream. No way could I ever be this happy." She smoothed down the delicate layers of champagne colored silk and lace clinging to her slim body. "I just wish my brother could have been here to give me away."

Meagan stepped forward, taking her by the shoulders. "Today's not the day for regrets, Sarah. None, whatsoever. You know he'd be here if he could, and he sure as heck wouldn't want you to be sad about it."

Sarah dabbed at the corner of her eye with a tissue. "I know, and you're right, Meg. No regrets, not today." She spun around, letting the dress flare out around her. "I'm so ready to marry Tanner. Is it almost time?"

A swift rapping on the door had them all pivoting in that direction.

"Is it safe to come in?" Daniel LeBlanc's voice sounded muffled through the thickness of the wooden door.

Tiffany McAllister headed to the door and opened it a crack for her own father. "As long as you don't have Tanner with you. I don't want him seeing his bride until she's walking down that aisle."

Daniel chuckled, tugging on his elegant black tux. "No, but someone almost as important to her. It seems I'm being robbed of my bride escorting duties for the day."

Tiffany released a shocked gasp a second before she pulled the door open for the U.S. Marine to enter the room.

Sarah flew to Mitchell and threw her arms around him. "What are you *doing* here, big brother?"

Mitch wrapped his sister in a bear hug. "You didn't think I'd miss your wedding, did you?"

Sarah laughed, straightening her dress as he finally released her. "I didn't think they'd give you leave again this soon. How did you manage this?"

He shrugged a sharply jacketed shoulder. "Turns out your timing was impeccable. I'm out, Sis. For good, this time."

Sarah waved her hands in front of her eyes, trying not to cry. "Seriously? I don't want to ruin my make up, but this would be so worth it."

Even through Sarah's tears and squeals of excitement, all Meagan could do was stare at the vision before her. Mitch Hebert in plain old jeans and a tee shirt had been a pleasure to behold nearly a year earlier during their first meeting. The sight of Master Sergeant Mitchell Hebert in full dress blues, complete with his cover and white gloves, was enough to turn her insides to liquid heat.

Out for good. Permanently. No more praying for his safe-keeping while he was in Afghanistan, without his knowledge, of course. *Maybe now she could manage to relax a little?*

A second later, his gaze found hers, pinning her to the spot.

Meagan's breath hitched in her throat at the perceptible widening of his eyes. *Maybe not.*

Red cleared his throat and spoke, breaking her out of her trance.

"Time to get this thing rolling, people. Father Carlos has another wedding in two hours."

Meg managed to slip out of the room without a word to anyone, and made her way to the pew reserved for wedding participants. Although Sarah only had one bridesmaid, Melanie Finley, she'd thoughtfully included her other friends for readings, gift-bearers during the communion for mass, or as witnesses. She'd chosen Meg as a reader for her favorite reading from Corinthians.

Meagan stood with everyone else in the church as Melanie and Red McAllister appeared, each carrying one of Sarah's twin daughters. Audible gasps of admiration rippled through the guests at the sight of the toddlers. Sarah's adorable girls, dressed in matching pink gowns, pristine white shoes, with their glossy curls framed in delicate flower braids, worked the crowd like the little hams they were. The gasps turned to laughter, as Sammi and Danni shrieked with delight upon catching sight of Leah and Daniel LeBlanc, seated in the first pew. For all intents and purposes, the couple filled in as welcome replacements for Sarah's deceased parents, and the twins adored them. Since generously opening their home to Sarah and her girls a year earlier, the Leblancs were the only grandparent figures they'd ever known, up until

Sarah and Tanner had begun dating. Now his parents claimed them as grandchildren as well.

The bridal march began and all eyes turned to where Sarah and her brother began their leisurely walk up the aisle.

Meagan tried…honestly she did, to direct all her attention on Sarah, the beautiful and glowing bride. She must have given up at some point, because her gaze zeroed in on Mitchell. Sarah's escort carried himself straight and tall beside his sister. Already agonizingly handsome, his impeccably clean shave and neat uniform gave him an air of masculine elegance that called forth heroes from decades gone by.

She hadn't even realized her mouth had fallen open until his soft brown eyes found hers, rooting her to the spot. She blinked, and closed her mouth in order to swallow a groan of appreciation at the sight of him, all six feet of him, buff and sexy as hell.

Meagan watched his approach—close—closer still. Close enough to notice a scar at his left temple, just missing his eye. Had that been there before? She didn't think so. What horrors had he seen since he'd been away? What horrors had he survived in his twenty years in the Marines?

Survived. A cold sweat overcame her at the thought. She'd spent weeks tracking down Christopher's brothers in arms, hoping to find someone who could fill her in on the last days of her fiance's life. No one else had understood her need to know, but at the time, it had been important to her. In the end, she'd heard more than she should have heard, seen more than she should have seen. Everyone else injured in the same incident had survived, in one form or another. Some without limbs, but with enough strength of character to bear their losses well. Others, either with more severe injuries, or with more psychological than physical damage, hadn't coped so well. One man had called *her* dead Marine, the lucky one.

During the months that followed Christopher's death, pregnant with his child, heartbroken and alone, she'd even found herself agreeing with him occasionally. Until the night she'd given birth to her son.

She pictured her handsome little boy, with his mother's dark hair and blue eyes. That's where her genetic similarity ended, though. Once she'd set eyes on him, she knew Chris hadn't left her completely. He was there, in the shape of his son's head, to his ears, chin, and shape of his nose. He was Christopher made over, only with her hair and eye color, and he'd been her reason for battling her way out of the darkness.

All too soon, it was time for Meagan's reading. She approached the wooden lectern on shaky legs, suddenly terrified at having to read in front of the church full of people. She took a deep breath and tried to relax her shoulders. What was *she*, an unwed mother, doing up here in a church about to read from the holy bible? Where was that archangel—the one on the lightning bolt committee? Any second now, he'd throw a bolt in her direction, just for being present in God's house.

Heat infused her face through and through, accompanied by a feeling of complete unworthiness. She managed to look up, intent on finding an escape route, but instead found Mitchell. He sent her a nod of encouragement from his seat directly in front of where she stood shaking in her three inch heels. For some reason, it helped to know he was there. She took a deep breath and found her passage.

"Love is patient. Love is kind. It does not envy, it does not boast, it is not proud..." She continued, making a conscious effort to read slowly, steadily, with full range, finally reaching the end. *"And now these three remain: Faith, Hope, and Love; and the greatest of these is love."*

～

She stood with everyone else, applauding the newly married couple, and grinning from ear to ear as Sarah and Tanner clasped hands and headed down the aisle, practically at a run. Red, the best man, took Melanie's arm to lead her out, leaving Mitchell standing alone. Meagan met him at the center aisle and he smiled down at her, placing his hand at her lower back to lead her out of the church.

"Well done, Meagan."

"You think so? Lord, I have never been so terrified in my life. I seriously thought I was going to lose it up there until I saw you."

Laughter rumbled in his chest. "I was channeling courage in your direction. Did you feel it?"

She chuckled. "I believe I did, Mitch, thanks for that."

"Glad I could help. Where do we go from here?"

She craned her neck, barely able to see Sarah and Tanner standing off to the side, surrounded by well-wishers. "I'm sure you'll need to stick around here for pictures, but the reception is at Red and Tiffany's ranch, at the pond out back by the pavilion."

He gave her a curious lift of one brow. "Will you be there?"

"For a while. I have to go pick up my son first. My roommate watched him during the ceremony, but she has other plans tonight."

"Oh…yeah. Your little boy."

She shouldered her purse strap, trying not to feel hurt at the immediate change in his demeanor—the tightness in his face, tension in his shoulders she couldn't ignore. "That's right—my son, Buck. I'm glad you could make it in for this, Master Sergeant. I know it meant the world to Sarah." She headed off in the opposite direction without another word.

∾

Jesus, she can't get away fast enough. He knew he'd upset her, though he sure as hell hadn't meant to. He'd barely laid eyes on her, and just for a few moments, he'd forgotten about the kid. The son…*her* son…Buck. Totally disgusted, he asked himself how the hell he could have forgotten the existence of a child.

"Jackass—" he mumbled to himself with a sharp shake of his head. Unfortunately, that was just the first of many reasons he wouldn't be good for her.

After enduring twenty minutes of a photographer barking orders like a sharp-tongued drill instructor, the group headed over to the reception venue.

Against all good reason, Mitch began searching for Meagan as soon as he arrived on site. Not so much to hang out with her, as for observation purposes. The soft drawl reached him even before he spotted the bluest eyes in this part of the state. Settling at the portable bar across the dance area from her, he accepted a beer from the guy tending the drinks.

Meagan's son, Buck, had grown a good several inches since he'd seen him last. His face had thinned out, giving him more the look of a little boy, rather than a toddler. Despite his mom's best efforts to rein him in, the boy wanted to cut loose. Meagan knelt in front of him, pointing to the pond in the distance before poking him gently in the belly, most assuredly warning him about going near the water. The child took off toward a group of other children, most were older, but a few a little younger than himself, including Mitchell's own nieces, Sarah's twins.

He sat through his sister and new brother-in-law's first dance as a married couple, and then danced with the bride. After handing her back to her new husband, he found himself touring the floor with the maid of honor.

Melanie Finley's eyes creased with secretive laughter. "Hello Marine. How've you been?"

"Since you left me alone in a Lake Coburn hotel last year, letting me wake up to a post-it note on the pillow, you mean?"

She gave her head a quick shake. "It wasn't a post-it note, it was a deposit slip from my checkbook, and it had my info on it…which you did *not* use to contact me, I might add."

"Oh. I didn't realize that."

Her face blanched. "What did you do with it?"

"What? The note?" He shrugged. "I think I just left it where it was."

She paused their dancing to stare up at him. "Seriously? Well, that's just great. Whoever found it knows I had a one-night stand with a Marine, not to mention my name and all my contact info."

He laughed softly at the look of horror on her face. "I wouldn't worry too much about it. I saw the housekeeper. She was seventy if she was a day and barely spoke English. I doubt seriously she could read it." He nudged her into continuing their dance. "Besides, that was nearly a year ago. If she wanted to steal your identity, I'm fairly certain it would have happened by now." He stopped suddenly and stared down at her. "You don't have any other surprises for me do you?"

"Like what?"

"Like 'Guess what? The condom broke and you're the father of a bouncing baby... whatever...'"

She looked serious for a moment. "Come to think of it, I did receive a blessed little addition to my household as of one month ago."

Mitch felt the blood drain from his face as he stood there contemplating the weight of her words. "You're serious, aren't you?"

She nodded. "Absolutely."

"Is it...he or she...mine?" He felt as though he'd be sick at any moment.

"He, and I named him Shots, you know, like 'shots' of tequila."

He pictured her as she was that night at the bar, downing shots of Patron with salt and lime. "You named my kid after booze?" he seethed, suddenly furious at the indignation of it all.

"Hold on, now, Marine. I haven't said he's yours. Although, now that I think of it, I guess he could be. I mean....we did do it doggy style..."

"What? What the hell does that have to do with..." He stopped as she burst into laughter.

"Oh God, your face! I got a new puppy, Mitch!"

"Ohhh...oh shit, Mel. I think I'm gonna puke." He rubbed at his belly, shaking his head at the woman doubled over in laughter. "Man, that ain't cool, Detective. Not cool at all."

"Maybe not," she finally managed to spit out between ladylike snorts. "But it was funny as hell."

He took her in his arms again, determined to finish the dance with some nuance of dignity. "Says you…shithead." He managed to smile as her joviality finally faded to soft chuckles. "You realize, of course, this means I owe you one."

Melanie made a fist and punched him playfully in the chest. "Well, you go on and give it your best shot, Marine. You've already taken out the element of surprise. I'll be waiting for it, now."

"You'll never see it coming, Detective. *That*, I can promise you."

∼◦∽

Meagan laughed as Tanner regaled them with how his mom used guilt to persuade him and Sarah into having a larger wedding than planned.

"I told Sarah she'd do it, gave her plenty of opportunity to get her anti-mother-in-law mojo brewing, so she could resist her. Did it do any good? Noooo! We could have been married a month ago, if she had."

Sarah slipped an arm around Tanner's waist. "Oh, it wasn't that bad. You barely had to lift a finger. Besides, she started out insisting on a society wedding in Houston that would have taken a year to plan. I held her to one month and convinced her how beautiful it would be here at Red and Tiffany's ranch. I'd already seen the pictures of Giselle and Jackson's wedding here, with the pond all lit up at night. It was gorgeous! I wanted a church wedding but I knew I had to have the reception here."

Tanner gave his new bride a resounding kiss on the mouth. "Ours is beautiful too. I've got to hand it to you, babe, my mom isn't easy to sway once she sinks her chops into an idea. Society weddings are important in her inner circle."

"Not nearly as important as keeping my new daughter-in-law happy." Heads turned as Celine Collins joined their circle, carrying one of the twins. "As much joy as she's brought into our lives with these two angels, it's the least I can do."

Tiffany stepped forward with Sarah's other twin. "Besides, after this, all of Ms. Celine's Houston friends will probably decide that outside fall receptions are the thing to do. It really is lovely."

"Oh thank you, Tiffany. I had such fun planning this. Maybe I ought to do it for a living. It'll keep me from sitting around and growing old in between visits with my new granddaughters." She leaned in, speaking in a loud whisper. "Along with any future grandchildren they decide to bless us with one day."

Meagan listened half-heartedly, while keeping one eye peeled on her child. All this talk of grandchildren and their doting grandparents made her a little sad for her own son. Sarah's parents had died, but no doubt, they would have loved to be around their granddaughters. Poor Buck had four living grandparents, none of whom wanted a thing to do with him.

Sometimes life just sucked.

Who would he have to teach him the things her own grandparents had taught her? Things like when to plant your vegetable garden so the plants don't get frost-bitten, how to cook popcorn the old fashioned way...in a kettle, not a microwave, and how to season a black iron pot?

Misty eyed with old memories and a sudden feeling of homesickness, she saw Buck pull to a sudden stop in the middle of chasing a balloon. She smiled, recognizing that look on his face—Christopher's look—the look he got when he saw something he couldn't resist. He started a slow walk toward whatever had garnered his attention. Meagan's vision tracked ahead to see what it was and froze at the sight of the lure.

Warning bells went off in her brain, but she couldn't seem to move. What the hell? Had she traded her heels for lead boots since the ceremony?

"Oh God, no," she whispered, finally taking a step, then several more, but not before her son made it to his destination.

~

Mitch felt a slight tug on his jacket and looked down. Meagan's little boy stood there, his face cloaked in childlike innocence and wearing a look of awe. "Hey there, buddy. How ya doing?" No training, military or otherwise, could have prepared him for the single question uttered by the boy.

"Are you my daddy?"

Mitch contemplated the strange question, as he studied the face so much like his mother's, but then again, not. He obviously bore a heavy resemblance to his father. His father…Meagan's Marine. He'd just made the connection by the time Meagan reached the two of them.

"Buck! Hey! There you are. I've been looking for you. I bet you've been having some fun playing with all these kids, huh?"

Her breathless, overly enthusiastic act fooled neither Mitch, nor her son, obviously. After casting a glance toward his mother, he looked up at Mitch and repeated the question.

"Are you my daddy?"

"No! Buck...No! He's *not* your daddy. He's just a friend of mine." Meagan knelt beside her son, obviously struggling to stay calm in a situation she'd never found herself in before. "His name is Mitchell, and he is a Marine, like your daddy was."

"Is." The word left Mitchell's mouth before he could stop it.

Two sets of identical, blue-eyed gazes landed on him.

"What?" Meagan asked—her eyes wide with worry as Mitchell knelt before her child.

Mitch looked from the mother to the son while keeping his tone steady and calm. "No, I'm not your dad, but I want you to know something. Even though your dad isn't where you can see him every day, he still *is* a Marine, Buck. One you and your mom can be very proud of." He took his cover off and played with the brim. "I bet you have a picture of him at your house, and he's dressed like I am, huh?"

Buck gave him a shy smile and a vigorous nod. "It's in my woom."

Mitch chuckled. "In your room, huh? I figured as much."

Buck gave him one more nod. "He looks like you," he said, reaching out a chubby finger to touch a shiny brass button. "You look like him."

Mitch swallowed hard, suddenly aware of the presence, the man that the ugly side of war had taken from this child's life, permanently. He offered his hand slowly. "I'm Mitchell, Buck—Master Sergeant Mitchell Hebert. It's real nice to meet you. And it's an honor to meet the son of a fellow Marine."

Buck looked up at his mother to get her approval before offering his own pudgy hand to return the handshake. "I'm Buck. I gotta go." In an instant, he was gone, off chasing another balloon, leaving the two adults staring after him.

Mitch rose slowly to his feet, even as Meagan began muttering apologies.

"I'm so sorry, Mitch. I didn't mean for that to happen."

"No apology necessary, Meg. It wasn't difficult to figure it out. The dress blues are designed to make an impression, but to a little kid, we must all look alike. How old is he, anyway?"

"He'll be four in two months."

Mitch nodded. "So, his dad never—"

"Chris died before he was born," she rushed, before he could finish.

He stared off after the boy. "That's too bad."

"Yep." She crossed her arms as though to ward off a sudden chill.

"Are you cold?" He started to take off his jacket to offer it to her.

She raised her hand to stop him. "No, I just get this feeling every now and then when I talk about him. My granny used to call it 'knocking on a coffin'. It's almost as though I can feel his presence." She ran her hands up both arms. "You'd think I'd feel comforted, but, for some reason, it freaks me out a little. I never was good with ghost stories and things like that."

"Yet you like to watch scary movies, like the one we watched at the theater last year."

"I don't have a problem with Hollywood spirits, Mitch. It's the real ones that give me the heebie-jeebies."

"You believe in that stuff?"

"Oh sure. My granny had too many stories and real life experiences of her own for me to be a non-believer."

"You don't think they were just that…stories?" He knew he sounded skeptical and there was good reason. There was no such things as ghosts and spirits.

She lifted her chin. "You know, I'm not trying to persuade you to believe. It makes no difference to me one way or the other what you think."

A second later she'd left him standing there, with the realization that he had, once again, shitified the entire situation.

"One of these days you'll learn to shut the hell up when you need to, you dumb son of a bitch," he grumbled while heading to the opposite end of the reception area. He finished off his beer, deciding it was probably for the best she'd high-tailed it when she did.

CHAPTER 3
The Sad Man (Part One)

Meagan arched her back, stretching her tight muscles, then attempted to work the kinks out of her neck with one hand. She swiveled in her chair at the light shuffling sound in the hallway, already suspecting what she'd find. "Hey buddy, you okay?"

Buck stood in the doorway, one arm wrapped around a purple and gold stuffed LSU "Mike" the tiger, while rubbing his eye with his right fist. "I can't sleep, mommy. The sad man keeps staring at me."

He shuffled to her outstretched arms and she lifted him onto her lap. "Aw, sweetie, we've talked about this before. The man in the picture isn't sad, he's just being serious for the camera, and he's your dad. You're not afraid of him, are you?"

Buck tried to suppress a huge yawn and failed. "It's not daddy. It's another sad man."

"Another sad man–what do you mean, Buck? You see someone in your room, someone that's not in daddy's picture?"

Buck nodded adamantly. "He's in my woom wight now."

Meagan hugged her boy closely, amazed at such a vivid imagination in a child under the age of four. Any day now, he'd be coming up with imaginary friends, just as she did when she was little. "You just dreamed about him, sweet boy, that's all. Daddy's just watching over you while you sleep."

"But I'm not asleep anymore."

She pushed his wayward curls back from his forehead. "No, you certainly are not."

"He's still in my woom, and it's too cold."

"Okay, let's go say good night to him together, then." She saved out her report on the differences between alkanes, alkenes, and alkynes on her roommate's PC before shutting it down. If her laptop hadn't crapped out on her, she'd have been working on it in the comfort of her own bed. She struggled to her feet while hefting her son onto one hip, his feet dangling nearly to her knees. "Pretty soon, you're gonna be too big for me to carry you around, Buckaroo. You're almost as tall as me now."

Meagan entered the room, somewhat shocked at the chill in the air as she turned on her son's Thomas the Tank table lamp. "Mommy is so sorry, baby. I must have left the window open in here." She placed Buck in his bed and tucked the covers tightly around him, then turned to shut the tiny room's only window. Halfway between her son's bed and the window, a wall of frigid air hit her, vaporizing her warm breath into hazy puffs. Jolted to a halt, she stood there, staring at the closed window. Icy breath on her neck had the hair standing up at the base of her scalp, goose bumps raised on her arms. She whipped around, but no one else was in the room besides her and Buck.

She pivoted her head slowly to stare at her son. Buck was still tucked tightly in his bed, but watching her, his eyes large and round.

"Buck?" He didn't answer but continued to stare at her. No. Not at her, but at the empty spot beside her. "Buck?" she repeated.

Without a word, he freed his left arm from the covers, lifted it slowly to point at the spot.

"There he is." His whispered reply was barely audible over the thudding in Meagan's chest.

Pretending to be calm for his sake, she steadied her voice. "Who, baby?"

"The sad man, Mommy. He's wight there. Wight next to you."

Meagan turned slowly to her right and stared at the vacant spot. She lifted her hand, encountered nothing—or she supposed it was nothing. Though why it had every fine hair on her arm standing at attention, she'd probably never know. "Oh my God!" She screeched, as she jerked her hand back and clenched it tightly to her chest.

Footsteps in the hallway preceded her roommate, Niki's frantic call from the door opening. "What is it? What's wrong?"

Meagan couldn't keep the terrified trembling from her voice any more than she could stop the onslaught of goose bumps from covering her entire body. "You don't see anyone besides Buck and me, do you?"

Niki stepped into the room and shivered. "No, but why is it so damn—*darn*—cold in here?" She made a face and mouthed the word 'Sorry' to Meagan.

Meagan felt the change immediately. Whatever it was that Buck had seen, and she had felt, dissipated the instant Niki crossed the threshold into the room. In seconds, the temperature returned to normal. She searched her son's face for clues. "Buck?"

"He's gone, Mommy."

Niki's wide eyed gaze travelled from Meagan, to Buck, then back to Meagan. "Who's gone? Someone was in here?"

Buck yawned and rolled over onto his right side, facing the wall. Within seconds, his eyes had closed. Meagan took a shaky breath and walked softly over to adjust his blanket. She touched his forehead, more for her own need, and fought the urge to scoop him up so he could sleep with her for the night. That too, would be more for her than her son. The fact that Buck fell asleep so quickly was a sign that he didn't feel the least bit threatened.

She turned off his lamp and straightened to follow Niki out of the room. Her friend turned on her when they got to their tiny living room.

"What the hell happened in there, Meg? Did I miss something?"

"I can't be sure, but I think Buck sees his daddy." Niki's eyes grew huge as Meg related the story to her friend.

"Seriously? The sad man. That would make all the sense in the world, don't you think? He'd have to be sad at having to leave the two of you behind."

Niki spoke in a low, reverent whisper. "So what was it that made you scream?"

Meg's heart pounded in her chest, her adrenaline rushing at the thought of it. "You may not believe this, but it felt like someone's fingertips brushed the back of my hand, Nik. The air was so thick, dense, and cold…icy cold. And there was this faint odor or something…I don't know…old, maybe? Decaying?" She paced the room, nervous and agitated. "I don't have enough to worry about right now? My son sees the ghost of his dead father? Really?"

"Maybe Buck seeing his dad isn't something you should have to worry about, Meg. Maybe he's just watching over the son he never got to meet. Buck has his own, personal, military sentinel. Try to think of it that way."

"You really think it's Chris?" Meagan needed to hear the words from Nik's own mouth, for some reason.

A gentle hand on her shoulder accompanied her answer. "I do, Meg. I doubt seriously there's anything to worry about, but I know someone who may be able to verify it for you. Would that make you feel better?"

Meagan nodded, knowing she'd never be able to relax unless she got some answers. "I hope so. Who is this person?"

Niki winked at her and grinned. "You just leave that to me."

CHAPTER 4
Bartending Tricks and Feeling Like a Dick

"Hey, beautiful! I've got a twenty for you if you can show me some fancy bartender tricks."

Meagan grinned at the cowboy who'd been trying to get her number all night long. "Is that all it'll take to make you happy?"

"For now." Mr. tall, dark, and ripped placed his Stetson onto the bar and sat back with his arms crossed over six pack abs his tight tee-shirt did little to hide.

More than happy to do something to cut the monotony, Meagan pulled a quarter-full bottle of Bacardi from behind the counter and flipped it a couple of times in one hand. The simple trick drew a quick response as the attentive cowboy whistled in appreciation.

"You like that?" He gave her a nod then guffawed as she flipped the bottle, end over end, over her head from one hand to the other, then back again. After a couple times at a single rotation, she eased into a double rotation of the bottle. Even though she found it as easy as walking and chewing gum at the same time, she knew how impressive it looked to customers. She caught the bottle by its neck and threw it straight up, bumped it with her elbow then caught it again.

Cowboy, along with a few others, broke into applause, cheered louder when she pulled a second bottle from under the counter. She juggled the two bottles, eliciting raucous hoots and whistles from the growing crowd of spectators. She caught the eye of her co-worker and tossed him one bottle. He caught it mid-air, and they spent the next minute exchanging spinning bottles of alcohol to thunderous applause. She caught both bottles, raised them in victory and bowed for the crowd.

"Well, hell, girl! I'm impressed—and you earned this." He threw a twenty on the bar.

"Thanks. We appreciate it." Meagan stuffed the twenty in the communal tip jar on her end of the bar and grabbed a towel to wipe up someone's spilled drink. That's when she caught sight of him, sitting alone at a corner table, his back to the wall, of course.

"Two more of these, please Meagan."

She nodded at the request from one of her regulars as she pulled two icy beers from the cooler and popped them open. She added the drinks to his tab then turned to the second bartender. "Hey Chuck, watch this end so I can go check on that guy, will ya?"

"You know it, Megs. I wish I could work with you every night. I always make double in tips when you're around. They love watching you flip those bottles."

"Glad to do it! Makes the night go by faster." She eased her way to the corner table, relaxed and ready to face Mitchell again.

"Hey there. You must have slipped in while I was on break." She pointed at his beer. "You ready for another one of those?"

He lifted his brew, giving it a slight shake. "Naw, I ain't even halfway, yet. Better hold off on that. Besides, I've got something to do tomorrow and I need to be sharp."

"Oh yeah? Well, okay then. Good luck with that." He grabbed at her hand as she turned to leave.

"I wanted to apologize to you, Meagan. I always seem to be pissing you off for one reason or another, and I honestly don't mean to."

She frowned, and gave him a curious tilt of her head. "You don't piss me off. What gave you that idea?"

"The fact that you haul ass and leave me standing alone like I've got an infectious disease is a pretty strong indication."

She gave him a careless shrug. "That doesn't mean I'm pissed off, it just means I'm out of patience. I don't have a lot of free time, you know. No use wasting it on a lost cause. Give me a holler if you need anything."

"But—"

Meagan spun on her heels without another word, cutting him off sharply. She'd thought the conversation had ended, so it shocked her to turn at the bar and find him hot on her trail. "That was quick—"

"What the hell is it with you, lady? Do you enjoy making me feel like a dick?"

~⁓

Her mouth fell open as she blinked several times.

"I'd like an answer, please, ma'am."

"And I'll give you one as soon as I figure out how it is I make you feel like a dick."

He released a frustrated breath. "I told you, Meagan. Every fu—*flippin'*—time I try to talk to you, you leave me standing there feeling like a—"

"A dick. I know. You said that already. What I don't know is why you should feel that way when I just *told* you the reason. I'm a busy person. I have things to do. A child, a job, a child, classes, a child, homework, a *child*, Mitch...a fatherless *child*. I don't have the time or finances to visit bars and try to create small talk. I'm sorry if you can't see the relevance, but exactly what is it you've done since you left the Corps that enables you to criticize me for not having enough hours in my day?"

Meagan threw the dishtowel on the counter, visibly flustered for the first time in his presence, her face lined with stress, her eyes shadowed by dark circles. Something was off, here. Before he could apologize, she stopped and lifted her gaze to his.

"I'm sorry. I had no reason to speak to you that way, and I'm sorry if I make you feel bad. I have...there's a situation...I'm just a little bugged right now, is all."

He reached out, placed a hand over hers. "What's wrong? What are you keeping from me?" Mitch could see how badly she wanted to share whatever it was with him, or with someone, anyway. Eventually, the part of her that refused to let her shields down won out. She pulled her hand out from under his and picked up the dishcloth again.

"It's nothing, Mitch. School is stressing me out, that's all."

"Meagan."

She gave him a brilliant smile, without the slightest trace of anger or attitude. "You ready for that beer, now?"

"Yeah, I'll have another one, please." He settled upon the barstool in front of her, deciding to let it drop, for now.

When she grabbed her purse to leave the bar at midnight, he met her at the end of the counter. "You're not closing up tonight?"

She found her car keys and looped her purse onto her neck and shoulder. "No. Red doesn't ask me to close during school."

"Can we talk, please?" He shrugged at her curious stare. "I'd like to clear the air. Can I meet you at your place?"

Taking a few seconds to mull it over, she gave him a quick nod and headed out the back exit.

CHAPTER 5
Marine 1 and Marine 2

After following her home, he parked on the street and met her just as she'd unlocked the front door.

"Have a seat," she said, pointing to the couch. "I'll be right back."

She disappeared into a room down the hallway for several minutes. He heard soft murmurs, one voice definitely childlike. Meagan came out of the room, rubbing her hands up and down her arms as she approached him. Her face at least a shade paler than when she'd gone in.

He stood quickly, reaching for her. "What is it? Is Buck sick or something?" The icy cold of her skin startled him. "What the hell?" The look on her face had his hackles up, even in the warmth of the small living room. "Why are you so cold?"

When a quick glance back at the hallway elicited a violent shudder from her, he decided to check things out for himself.

"Mitch, no!"

She grabbed at his arm, but he was determined. He strode down the corridor and stopped in the doorway of the room—Buck's room, obviously. Everything *looked* normal, from toys lined up or stacked neatly on a shelf, to a small train and track set-up on a child-size table. The second he stepped into the room, things changed.

The hair on his arms stood straight up as he encountered a wall of frigid air. Ice cold air, with no hint of a breeze anywhere to account for the abrupt drop in temperature. He took a deep breath and released it in a visible puff of vaporized air. He froze in place, instantly overcome by the all too familiar smell of overheated shell casings and gunpowder.

Mitch glanced over at the child snuggled under the covers and suppressed the need to curse long and loud. Instead, he took two large steps back into the hallway and turned to find Meagan's wide-eyed gaze on him.

"Jesus Christ on a popsicle stick," he hissed. "What the hell was that?"

She shook her head, tried to turn away. "I don't know what you're talking about."

He reached for her. "Hey."

She shook off his grip and walked back to the living room, with him following closely behind her.

"I think you need to go. I just remembered I've got some studying to do."

"Why don't you tell me what's going on?"

"I would, but the truth is, I don't know how to answer that." She walked to the front door and held it open for him. "Good night."

He met her at the door. "Barring what happened in your boy's room just now, *whatever* the hell that was or wasn't, we still haven't cleared the air between us."

Her eyelids closed as she muttered a mild oath under her breath.

"But, I can see you're too tired for any of that, so I'll leave you alone *if* you agree to reschedule our talk." Simply telling himself she looked tired would have been the mother of all understatements. The girl looked as though she hadn't slept in weeks.

"I've got an exam to study for and I'm taking Buck to Lake Front Park tomorrow afternoon. Sunday is my only day off all week." She lifted one brow at his grunt of disappointment. "I told you

I was busy. Now do you understand why I can't waste time? I don't have any."

"I understand," he conceded. "What time should I be there?"

"Where?"

"The park. You mind if I hang with y'all a bit?"

She shrugged. "It's a public park. You have as much right to be there as anyone, but I value my playtime with my son."

Mitch turned, released his breath in a huff and headed down the steps mumbling. "Well, I've had about all the rejection I can take for one night."

"Around two!" she called after him.

He stopped and faced her again, ready to fire off a 'don't do me any favors' comment, but her angst-ridden face stopped him. More than anything, he was thankful she'd relented. "I'll be there."

He drove to his recent rental, a sparsely furnished two-bedroom house, still thinking about the encounter with whatever the hell that was.

Later, he lay in bed, trying to recall everything he'd experienced in Buck's room. The frigid temps that turned his breath as frosty as an Arctic front, the heaviness in the air, and above all...the smells. The distinct odor of sand, dust, grit and grime. He hadn't dared close his eyes in that room, sure if he had, he'd have been transported back to the sandbox—back into the thick of Afghanistan. Whatever went on in that place had a negative effect on Meagan, and maybe her son, too.

He tried to sleep, but every time he closed his eyes, he imagined the icy cold sweeping through him.

He swung his legs out of bed and pulled on a clean pair of jeans to pace his apartment. Recognizing defeat when it bitch-slapped him, he grabbed his wallet and keys and climbed back into his truck. Ten minutes later found him parked in the driveway of the empty house next to Meagan's place, the one with the real estate agency's FOR SALE sign planted in the front yard.

There couldn't have been more than thirty feet between the two homes, and less than that from where he'd parked his truck to what he figured was the window of Buck's bedroom. He turned, stretching his legs out on the bench seat of the Chevy work truck he'd purchased from a friend. With the passenger window down, and his back propped up against the driver's side door, Mitch knew he'd hear if anything went wrong during the night. This was actually a hell of a lot more comfortable than the hide sites he'd dug into in his earlier years with the Corp, before promotions had him in on the planning, rather than executing, missions.

That single night of surveillance shed some serious light on Meagan's situation. The lamp in Buck's room flipped on for a short period at least three times during the night. Through the curtains, he could see the shadowed figure of someone in the room seconds before the light went out again. Meagan, no doubt, up and checking on her son. No wonder she was exhausted. Whatever was going on had totally disrupted her life.

He managed to sneak off a little before 5:00 a.m., hopefully before she saw his truck parked next door. He crawled back into his bed for a couple hours of sleep, wondering how best to get the truth out of her at the park later in the day.

CHAPTER 6
Kites and Confessions

Mitch found Meagan's car at the park's entrance, near the playground. He pulled into the empty spot next to hers, grabbed a bag from his truck seat and swung it over his shoulder.

It didn't take long to find the two of them, spinning on the merry go round. Meagan pushed with one leg while she held on to Buck, tucked protectively in her arms. Judging by the huge grin on Buck's face, the kid was having a blast.

"Hey buddy!" Buck said, between giggles.

Mitch chuckled as he set the bag down on the nearest table and approached them. "Hey yourself, buddy boy! Do you want to go faster? Hang on tight, mom."

Meagan lifted her foot and grabbed onto the bar for security as Mitch put some muscle into his spins.

Even the near-blurred glimpses he caught of her face revealed her exhausted state. Her eyes, shadowed by dark circles told the tale of too damn many sleepless nights. After several high-speed spins, he heeded her plea to slow down to a more comfortable pace. Several more minutes passed and he slowed it down enough to jump on with them. He continued pushing slowly as he faced Meagan and her son.

"How's it going?"

"In circles, right now." A tired smile accompanied her comment. "Buck, do you remember Mitch?"

Buck studied him before nodding. "Yeah, but you don't look like my daddy today."

Mitch gave his head a slow shake as he smiled down at the boy. "No, buddy. I'm just dressed regular today."

Meagan put one hand to her face and released the barest hint of a groan.

Mitch slowed the contraption until it came to a gradual stop. "I think that's enough merry go round for one day, Buck. We don't want you getting sick on us or anything." Buck's protest came to an abrupt halt when Mitch added. "Then you wouldn't be able to help me fly this cool thing I brought with me." He pulled out a large kite painted to look like one of those prehistoric bird dinosaurs. He had an entire explanation at the ready, when Buck took the wind from his sails with his reaction.

"Look, Mom, it's a te-wo-dactyl!"

Meagan laughed as Mitch's jaw dropped open. "He knows what a pterodactyl is already?"

"Not only that, but wait. Buck, can you spell pterodactyl for Mitch?"

Mitch's mouth dropped open even further as the toddler proceeded to spell the word out for him. Mitch nodded in approval. "That's close, buddy, but I'm not sure about that P at the beginning."

Meagan released a soft chuckle as she nodded at her son's questioning gaze before turning to Mitch. "There's a P, believe me. That boy is obsessed with dinosaurs and that's about his favorite. How'd you know?"

Mitch shrugged. "I didn't. It was between that or a bat, or a pink princess. The choice was obvious." He leaned in closer. "Are you positive about that P?"

She put her head back and laughed. "Let it go, Marine. There's a P, I promise."

With the brisk October breeze blowing, the kite was soaring high in the air in a matter of a few short minutes. Mitch lifted Buck to his shoulders and gave him the reel with the string on it while he held tightly to the boy.

He pointed to the bag on the table. "I have another surprise in there if you want to go take a look. I didn't want to break it out before getting your approval, Meagan."

Her eyes lit up as she pulled out packages of cotton candy. "Oh I love this stuff." She held up the two bags, one pink and one blue. "Buck, look what Mitch brought us."

"Oh, can I have some, Mom? Please?"

"Do you promise to eat all your veggies during supper?"

"I will, I promise. Except not spinach."

"Even in a salad?"

Mitch could tell by the boy's movements that he was nodding.

"It's a deal," she said, tearing into the bag of pink stuff.

"I don't want the pink, Mom. I want blue."

"There's no difference. It tastes exactly the same."

"I'm a boy, I want the blue stuff."

"Yeah, pink is for girls," Mitch agreed. "And we're boys."

Meagan shrugged. "Fine by me, that means I don't have to share with either of you. I get a bag all to myself."

The kite lasted another hour before a nose-dive to the ground snapped its spine. As they stood around examining the toy, Buck asked Mitch if he could fix it.

"Not without some spare parts, buddy. I'm sorry."

Buck reached out for it. "Can I hab-bit, mama?"

"*May* I *have* it?" she reminded him as she ruffled his hair. He nodded. "I'd say you need to ask Mitch."

The boy turned large blue eyes toward Mitch, his voice pleading. "May I have it, Mitch?"

"Sure you can. You want to try and fix it?"

"No, I just wanna habbit. Thank you." He grabbed the kite and took off running, making a squawking sound, with it raised high in his arms.

Meagan stared up at Mitch. "You didn't have to do any of this, you know, but it was a nice gesture."

"I loved flying a kite as a kid. I figured he would too."

"Well, you did well with the one you chose, that's for sure. He's a dinosaur freak, just like his daddy was. Chris had dozens of books on dinosaurs. Loved reading all about them."

"Books are always a good legacy, something to bring him and his father together when he reads them."

She nodded, slowly. "It would be if I had them, but they all stayed in Texas at his folk's place. Our parents...they...when we left home together, they refused to give us anything that we could have remotely considered help, or even a comfort. Their collaborative goal was to have us crawl home, penniless, disillusioned with life, and each other, so they could continue to mold us into whatever they wanted. It irked them that we actually made a go of it."

The back of her hand plastered to her forehead, Meagan performed a typically dramatic rendition of Scarlett O'Hara. "We were a shameful reminder of their 'failure' as parents."

Mitch grinned, filling in as the cultured southern gentleman. "Why, Miss Meagan, you surely do make a lovely southern belle."

Her low chuckle reverberated as she seated herself in one of the swings. "Our parents are all friends, upper echelon members of this huge non-denominational church in the next town over. You know the kind, where the preacher judges you on how much you contribute to his bank account? His 'services' are so staged, set-up, to play on the emotions of everyone in there…it's ridiculous…but they never saw it that way."

She shook her head. "The preacher and his wife drive fancy cars and live in a flippin' mansion, while his 'flock' has to tithe outrageous amounts and barely keep their heads above water. Makes you wonder what God thinks of people like that."

Mitch grunted his disapproval. "Hm, giving to the church is fine, but what's that old saying about charity beginning at home?"

Meagan nodded her head vigorously. "Exactly, but it turned out all four of them were good at the same thing. Holding grudges and belittling their children."

"That seems kind of harsh. Were you already pregnant when you and Chris left town?"

"Nope."

"So, what'd the two of you do? Elope? Get married without their knowledge?"

"No. Chris and I never married."

"Oh, sorry. I guess I just assumed you had."

"He tried to talk me into it. Especially the last time I saw him, for his pre-deployment leave."

"You should have married him Meg. You and Buck would have been taken care of."

"Hindsight's twenty-twenty. At the time, I didn't want to get married without our parents there. I just knew they'd soften up and realize how much we all needed each other. I even called our folks to plead with them to reconsider." She looked off toward the slowly setting sun in the west, wiping at a tear in the corner of one eye.

The sight had Mitch wanting to pull her tightly against him, just to comfort her. Nothing else. "I gather they wouldn't consider it?"

A snort accompanied her sharp comeback. "My own father hung up on me, just before telling me he didn't have a daughter." She released a hysterical little laugh. "Even after that, I still insisted on waiting to marry Chris. I told him God wouldn't smile down on our marriage if we did it without our parents' approval." She sniffed loudly and kicked at a pebble.

"Do they know they have a grandson?"

She stared straight ahead, her eyes darkened with anger. "Chris had me listed as the contact for the Marines, so when I called his parents to let them know he'd died, I told them I was pregnant. It didn't change a thing. They even blamed me for Chris enlisting instead of going to college as they'd planned for him." She swiped at her eyes. "Hell, I didn't want him to go. Did they think I enjoyed worrying about the man I loved? Did they think I haven't wished thousands of times he'd listened to me and gone to college instead? We could have made it just as easily, both working part-time jobs and taking a few classes."

He already suspected how she'd answer his next question. "And your parents?"

"They weren't any nicer. My mother even asked if I was certain the child was Christopher's." She gave her head one final shake before lifting her chin. "I told all of them they could take their holier than thou values and stick 'em where the sun didn't shine. Told them my child was better off without grandparents who were such huge hypocrites." She sniffed. "Turns out I'm pretty damn good at holding a grudge, myself."

"Can't say that I blame you, Meg. Seems like they all had it coming." He shook his head, remembering all the wonderful times with his parents. "I can't imagine my parents treating either Sarah or me that way. I know it's none of my business, but had you or Chris given them trouble at home? Were either of you teenage terrors?"

Meagan snorted. "Both of us straight-A students, who never smoked, drank, or did drugs. Neither of us ever in trouble with the law, and did whatever they asked without any backtalk. Chris used to say that instead of them spoiling us, we spoiled them. The very first time we stood up to them, they bailed, couldn't take it."

He grunted, still trying to grasp how a parent could abandon their child. "How difficult could it be to reach out to their daughter or the mother of their future grandchild?"

"Apparently impossible for the four of them." She turned to watch Buck climb his way up the tallest slide on the playground, then slide down, still hanging onto the kite. "I got the best part of that deal. The very best part of Chris. Our son. I'm so thankful for him."

"I imagine Chris was pumped up when he found out you were pregnant." He stepped closer, seeing her eyes tear-up suddenly. "What is it?" He could have kicked his own ass for making her cry.

"He never knew." Meagan clamped a hand over her mouth to smother a sob, but soon recovered and wiped hastily at her eyes. "I sent him an email with a picture of the ultrasound. Buck was just a tiny little bean." She wiped at her eyes again with the hem of her light jacket. "He never got the chance to see it. I was notified a few hours later."

"How?"

"A personal visit…one was a chaplain." She glanced up at him, her lashes heavy and wet with tears. "If there is any moment in this world that's worse than opening your front door to three Marines carrying a single envelope, I hope I never experience it."

He placed a hand on her shoulder as she kicked nervously at some pebbles on the ground. "I've never been on that end of it. I've had to report Marines down to CO's, but never family members. I've also visited the widow of a Marine brother, along with a few other guys once we got leave. We couldn't attend his funeral so we paid our respects when we could."

He sucked in his breath and cringed at the memory of Bobby's wife crying, hugging each of them in turn. Touching their faces, their shoulders and chests as though she could somehow connect to *her* Marine through them. "That was almost as difficult for us as the day Bobby lost his life from that IED." He snorted. "You know, for years, it was good enough to call those damn things what they were, pipe bombs or roadside bombs, or whatever. One day we were told to call them IED's, an acronym for Improvised Explosive Devices. Different name, but they kill just the same." He shook his head slowly. "I sure am sorry for you and Buck, Meg. I truly wish Chris had made it back home to you."

"He made it back, all right, just not as I'd hoped and prayed." The chain from her swing bounced and jangled as she stood abruptly. "I'm still a little angry at God for that. I've attended a couple of church weddings since then but still haven't stepped inside my church on a Sunday since he took my Marine from me." His grunt had her turning to face off with him. "Does that disappoint you?"

Mitch studied her. The tortured look in her eyes, the tears that threatened to spill at any second, the arms crossed tightly against her slim torso. He shook his head and smiled down at the stubbornly brave woman who was trying her damnedest to keep it together for her boy's sake.

"I don't know that you could ever do anything to disappoint me, Meagan." He approached her slowly, reached out to smooth the furrows on her brow. "I don't think you've lost your faith in God, simply misplaced it for a bit."

Her hand closing around his fooled him for just a second. Had him believing she longed for his touch as much as he longed to touch her. Instead, she pushed it gently away.

"I haven't lost my faith, Mitchell. I just can't face God in *his* house right now. I talk to him, I pray and I teach my son to do the same, but it's on my terms, my turf, in *my* house. What God did to me…that was a deal-breaker, you know? Hard to take. I figure, if I'm still speaking to him and believing, he shouldn't hold that against me. I'm doing the best that I can right now."

Mitch fought the urge to take her in his arms, to give this poor woman some kind of comfort. Instead, he reassured her the only way she'd want him to. "God doesn't hold that against you, Meg. He wouldn't dare." Her quick response—the instant raise of her blue-eyed gaze locking with his, and the accompanying lift of the corners of her mouth in the slightest of smiles—told him he'd succeeded.

Just as quickly, Meagan seemed to shake it off. She wiped her eyes and took a deep breath. "That's enough about me and Chris. What about you? No high school girlfriend waiting for your call? No girl you met while stationed in some other country? Or are you one of those men whose mistress *was* the Marine Corp all those years?"

He threw his head back and guffawed. "Damn, I wouldn't call the Corp a *mistress*. More like a hard-assed task master, always there to whip my butt into shape if I relaxed too long. But no, there's no woman anywhere waiting for me to call her, I can assure you of that."

"Do you miss it?"

"Being in the Corp? Sometimes I miss the order. The structure. I always miss my friends, my Marine brothers. Some I've known for two decades. Like Tex."

"Some of Christopher's closest friends were those he went to boot camp with. Did you and this 'Tex' have that in common?"

"Yep, we plowed through boot camp together, but went our separate ways after that. It wasn't until nine-eleven threw us together in Iraq that I saw him again. But, I've seen that son of a bitch nearly every damned day since then. He couldn't be more of a brother to me if we were related by blood. He lives in small town east of Beaumont."

"Did he get out too, or is he trying for thirty?"

"He's out too. We decided together we'd had enough. The corps has changed an awful lot since we enlisted, some ways good, some not so good." He started to sound off, but thought better of it, and snapped his mouth shut instead.

She nodded, let her arms drop, her shoulders relaxed just a little. "Did you lose many friends over there?"

He nodded. "Enough."

"How?"

"Mostly IED's…like your Marine, some in vehicular one's set off with a detonator, some by sniper fire."

"You ever been wounded?"

"A couple of times, but nothing serious. Got shot in the ass once." He started playing with his belt buckle. "Want to see my scar?"

She lifted one hand in front of her face. "That's quite all right, Forest…Forest Gump." Meagan smiled as she continued her line of questioning. "So this Tex, does he have a real name?"

Mitch grinned. "Matthew Houston Broussard. Just in case you're wondering, he was born *before* Lee Horsley brought the role of Matt Houston to the small screen." Meagan's confused look lead him to further explanation. "You know, 'Matt Houston', the television series?"

"Never heard of it."

"Come on, it only ran from 1982 to '85, but I grew up watching the re-runs."

"I was born in 1985, Mitch, and my parents didn't let me watch much television."

He did the quick calculation in his head. That put her at twenty-seven or eight, depending on her birthday. "So, you're twenty…"

"Twenty-seven until November 27th," she finished for him.

"Huh." He turned away from her. "Wish I was twenty-seven again."

She scuffed her shoe on the grass. "I'm sorry if I made you uncomfortable by asking all those questions. I'm just realizing that maybe you didn't want to dredge up some of those memories."

He waved off her apology. "It's okay. It actually makes me feel good to talk about it. Kind of lightens the load, you know?" He did a couple of easy chin-ups on the crossbar of the swing set then stopped to meet her gaze. "You sure you don't want to lighten your own load some, Meagan?"

The widening of her eyes told him she knew what he meant. She didn't even bother playing dumb, but did remain silent.

"So tell me, what the hell is going on in that house of yours? You can trust me."

She studied his eyes and finally gave him a slow nod. "It all started when Buck told me 'the sad man' was watching him."

Mitch listened to her tale, fascinated at numerous events that had taken place in such a short period of time. It made him curious to know how she hadn't lost her flippin' mind over some of the episodes.

"One day I walked into Buck's room to find Christopher's Marine portrait frame face down. I picked it up and checked the frame—the stand is solid, perfectly sturdy. Next time I walked in it was laying on its back."

"You think Buck knocked it over?"

"No." She shook her head vigorously. "This happened several times the afternoon Niki took him to the park for me so I could study for a test. I was doing a week's worth of laundry at the same time, and every damn time I walked in that room the portrait was in a different position." She turned to him and stepped closer, her voice dropped to a menacing whisper. "I swear, Mitch. One time I even left it on its back as I'd found it. When I walked by the room again, it was face down." She raised her hands in a helpless gesture and dropped them. "I don't know what to do anymore. If I insist Buck sleeps with me, it'll only make him suspicious because I've tried never to do that unless he's sick or something. So I get up at least a couple of times a night to check on him."

Mitch cleared his throat quietly, thinking, a couple of times or *more*, from what he'd witnessed. "I'm amazed you can bring yourself to stay there. Most people would have performed a drop and smoke by now." Her curious look had him explaining the military terminology. "That's what we do when we have someone injured. We call for helo transport. When it gets close, we drop what we're doing, throw lots of smoke grenades to hide the medics carrying the wounded."

She nodded halfway through the explanation. "The fact is, Buck doesn't seem the slightest bit afraid. I can't afford to move, but if he was terrified to go to his room, I'd find a way to get the heck out of there." She crossed her arms again and leveled a glare at him. "I suppose you don't believe any of this, you not believing in spirits or ghosts or anything."

"You're right, I didn't believe…but I do now," he found himself admitting.

"You believe me?" she asked, eyes wide, arms dropping to her sides, and shoulders visibly relaxing.

"I'd be a damn fool not to after what I experienced that night."

She dropped her head forward as she pushed her hair out of her face with one hand. "So, uh…What exactly did *you* feel the night you went into Buck's room?"

He hesitated, until he caught her glancing furtively up at him through lowered lashes. "It was cold…like the desert at night cold—cold enough to make my breath smoke. But that's not what got me." He paused trying to decide how to put into words what he'd experienced that night.

"Please. Tell me. Please, Mitch."

He released a long, slow breath. "God, Meg…it was the assault of odors. The smell of desert, hills of rock hard dirt and compacted sand, and dry heat. I've never been able to describe the smell of that place other than it smells like decades of decay…of a land just rusting away." He leveled his gaze on hers. "I smelled fighting. I smelled war. The overpowering odor of gunpowder, overheated metal casings from used ammo, and that distinctly metallic smell of human blood."

He shook his head, clenched and unclenched his jaw before continuing. "At one point, I thought that if I closed my eyes, I would have been back there, in the heat of it. I could practically feel the sand on my skin, the grit in my teeth, the all-encompassing grime that accumulates on anything exposed to it. It *was* Afghanistan."

He gazed into her eyes, knew she believed him. "If Warren flippin' Buffett had offered me a million bucks to close my eyes in that room, I'd have turned it down. That's how serious that shit was for me, Meagan."

She swallowed loudly in the ensuing silence.

"So, it's not just me. I'm not crazy." A statement, not a question.

"Hell no."

She nodded several times. Stopped. Nodded again before releasing a nervous laugh. "You have no idea how...*liberating*...it feels to let someone else in on this. My God!"

"The question of the hour is what the hell can you do about it?"

"I don't know. I mean, I can't exactly call in Ghost Busters."

"Hey, there's always *Deep South Paranormal.* I was watching a little bit of that on the tube last night. You know that oldest guy used to be a technician for NASA?"

"You lost me. I've never seen it."

"Seriously? That's some funny stuff!"

"No time, remember? But Niki has a friend who's supposed to come over when she gets back from vacationing in the Bahamas. Nik claims she's a medium or empath or something."

"An empath?"

"Someone who's hypersensitive to spiritual occurrences, I'd guess."

Before Mitch could open his mouth to speak she put up her hand to stop him.

"Don't say it! I know. I don't put much faith in people claiming to be psychics either, but it can't hurt at this point."

He thought about it, realized he couldn't argue with her reasoning. "Can you call me when she goes? I'd really like to be there, and not to make fun of her." He raised a hand and slapped it over his heart. "I promise, and when a Marine makes a promise, he keeps it."

The bittersweet smile she sent him nearly broke his heart.

"Unless it's beyond his control," she whispered.

Mitch realized, too late, that her Marine must have promised to return. "Meg. I'm sorry."

"It's okay, Mitch. I'll call you."

CHAPTER 7
Two Jarheads and a Cowgirl

Bam! Bam! Bam! Bam!

Mitch jumped at the pounding and spewed a steady stream of curses as hot coffee spilled down the front of his bare chest.

"Hold on!" he yelled, jumping up to wet a paper towel and wipe his chest. Growling under his breath, he grabbed a white tee shirt off the back of the chair and slipped it over his head.

Bam! Bam! Bam!

"I'm comin' dammit!" He ran one hand through his hair to smooth it down and jerked the door open, fully prepared to chew somebody's ass out. The sight of a pretty, young thing, a woman in her late teens or early twenties, had him swallowing the curse he'd worked up. She stood there, one hand on her hip, her long, honey-brown hair pulled up in a high ponytail, and staring up at him with big, beautiful, brown eyes.

He finally managed a feeble response. "Oh…Um. Yes ma'am, can I help you?"

She crossed her arms, cocked her head to one side. "It depends."

Mitch weaved a little from one side to the other, trying to make sure no one was hiding behind her. He sensed a set-up, sure as shit.

"Depends on what, little lady?" Her right brow lifted delicately, just as he caught the sparkle in her eye.

"I'm looking for a Jarhead. You happen to know where I can find one around here?"

By the time she posed the question, he knew who she was. Her voice, dripping with east Texas drawl, one he'd heard every day for over a decade, had been the deadest give-a-way of all. Tex's sister, Haley, had been out of town for her brother's coming home party, but he remembered that pixie grin of hers from years earlier.

"Yes ma'am, but only if you tell me where that no-good brother of yours is."

Her left forefinger straightened to point to the area off to her right as she gave him a small nod. "I'm sure I don't know what you're talking about, Mr. Jarhead."

As expected, Tex stepped into sight. "What's up, Cajun Heat? How in hell did you recognize my baby sister? You've only seen her once, and that was nearly ten years ago."

"Maybe so, but I've heard that distinctive twang a lot longer than that. What's up Tex?" He clasped the arm Tex offered and pulled him in for a brotherly hug and good-natured slap on the back. Mitch released him and gave his sister a good look. "This can't be Haley. She's far too grown up."

"It's me, all right. How ya doin', Mitch?"

He lifted the girl and swung her around in a circle. "Man, I can't believe it!" He put her down and stood back. "Look at you, girl. No freakin' way can that ugly SOB have a sister this damn good looking. Last time I saw you, you had a face full of freckles and a mouth full of metal."

"Yeah, and back then I wanted you to wait for me so I could marry you. Sooner or later we all have to grow up."

Mitch gave her a conspiratorial wink. "Really? You still up for that? I'm not that crazy about having Tex as a brother-in-law, but I could get past it for someone as drop dead gorgeous as you!"

"Watch it, asshole," Tex growled from behind him. "No way are you gonna contaminate my fine Texas bloodline with that cur lineage of yours."

"Excuse me, but your last name is Broussard...I think it's already been contaminated."

"Yeah, but that was decades ago and we're still tryin' to breed that Crazy Coonass out of us," Tex snorted.

"Every bloodline can do with a little Cajun spice, don't you agree, Haley?"

Haley wrinkled her nose at the two men. "I don't have a problem with the spice, but I do have some concerns with the age of the pepper."

Mitchell's jaw dropped. "Are you insinuating I'm too *old* for you?" He turned to stare at Tex, who stood off to the side hooting with laughter.

Haley raised one hand. "No offense, but if and when I settle down, it'll be with someone a little less long in the tooth, if you know what I mean."

Mitch coughed several times while pulling an imaginary dagger out of his heart. "No offense? Kind of late for that, don't you think? Damn girl, you act like I'm ready for a retirement facility and I'm not even forty yet!"

She put her head back and giggled. "Sorry, Mitch. Besides, I will *never* fall for anyone in the military. I want a man who's around when I need him, not on the other side of the world."

Tex shook his head at his little sister. "I feel sorry for the poor son of a bitch already. I think somebody's still got a little growing up to do."

She flipped her ponytail with one hand and rolled her eyes. "That's okay, big brother. I'd rather be on the needing end of growing up than the receiving end of growing old…like *you* guys." She edged by Mitch to step into his apartment. "Nice digs, Marine. Needs a woman's touch but it's entirely livable and very spacious."

"Thank you, ma'am. It's so nice to have you approve of *something* pertaining to me." He laughed as her brown eyes sparkled with amusement. "What brings you two to this area, anyways?"

"I've got a competition this afternoon." Haley slipped her hands in the back pockets of her jeans and spun on her boot heels to face him. "And after that, I want my two favorite Marines to buy me my first beer in a *reputable* club of your choosing, here in Lake Coburn. As of 6:45 this morning I'm twenty-one!" She leaned in closer and whispered behind her hand. "Guess whose idea it was to throw in reputable?" She nodded toward Tex, who stood there, glowering at her.

"Well, Happy Birthday, Haley, but first beer?" Mitch chuckled. "Excuse me, but I find that a little difficult to believe."

Tex approached the two of them, pushing his sunglasses up to rest on his high and tight. "No doubt, she means her first *legal* beer. But I can't say too much, being as I joined the Marines to get my butt out of trouble from having too many *illegal* beers. I can only hope she shows more good sense than her considerably wiser brother."

"You mean older, don't you, big brother?"

"Yeah, well, with age, comes wisdom, Haley girl. You might want to keep that in mind."

"I will, Matty, don't worry. Besides, I've got a plan for my life that doesn't involve DUI's and barfing on cops."

Mitchell's bellow of laughter rang out through the room. "You hurled on a cop, Tex?"

Tex grabbed uncomfortably at the back of his neck. "Not one of my finest moments."

Mitch choked back the laughter. "What the hell did he do?"

"He was about to arrest me, and I begged him not to. Told him I was having one last hoorah before enlisting in the Navy the next day. You know this story. He said if I made it the Marines he wouldn't throw my ass in jail."

"I know a story about a speeding ticket and DUI. This is the first I hear about you hurling on a cop! What'd you do? Barf on his feet and ruin a brand new pair of boots or something?"

"I'd say it was a little more serious than that." Haley gave a throaty chuckle.

Mitch leveled a questioning gaze on his friend. "So, what happened?"

"Projectile…" Tex closed the gap between himself and Mitch. "That dude was about two foot from my face. When I spewed, it covered him…from head to toe. I'd lied like a rug about joining the Navy, but after that little incident, I was extremely glad to join the Marines. Hell, I'd have done anything to get out of Beaumont and away from that cop."

"Oh man!" Mitch wiped tears of laughter from his eyes as he tried to catch his breath. "I wish I could have been around to see that. You ever see that guy again?"

Tex laughed and nodded. "Just about every damn time I come in. We've had some good laughs over it. I've thanked him for forcing me to make the best decision of my life, and he's apologized. Said he'd always worried I'd bite the bullet in the Middle East and he'd be responsible. Truth is, considering where I was headed he probably saved my worthless butt."

"You're probably right. Now how long will you two be in my glorious state?"

Tex hooked a thumb toward his sister. "Annie Oakley here's got a race tonight and tomorrow, so we'll be heading out on Sunday."

Haley spun around to face her brother. "Who the hell is Annie Oakley?"

Tex stuck his finger in her face. "Watch your mouth."

Haley's mouth fell open. "You're joking, right? For saying the word hell?"

He flicked the tip of her nose. "Nope, for not knowing who Annie Oakley is. You being' a horsewoman and all, you should know everything there is to know about her."

"Oh please…"

"So!" Mitch interrupted the bickering siblings. "You've got a horse race at Delta Downs? You betting or riding?"

Haley's brow furrowed in a pretty, little frown before she and Tex burst into laughter. "Not horse racing, Mitch. Barrel racing. The only thing I race against is the clock."

"That's right! I heard there was a rodeo at the coliseum this weekend. Barrels—Is that where they do that figure eight thing in an arena?" Mitch waved his finger in a figure eight pattern in the air.

"Three barrels, so it's a cloverleaf pattern."

He nodded, pointing at her. "I was watching some of that the other day. That stuff can get dangerous."

"Not if the horse and rider both know what they're doing. Barrels are Dakota's favorite thing to race."

"You ride a male horse?"

"A gelding, you mean? I have, but Dakota is short for Miss Red Dakota. She didn't care for roping calves, and barely tolerated poles and break-a-way. But if she sees a barrel, I have to hold her back. My event starts at two o'clock, and I need all the support I can get."

"I'll be there." Mitch nodded, wondering if Meagan and Buck would enjoy watching something like that.

～

Mitchell watched Haley's race, amazed at the speed and agility of both horse and rider. Haley and her Miss Red Dakota operated as a single unit, leaning and turning as one, building speed and slowing to circle incredibly close to the barrels, missing them by a hair.

Tex whooped loudly when his little sister rounded the last barrel and sped back to the starting point. "That's what I'm talkin' about, Haley girl! That was a clean ride and slick as a greased pig. Damn, that girl can ride, can't she?"

"Yes sir. It looks like she's been doing that all her life."

"Close to it, I want to say she first got on a horse at two and they've been her life since then. I think if mom had let her sleep in the stables with them, she would have."

Being that Haley was the last to ride in her group, they didn't have to wait long to hear she'd won that round of the barrels competition. After rousing applause, he stood to follow Tex down the metal steps of the bleachers.

CHAPTER 8
Birthdays, Brawls, and Brothers in Arms

The three of them entered Red's club around eight p.m. at Haley's anxiousness to get her evening of legalized drinking started early.

Mitch led them straight to Meagan's end of the bar, just in time to witness an unruly customer giving her a hard time.

"Come on baby, what other tricks you got up your sleeve?"

"I'd be willing to show you more but I have customers," she said, sounding apologetic. He grabbed her arm, jerking her to an abrupt halt as she turned away from him.

She turned slowly toward him. "If you don't want to be banned from this place for life, you will take your hands off of me right now."

He released her immediately and raised both hands. "All right. No harm done!" He spun on his barstool and walked away, grumbling to himself.

Meagan shook her head and grinned at Mitchell's approach. "I almost hate to start the bartender tricks. There's always one guy looking for a little more than I have time for."

Mitch's gaze followed the dude she'd just chased away. "I think that one wants something more substantial than a flame throwing orange."

"Oh yeah? Well, you should know." A slight lift of one brow accompanied her comment. She shrugged. "Besides, he's harmless. Who do you have here?"

Tex didn't waste time on a third party introduction. He flipped his hat off with a flourish and reached for her hand. "Matthew Broussard, ma'am, and it is truly a pleasure to meet you, especially you having such a lovely accent and all."

Meagan laughed, putting things together. "You're Tex, Mitchell's buddy from Beaumont! I've heard about you, but he sure as heck left out the fact that you were so darn good looking. Blonde hair, blue eyes, and dimpled, to boot…Good God all mighty, you must have to fight the women off with a stick!"

Tex winked at Mitch. "A woman with excellent tastes. I like this girl."

Mitch felt Haley's eyes on him and faced her. He could only assume his features revealed the sheer terror he'd felt at the sight of Tex towering over Meagan. Whatever she sensed had her stepping up to nix her brother's onslaught of pure Texas charm.

"Haley Broussard." She extended her hand. "I'm his sister," she said, pointing at Tex.

"Nice to meet you both. What can I get you guys? And darlin', if you're ordering alcohol, I'll need to see some ID."

"Gladly!" Haley whipped her driver's license from her pocket as though she'd been waiting all her life to do that very thing.

Meagan studied it for a second before her face lit up with anticipation. "We've got us a birthday girl!" she shouted out to the bar patrons. "You know what that means don't you?"

"First drink's free!" about a dozen people shouted.

Meagan climbed the ladder behind the bar, bringing a large brass cowbell with her. She began clanging it loudly until she had everyone's attention. "Not only is it this young lady's birthday, but it's her twenty-first birthday…and y'all know what *that* means don't you?"

About fifty people shouted in unison. "Second drink's free!"

"What number is that, Meagan?" a guy shouted from the back.

One of the other workers handed Meagan a small dry eraser board from behind the bar. She beamed as she erased the #99 from the board and wrote a big fat #100 then lifted it for all to see. The bar filled with whistles, cheering and hoots.

"What does that mean?" Haley called to Meagan over the din.

Meagan stood as tall as she could on the ladder and quieted the crowd. "She wants to know what it means. Shall we tell her? One…Two…Three…"

The entire club bellowed, "Free shots…all night long!"

Mitch had to laugh at the sour face Tex produced at the news. "Come on, bro! You know she's earned it just for being your sister for twenty-one years."

"I don't want her sick as a dog. She's got another race tomorrow." He leaned over to address his sister, who was listening to Meagan. "You haven't forgotten about tomorrow, have you?"

She turned on her brother. "Jeeze Matty, give me a little credit, would you? Meagan was just telling me that I get a complimentary bottle of my choice of whatever I want. I was just about to ask her if she'd hold it for me until tomorrow night since we'll be back then and I don't have to race on Sunday."

"Absolutely! Just make sure you have a designated driver with you. Red has a strict policy that no one leaves here with keys if they're too drunk to drive. We've got Big Man at the door to stop them if they try to leave." She indicated the huge bouncer they'd passed coming in. "So, have you decided what you'll be shooting tomorrow night?"

"Mm…how about Jagermeister?" Groans from the two men had her spinning around. "What's wrong?"

Tex shivered in revulsion. "Bad drunk, sis. Believe me, I know."

"Okay then, Hot Damn!" This time Meagan's groan caught her attention.

"Even worse. Want my advice? Keep it simple. You can't go wrong with Crown, JD, or a good brand of tequila. On the other hand, you could try the new rum made right down the road from here. Bayou Rum is made from Louisiana sugar cane grown by area farmers. Smooth enough to shoot straight and it's got a real fine aftertaste."

Haley seemed to consider her words. "Hmm…I'll have to think about it. For tonight, I'll just have a beer please. Why don't you surprise me? My brother's paying."

Tex balked. "I am? After you walked away with first place in barrels today?"

"College money, big brother. Mom says I can't use it for any other purpose but college."

He frowned at his sister. "Oh sure, bring mom into it to make me feel guilty as hell."

Mitch laughed at the siblings' antics, wishing his own mom was around to make him feel guilty. His mood took a dark turn, remembering he already had plenty enough reason to feel guilty where his parents were concerned. He'd never really been there for either of them during their illnesses. Sarah had shouldered their health problems alone.

∽∾

Meagan glanced at Mitchell, taken back by the look of dark brooding covering his face. She placed an icy cold bottle of Dos Equis with a slice of lime tucked into the neck in front of Haley. "Here you go, sweetie. Enjoy your birthday, and I'm honored to hand you your first legal beer. And take my advice…if you're going to drink alcohol, drink responsibly and always have a designated driver who isn't drinking."

Haley lifted the beer and tipped it at Meagan. "I certainly will, and thanks." She sipped the beer, closing her eyes in appreciation. "Mmm…good and cold. I like the lime."

Meagan planted a second bottle in front of Mitch. "A beer for your thoughts, Marine."

He cocked his head at his companions. "Thanks, but after this it's water or soda for me. You're looking at their designated driver for the night."

"What's on your mind, Mitch? You look kind of sad."

He gave a casual shrug. "I was just thinking about my own folks…wishing I'd been man enough to be there for them when it counted, instead of letting my baby sister do all the heavy lifting." He scratched at the corner of the label. "It's too damn late for anything but regrets."

"It's never too late to make up for past neglect, even though I doubt anyone else sees serving in the military as neglecting your family. Even if the people you think you neglected aren't around anymore, just do unto others. And I know, for a fact that you have been." Meagan placed a hand on his arm. "Have I told you how grateful I am for you showing up at the park the other day? Buck had so much fun."

"Aw, hell. I had as much fun as he did. It was nothing."

"It was a lot for a kid without a dad. That boy is still toting that kite around the house…climbs up on the couch and jumps off so *Mitch* can fly." She laughed as Mitchell's brow furrowed. "Yes, he named his pterodactyl kite after you. There is simply no way to interpret the thoughts or actions of an almost four year old boy." She grinned when his face lit up with the news.

"Thanks for telling me, Meg. It's nice to know I made an impression. Buck's a great kid."

"I think so," she beamed at the thought of her son, and turned away to wait on a fresh group of customers. She couldn't help but think about the butterflies in her stomach at her first sight of Mitch tonight. *He's just a friend.* The good Lord knew she was juggling too much as it is. No way…no way in hell could she add a relationship to the mix.

A packed house always made for a time-flies-by kind of night, and tonight's crowd had the building almost at capacity. As a result, she barely got to visit with Mitch and his friends. A full two hours later, a prickle at the back of her neck made her look up toward the dance floor. Just in time to see Haley, struggling with a guy who seemed to have eight hands…and every one of them was all over her. As soon as she'd push one off her breast, another landed on her butt.

Meagan scanned the area searching for Mitch or Tex, with no luck. Just as she was about to radio the bouncer for back-up, she saw a much taller young man place a hand on the shoulder of the human octopus and say something to Haley. At her nod, the tall young man leaned in to speak to the other guy. Mr. Octopus shoved hard at Dudley Do-Right and grabbed Haley's arm.

Hoping to keep Haley's birthday from turning into a free for all if her brother caught wind of the situation, Meagan stepped around the corner of the bar. She approached the trio in time to hear the taller guy speak, his voice steely and determined, as though trying hard to control his anger.

"Let her go man, you don't want to do this tonight."

"What I wanna do tonight doesn't include you, so why don't you buzz on outta here before you get hurt...*junior*."

The guy had an iron grip on Haley's arm and, judging from the look of it, she'd have a bruise tomorrow. Megan stepped between the two and turned to the shorter, well-muscled stocky man. "Let her go then get on out of here. Your time here is up and if you don't want it to be forever you'll leave without another word."

He turned his icy glare her direction, seemed to consider saying something for a split second, but turned to Dudley Do-Right again. "You don't want a piece of me, bro. You Louisiana boys don't know dick about getting the better of somebody like me." He shoved hard at Dudley Do-Right's chest, his eyes widening perceptibly when his target barely shifted an inch.

The bouncer pushed his way through the gathering crowd's nucleus, packed tight with onlookers. "Break it up, now."

"Micky, that's the one causing all the trouble." Meagan pointed to the man still gripping Haley's arm. To her horror, she saw him take a swing at Haley's defender, who'd taken his eyes off Mr. Octopus for an instant. Before she could warn him, the taller man had grabbed the guy's fist, twisted it neatly with his left hand and whipped it around. As smooth as any dance move she'd ever seen, he'd pinned both of his arms behind his back, rendering him defenseless. He held him there as he spoke.

"I'm gonna let you go, okay buddy? Just go on home now and leave the lady alone."

"Yeah, okay!" the guy groaned. However, lacking the good sense God gave him, the second his captor freed him, he took a healthy swing at him.

Meagan winced, expecting to hear the thud of fist connecting with unsuspecting facial tissue. She heard the empty whoosh of a swing and miss, then a trio of lightening quick *pop...pop...pops*. Mr. Octopus groaned, and would have hit the floor if Micky hadn't been there to catch him.

"Can't say you weren't warned," Micky chided Mr. busted nose, as he ushered him toward the exit.

Meagan spun around to tend to Haley, but saw her rescuer guiding her away from the scene with a gentle hand to her lower back. The crowd parted for the two of them like the Red Sea before a staff-wielding Moses. He settled her into an empty chair on Meagan's end of the bar.

She pushed her way to the two of them. "Haley, are you all right? Did that guy hurt you?"

"She needs ice on this. I doubt if it'll stop it from bruising but it may keep the swelling down."

"Right away!" Meagan scrambled to fill a freezer bag with crushed ice and wrapped it in a dishtowel. By the time she returned, Haley and her rescuer were already deep in conversation. "Keep this on your arm. You sure it isn't fractured or anything? That guy seemed to have a pretty good grip on you."

"Ben says it's not, and it doesn't hurt like it's broken." Haley's eyes glittered with excitement.

"Ben?"

The man of the hour turned to face her, all big hazel eyes set in a chiseled, handsome face.

"Yes ma'am, Ben Bonin." He extended his hand, giving her a strong handshake.

Meagan winced at the title. "Well it sure is nice to meet you, Ben Bonin, but if you call me ma'am again I might have to hurt you. I'm Meagan and I'm only twenty-seven. You're what…twenty-three or so?"

"Twenty-two, ma'am."

"Meagan," she insisted.

"Meagan…ma'am." He stood straight, tall, and unapologetic.

She studied his haircut, military high and tight, the rod-straight back, the politeness…all so very familiar to her. "You're a soldier aren't you?"

His brow furrowed just a little. "No ma'am!"

She grinned, pegging him with one simple question. "Ah…then you must be a Marine."

"Yes, ma'am."

"Active or Veteran?"

"Active, ma'am."

She nodded, checking out the handful of friends who'd gathered around to come to his defense if needed. "Pre or post-deployment?"

"Pre-deployment." He opened his mouth and closed it again, seemed to ponder her familiarity with military terminology. "You have someone over there, ma'am…Meagan?"

Right on cue, the familiar tightness appeared in her chest, although not nearly as severe as in the past. "I had someone."

He stared at her for several seconds before nodding slowly. "I am sorry."

She smiled at him. "Thank you, but I'm glad you're here, Ben." Meagan couldn't help but notice Haley stealing glances at him behind his back. "I have a feeling she is, too. You gonna be around here tomorrow night?"

He cast a glance over at his friends. "I don't think so. I believe they have a pool party and a fish fry or something lined up at another buddy's place."

"FYI, Haley will be here tomorrow night to collect her free birthday shots. She can't do it tonight because she's competing tomorrow. Just sayin'." She gave him a wink and returned to her spot behind the bar.

The steady flow of customers didn't let up enough to enable her to relax for another two hours. At a quarter to midnight, Meagan finally got to sit for a few minutes as she readied to leave for the night.

"You out of here at twelve?"

She looked up at Mitchell's approach. "Sure am. Tonight flew by."

He gave her a hangdog expression. "No chance you could hang around just to visit with us for a bit?"

"I can't Mitch. I need to get home."

"Isn't your roommate there with Buck? I'm sure they're both asleep by now."

"It's not as simple as that. Niki doesn't care to st…" She stopped suddenly, knowing she'd said too much.

"Stay in the house at night," he finished for her.

"Well, not without me being there with her."

"The 'sad man' still making his presence known, is he?"

She bit her lip, thinking that maybe it wasn't such a good thing that he knew so much about her home life. "This isn't the place to be talking about this."

He opened his mouth to speak then snapped it shut again. After seeming to mull things over he finally spoke, breaking the uneasy silence between them. "Do you still have my number from last year?"

She pulled her phone from her pocket to check, and nodded. "I do."

"Don't hesitate to call me if something happens that you can't or don't want to handle alone. There's no shame in asking for help, you know. That's what friends do."

"I'll call if anything comes up." She hefted her backpack onto one shoulder and waved as she headed out.

CHAPTER 9
Fear of Flying Photos

As soon as she pulled into her driveway, she suspected there had been some trouble. If the fact that it was lit up like the Vegas strip didn't clue her in, seeing Niki curled up on the couch with Buck certainly did. Though Buck was sound asleep, Niki's eyes were wide open, glued to her as she approached.

"What happened?"

"Jesus Christ, Meg. Maybe you ought to ask what didn't happen."

Meagan lifted her son gently and walked down the hall, stopping to open the closed door of his room. She stood for a moment to check its condition before tucking him into his bed. She heard her roommate's sharp intake of breath at the doorway and met her gaze. "What Nik?"

"It's warm again." Niki, her voice shaky and faltering, stood at the threshold, stiff as a rod. "The last time I was in here, my nipples practically had icicles on 'em."

Meagan checked the room again. "It seems to be fine now." She walked over to the picture frame of Christopher lying face down on the dresser. She picked it up, startled to see the cracked glass covering his handsome face. "What happened?"

"It, uh…flew off the dresser and broke."

"You mean it fell off the dresser?"

"Hell no!" Niki hissed. "When I tell you that thing flew off the dresser, that's exactly what I mean."

Meagan caught her friend's reflection in the mirror and knew she was telling the truth. Nik's face was a masque of terror wrapped in a façade of nervous tension. Her thin arms hugged at her middle as if she struggled to keep from falling apart. It was as though it took every ounce of strength she possessed not to bolt in the opposite direction of Buck's room.

Meagan took one last look at Buck before approaching her friend. "Come on back to my room with me. I want to hear everything."

They stopped in the kitchen to pull a chilled bottle of cheap wine from the fridge and two glasses off the shelf. "I'm gonna need this to sleep tonight, hon," Niki said, twisting the cork out of the previously opened bottle. She filled her glass to the brim and took a huge gulp before settling on Meagan's bed.

Meagan filled her glass halfway and settled back against the headboard. She took a sip then faced her friend. "Tell me."

Niki took a deep breath as though to build her courage. "Everything was fine, Meg. I fed Buck his supper and gave him a bath, and he fell asleep watching *Prancer*. He didn't give me a bit a trouble, as usual." Her big green eyes seemed to grow even larger and brighter as she continued with her story. "As soon as I tucked him into his bed, all hell broke loose."

Niki gulped her wine and held the glass to her chest with both hands. "When I turned around to leave the room, the temperature dropped." She shook her head in a violent, jerky movement. "That doesn't describe it nearly good enough. It was more like running smack dab into a wall of icy air! From one second to the next I was blowing smoke, Meg. Then…that picture fell on its face. I went to pick it up and it slid all the way to the other end of Buck's dresser…a good two and a half feet, I tell ya. And fast!" She stopped long enough to throw back the rest of the wine and refill her glass.

"I went to pick it up again and the damn thing flew across the room, Meagan, I swear to God. It smashed right into the wall on the opposite side of the room. It about scared the life right out of me! I couldn't help it, Meagan. I screamed and it scared Buck. He woke up screaming. I picked him up and left the room with him. It took me a good fifteen minutes to calm him down. As for me, well hell I'm still trying to calm down, as you can see." Niki raised her wine glass and took another swallow before resting it on the nightstand. She sat in a ball against the headboard, hugging her knees to her.

Meagan groaned and reached out to rest a hand on her friend's arm. "Now I know why you closed the door of his room."

Niki shook her head. "I didn't. He did."

"Buck?"

Nik's eyes were saucer round and filled with terror. "No—*him*—the sad man. He slammed it closed as soon as I walked out of there with Buck…who told me he *saw* the sad man do it."

"Holy crap." Meagan lifted both hands to her face. "What the hell am I gonna do about this?"

"I called Elvinia and told her everything that's been going on."

"Who?"

"My friend, Elvinia. The one that's been on vacation? She made it back last week but has been too busy playing catch up to call me back. So, I called her. She'll be here the day after tomorrow."

"What do you think she can do, Nik?"

"I'm not too sure—communicate with him, maybe? Find out what it is he wants or needs from you. If you give it to him maybe he'll leave you in peace…go to wherever he should have gone after he passed on."

"What if what he wants is too much to give him?" Meagan shuddered at the one thought she was too afraid to put into words.

What if he wants Buck?

CHAPTER 10
Cowboys, Crowds and Competitions

The muffled thump of bass blasted to a driving beat as Mitch pulled open the door of Red's club. He followed his houseguests, Tex and Haley, along with Trevor, a dick with a perpetual attraction to pretty cowgirls, into the building. After a quick scan of the bar, he found Meagan in her usual spot, tending to the area along the east side of the establishment.

He took the lead as they painstakingly made their way to her.

Meagan looked up at them and grinned. "Hey, I'm glad to see y'all back."

Mitch pointed his thumb at Haley. "She's coming to collect her birthday shots."

"Ah, that's right! If my memory serves me, you wanted to think about it. Have you come to a decision, yet?"

Haley gave her a huge grin. "Actually, I believe I've decided to support the Louisiana sugarcane farmers. Ben said its real smooth."

Meagan beamed at her. "*Ben* would be correct. Its fabulous mixed with cola, but smooth enough to shoot straight. I highly recommend it. You want the Silver or Spiced?"

"Let's start with the Silver, please."

Meagan set out a large plastic tray, placed the bottle in the center and added a few cans of coke and four shot glasses.

No sooner had they taken the set-up to an empty table, than Mitch came back to the bar, asking for a beer.

"What's wrong, Mitch? Are you worried that rum's got too much bite?"

He laughed. "It does have a gator on the bottle, but no. I may have a shot or two, but I like my beer."

She nodded and handed him a beer. "What's the deal with the cowboy sniffing around Haley? He doesn't look her type."

Mitch leaned against the wall to watch the guy in question brazenly stare at a gorgeous blonde-haired woman making her way into the women's restroom. "He isn't, but they have the rodeo thing in common and she invited him to hang with her tonight."

Meagan frowned and sucked in her breath. "Oh damn, that's gonna break that big ole heart of *his*."

"Of who's?"

"His." Meagan's gaze landed on the tall Marine walking in their direction. "He's been bugging me for the last hour to let him know when y'all got here."

Mitch grinned as he shook Ben's hand. "Hell, yeah, just what that asshole needs—a little friendly competition."

Ben's brow furrowed. "Which asshole?"

"That one right over there." Mitch used his longneck beer bottle to point at what he considered an unwelcomed interloper. "She met up with him at the arena this afternoon. I think they used to date once upon a time and he's hoping to date her again." He sipped from his beer and shook his head. "Except every damn time she turns her back he's trying to pick up some other chick." He sent Ben a meaningful gaze. "I don't like him, and Tex has been ready to kick his ass since he showed himself."

"Maybe I should just leave," Ben said. "I don't want to stir things up."

"Trust me, as many times as I heard that girl mention your name today, she'd want you to stay. I'm looking forward to seeing you stir up a little shit with that jerk. Look, there he goes again," he said, as Trevor ogled another woman behind Haley's back.

Ben gave a snort of disgust. "What an asswipe."

"See what I mean? I think you sh—"

"Excuse me." Wearing a determined look on his face, Ben walked toward the corner table.

"Go get 'em, Jarhead!" Meagan called softly as Mitch swung around to face her.

"Jarhead? Ben is a Marine, too?"

"Well, yeah. Didn't you know?"

He stared after him, chuckling as Trevor got his first look at the competition. "He never said a word. Is he still active?"

"Yep, he's pre-deployment…not sure where he's going."

Remembering Haley's comment about not dating a military man, Mitch sipped at his beer and headed back to the group. "This should be interesting."

By the time he got there, Haley had just seen Ben.

"Hey! I thought you weren't going to be able to make it tonight," she said, her face lighting up at the sight of him.

"I didn't know for sure until this afternoon. I cancelled some plans to be here."

"Did you really?" She laid a hand on her chest. "I'm honored. Now, come shoot a round of birthday rum with me."

He grinned, bearing a beautiful smile that had surely cost his parents a small fortune in dentist visits. "I've already had a couple of beers, so I'll pass on the rum. But how about if I watch you shoot and offer to hold your head when you're hugging the porcelain throne later?"

Trevor stepped up and threw an arm possessively around Haley's shoulder. "Uh, excuse me, but that's what I'm here for, buddy."

Haley jarred Trevor in the side with her elbow. "Don't be a jerk, Trev. You don't own me. Trevor Jameson, this is Ben Bonin. I met him here last night. I ended up dancing with a human octopus and he rescued me." She left them to pour herself another shot of rum.

"So, you rescued the lady from a hands-on kinda guy, huh?" Trevor drawled. "Well, I've known Haley nearly all my life, Ben *Boner.*" He extended his arm for a handshake. "There's nothing for you here, so you can run along now."

Mitch held his breath to see if Ben would take the not so subtle insult or do something about it. It turned out that the younger Marine could be just as effective without being an asshole.

Ben took the mouthy cowboy's hand and spoke without cracking a smile. "The name's B-O-N-I-N, and pronounced Bon-ay—you know, like the letter "A". Then again, I'm bettin' you didn't see too many of those in school, did you, *Trevor?* You've got "D" for dumb-ass written all over you."

Trevor's face sobered as he practically sunk to his knees during the handshake and monologue. When Ben finally released his hand, Trevor flexed it as though trying to get his blood circulating again.

Haley returned from their table, totally unaware of the overflow of male testosterone crackling in the air. "Here's to being twenty-one!"

Mitch clinked his beer bottle with her shot glass. "And all the fireworks that go along with it."

"Here's to free booze!" Trevor brayed, reaching for a shot glass, only to have Tex pull it out of his reach while sending him a scorching look.

Ben clicked his own beer bottle to Haley's shot glass brimming with the clear liquid. "Here's to you, Haley. I hope you have nothing but great birthdays from here on out."

∿

Anything involving horses, cowboys and competitions equated to large crowds for the local bars and dance clubs. Red's always had admirable business, but his excellent selection of country bands and huge dance floors always made it a favorite with people in town for the rodeo. The last two work nights had nearly driven Meagan to exhaustion with the non-stop bustle of activity. That, coupled with events at home, and a severe inability to sleep the night through, had her feeling edgy and irritable. The guy across from her wasn't helping matters.

"Come on, honey. Do some of those fancy bartender tricks for me. I heard you're the best in here." He pulled a thick wallet from his pocket. "I'll make it worth your while."

"Sorry, sir. There's no time for that tonight. Do you see the line of people behind you waiting for drinks?" She wiped up a minor beer spill with the dishcloth and met his gaze. "Now, is there anything else I can help you with?"

"I don't *want* anything else, and I don't give a flying fu…"

"Sir!" She cut off what was sure to be a tirade of foul language and unclipped her radio. "Come in Micky! This is Meagan and I need assistance at the bar, please."

"Aw shit! There wasn't no need for that. Especially since you and me are from the same great state of Texas." He leaned across the bar to get close to her. "We could spend some time together after you leave this place tonight."

"Sir, I told you, I'm too busy for this. Would you please move along? You aren't the only person who'd like a beer tonight, you know."

A man spoke up from behind him. "Yeah dude, you're holding up the line."

The cowboy, a good 6'3", turned on the guy and leaned over to sneer in his face. "You might oughta get in another line, then buddy."

"Hey screw you, man. She said she didn't have time for your bullshit. I see you have your drink, now move on so the rest of us can order."

Cowboy reached for the man's shirt and Meagan reached for her radio again. "Micky, I've got trouble. Where are you?"

The bouncer appeared to her left. "I'm right here, Meg." Micky placed a beefy hand on cowboy's shoulder. "Okay, man, let's go. From the sound of it, you've had plenty of chances to back off."

Cowboy jerked out of Micky's grip. "Get your hands off me, you sonovabitch! I don't need to be lead anywhere like a prisoner. Let me at least take a swig of the beer I just paid for and I'll walk out on my own."

Micky lifted both hands and nodded. "That's fine, man." He turned to Meagan. "I think it'll be all right. He seems agreeable enou—"

Meagan had witnessed enough fights in her earlier bartending years to recognize the distinctive thud of a beer bottle hitting a skull. However, witnessing the aforementioned skull, cracking open with an accompanying gush of blood was an entirely new experience. She screamed as Micky pitched forward onto the floor like a pine tree in a hurricane.

She grabbed a clean dishcloth from the bar, dropped to her knees beside him and pressed it to his gaping wound, hoping to stem the flow of blood. "Somebody call 911!" she called out, even as a scuffle above caught her attention. She looked up just in time to see Mitch take the offending cowboy down in two swift moves. As he held him there, face down on the floor, arms locked in a tight grip, she wondered if there was anything Mitch couldn't handle.

Mitch met Meagan's gaze and yelled over the din. "How bad?"

"Bad enough. He's bleedin' like a stuck hog, poor thing. Did someone call for an ambulance?" she asked those nearest to her.

Kelly Broussard, an acquaintance who occasionally visited the club, waved her phone.

"They're sending an ambulance now, as well as the cops, Meg," she said.

"Thanks, Kelly." She increased the pressure on the wound and dropped her head, thinking they couldn't get there fast enough. When Mick groaned and tried to sit up, she pushed him gently back down. "Don't move, hon. You're cut open pretty bad. This will definitely need stitches."

"Son of a bitch, that hurts," he growled, flinching when she applied more pressure.

"Don't move, I said. Every time you do, I lose pressure on the wound and blood comes gushing out. You wanna bleed out on the floor of this club?"

"No, but damn that stings. You're pressing too hard, Meg!"

"Yeah? Well the fact that you're strong enough to whine like a big ole ta-ta tells me I must be doing something right. Otherwise, you'd be too weak to say a flippin' word to me."

"*Ta-ta?* No fair, Meg. You know I can't speak east Texas hick."

"I was trying to be nice, but since you won't let me, it's a *tit*, you crazy ass Cajun! I called you a big titty-baby. Now hold the hell still before I lose my supper all over the place." Her comment, meant as a joke, was closer to the truth than she wanted to admit.

She stayed there on her knees with him until another woman knelt beside her, holding out a hospital ID badge.

"Hey, I just walked in and they told me what happened. I'm an emergency room nurse. You want me to take over? You're looking a little green around the gills."

Meagan sighed in relief. "Dear God, please do! What's your name, honey?"

"April Fontenot, and I work at Lake Coburn Memorial."

Meagan waited for the EMT's out front and cleared a path for them and the local cops when they arrived. Though the cops left immediately with their charge, it took a good fifteen minutes for the technicians to get Micky loaded into the ambulance.

By then, Red McAllister, the club-owner, had arrived on the scene to check things out.

"Two fights…two nights in a row." Red shook his head. "You can always tell when the rodeo's in town."

"I'm sorry, Red. I was trying to keep an eye on the situation. I called Micky immediately, but he was busy at the door. By the time he showed up, that guy was all riled up. He decked poor ole Mick when his back was turned. I feel so *bad* for him!"

Red raised a hand. "This is not your fault Meagan. Like I said, when all these cowboys gather in one crowded space, sometimes their idea of letting off steam doesn't jive with ours." He gazed at the crowd, thinning now that the excitement was over, and then turned his attention on Meagan again. "And by the way, you did a great job tending to Micky. Thanks for jumping in there."

"Well, shoot, Red. I sure as heck couldn't let a co-worker bleed to death while I stood around doing nothing."

Red gazed at the other workers, all gathered around, their faces a study in concern. "Let's shut it down early for tonight. You'll all get paid your regular hours plus what you would have made in tips." He placed a friendly arm around Meagan's shoulder and turned her toward the bar. "And *you,* my friend, need to get cleaned up *now*, because you're covered in blood. I'll throw in a little extra to replace your jeans. Grab another work T-shirt from the stash and trash that thing you're wearing."

"Thanks boss. I appreciate that."

∽

Mitch watched Meagan disappear into the ladies' room then propped himself up against the door to wait for her.

Red approached him scratching his chin. "Now I've got to find someone to replace Mick while he's recuperating." He looked around. "Who took down the cowboy after he blind-sided my bouncer with a beer bottle?"

Mitch stepped forward. "I did."

Red's face stretched in a broad grin. "Oh, yeah—this is perfect! Please tell me you need a job here. I'll make it worth your while."

"It so happens I do, and I'd be glad to work for you."

Red reached out to shake his hand. "Done! You're a lifesaver, Marine. Come on into my office and we'll discuss the terms."

Mitch glanced at the door of the ladies' room, wanting to be there when Meagan exited. Something about the look on her face told him she was running on pure adrenaline. He wanted to be around when her supply ran dry. "Can it wait, Red? I'm not very concerned about the details. After the way you and your family have cared for my sister and nieces, I figure I owe you."

Red waved off his comment. "You don't owe me squat, but it can sure wait." He pulled out his wallet and handed Mitch a business card. "Call me in the morning and I'll get all your info. Thanks bro, you're a life saver."

"No problem."

Meagan pushed through the door several minutes later, all traces of blood washed from her hands and arms, and covered in a new *Red's* T-shirt. Her blood-spattered jeans still bore the evidence of Micky's injury, and no doubt, she wanted to get rid of them. She approached him, fidgeting as though she was about to jump out of her own skin.

"You okay, Meagan?"

The gaze she leveled on him answered the question…Definitely *not* okay. In fact, so far from it, she was about to lose it. She opened her mouth to speak, but instead, grabbed her purse from behind the bar and rushed out the back door at a run.

CHAPTER 11
The Normalcy of Para-normalcy

He didn't even try to stop her, but went out the front to his own truck and followed her home, keeping an eye on her erratic driving. That alone, told him she'd probably cried all the way home. He pulled up behind her and caught her before she entered her home through the side door.

"Come on in, Mitch," she said, not even bothering to face him, as if she'd expected him to follow her home. Once inside, she dropped her purse and headed to her room, coming out with a handful of clean clothes. She murmured something before disappearing into the bathroom.

He heard the distinct sounds of her showering, suspected how taxing it had been for her to wear clothing covered in someone else's blood. Remembering the dozens of times he'd been in that particular situation, he could definitely relate.

Eyeball-deep in thoughts of missions, sniper attacks, and IED's, Meagan caught him somewhat by surprise with her timely exit from the bathroom.

"Interested in a cup of decaf, Mitch?"

He nodded, wrenching himself from the painful memories of holding Marine brothers in his arms as they spoke their last words…took their last breaths. "But, only if I'm not keeping you from getting some sleep. I really just wanted to make sure you were okay."

"I'll live. I…I had to shower, though. And no, I doubt I'll be getting to sleep anytime soon." She waved her hand at the sofa. "Make yourself at home."

As soon as she disappeared into the kitchen, he quietly made his way down the hall to Buck's room. Half expecting to see a 'sad man' standing by the boy's bed, or at least having the room cloaked in icy temperatures, he was somewhat surprised at the normal atmosphere of the room.

Mitch walked over to the small dresser, picked up the portrait of the Marine in dress blues, noting its absence of glass. Now that he'd spent a little more time with Buck, he could definitely see some of the little boy in his dad's features. How sad that the kid would grow up never knowing his own father. Lots of kids lost their parents as children, but the majority had at least something to remember them by. Buck didn't even have a picture of him and his dad together. Not only that, but according to Meagan, Chris hadn't even known of her pregnancy when he died. That had to suck.

He placed it back on the surface, went to adjust its position, only to have it slide quickly to the other side of the dresser. From one second to the next the air turned icy, causing his breath to vaporize into visible puffs of smoke. His heart pounding in his chest, he reached out for the picture and jumped back as the damn thing flew into the wall on the opposite side of the room.

"Shee…it!" he hissed, making sure Buck hadn't awakened. That explained the missing glass.

The instant Meagan appeared in the doorway, he could tell that she knew what had happened. Furthermore, the blank look on her face said she wasn't a bit surprised.

He raised both hands. "I didn't do it."

She nodded and tucked the covers around her son. "I know. Coffee's ready."

She turned and walked out. Just like that, as though nothing out of the ordinary had happened. Sweet Jesus! Now he understood the seriousness of the situation. In the world she lived in, it was just a typical evening.

Mitch followed her out, glad to cross the threshold into normal temperatures. He sat on the opposite end of the couch from her and picked up a mug of steaming coffee from the cocktail table.

"I don't know how you do this every day, Meagan." He sipped from his cup and sat back on the sofa, crossing one booted foot over his knee.

"You mean drink decaf?" She leaned back against the arm of the sofa, facing him, and stretched out her jeaned legs on the cushions.

"Yeah, that's exactly what I'm talking about, smart ass." He reached over with one hand to caress a bare foot. "Damn girl, your feet are ice cold." He warmed both hands on his mug then set it aside. He reached for one of her feet, rubbing it briskly between his hands. She rewarded him with a low groan of appreciation.

"Oh, God. You can do that all night long, Mitch, and I wouldn't complain...not one...little...bit." She let her head fall back against the padded sofa arm and closed her eyes.

Mitch leaned forward to warm his hands on the mug again then reached for her other foot, treating it to the same warm administrations. He smiled as she gave him an equally appreciative groan of pleasure. "Your dogs must get pretty tired by the end of the night slinging drinks at Red's. That place pulls in some business."

"That's because it's a nice place. My *everything* gets pretty tired by the end of every day," she murmured. "Even when I don't pull a shift at Red's."

"I imagine so, with all the chasing after Buck and school work." He warmed his hands on the mug and picked up the opposite foot again. "And that's not taking into account the paranormal activity going on in this place. I don't know how you do it, Meg."

"I try not to think about it."

"Then I won't make you talk about it, unless you want to."

Nearly a minute had passed with neither of them speaking. He thought she'd fallen asleep when she finally broke the silence.

"It took everything I had to keep from screaming when Mickey got hurt. I kept imagining it was Christopher's blood all over me. I kept asking myself if someone had to do the same thing for him when he got hurt." She swallowed loudly. "Was someone there to apply pressure to his wound to keep him from bleeding out?"

His hands stilled as she voiced the most personal of questions.

"I'm sure his Marine brothers did whatever they could for him, Meg."

She shook her head. "Then I remembered there wasn't enough of him left to work on, so probably not."

He froze, wondering what he could possibly say to that. "Did they bring him home?"

She lifted her tear stained face to gaze at him and gave him a slow nod.

"Then they did what they could for him. I assure you, they treated Christopher with the utmost respect. It happens, and when it does, we can't help but think it could have been *any* of us. So, you care for your dead brothers the same way you'd want them to care for you if it ever happens." He watched a tear break free to make the journey down her cheek in a long, slow, torturous path until it dripped from her delicate chin. God, he wanted to hold her—hug her to him until all traces of sadness were completely gone. He settled for beginning the gentle foot massage again.

Her next words were a reverent whisper. "Do you think they said words over him when it happened?"

"It depends on the situation," he said, striving for total honesty. "If they weren't being fired upon, they probably did say something over him. If they were, they probably waited until they were in a more controlled environment. Did you ever get the chance to meet any of his buddies?"

"Not while he was alive. I met a few of them afterwards. Some were being rehabilitated at McGuire Veterans Administration Hospital in Richmond, Virginia. I drove all the way over there to talk with them."

He gave her another slow nod. "I assume you went with questions. Did you get any answers?"

She lifted one thin shoulder. "Some, but I couldn't bear to ask some of the questions I'd gone over there to ask. I realized those men had already lost enough, and I didn't want to dredge it up for them again."

"What did you discover, Meagan? What did you gain by making that trip, by meeting those men?"

"Well...I met one man who wished he could switch places with Christopher, because he'd lost his hand and couldn't play the guitar anymore. He said it was his life, all he'd ever been able to master and it was a gift he'd inherited from the men in his family for the last five generations. And then I met another who'd lost both legs and said it gave him the perfect opportunity to build his upper body strength."

She wiped away her tears with the back of her hand. "I'd thought that I wouldn't have minded Chris coming back with no limbs, just as long as he came back alive. But seeing those men, talking to them and their families..." She released a long, drawn out sigh. "I realized that maybe Christopher wouldn't have handled a disability so well. He'd hardly ever been sick, never had a broken bone or an injury, was an excellent athlete. His grandfather came back from WWII missing an arm and he took to drinking. His grandmother told me once that he had the strength of two men in that one arm, and she felt it every time he hit her, which was nearly every time he drank. Alcoholism ran rampant in his family and so did mean drunks. That's why Chris never drank. He knew he had the genetic tendency."

Mitch used the thumbs of both hands to massage the pad of her foot. "So, you think maybe if he'd survived with a disability maybe he'd have been a mean drunk, too?"

She shrugged. "I'm saying it's a possibility. Maybe that's why God took him when he did, and as suddenly as he did. Maybe this *was* the only way I could remember all the good in him, to tell his son what a good man he was. I'm just sayin'...maybe that was God's reason all along and I've been wrong for being mad at him for almost five years."

"I suppose it could be," he whispered, bothered by the thought of a bitter, angry Chris coming home to become an abusive alcoholic. Somehow, he knew that if there were any way Chris could have chosen to die rather than become that kind of man, he would gladly have sacrificed himself. "Maybe you're looking at it the wrong way. Maybe God didn't make that choice. Maybe Chris asked to be taken rather than to have it happen that way."

Meagan sat up straight and stared at him. "I guess anything's possible, but it'd be nice to know for sure, though."

He grinned at her. "Did that psychic chick ever show up to check things out?"

She rolled her eyes at him. "She's coming tomorrow. Or rather, today," she added, glancing at the clock.

"Maybe she can get an answer for you."

She nodded. "I hope she can get more than one."

"You mind if I tag along?" The curious cock of her head had him explaining. "You know, when she comes over to do whatever it is she does, can I be here? Is that okay?"

"I don't have a problem with you being here. I guess I'm just curious as to why you'd *want* to."

He pondered his own reasoning. "I kind of feel as though I have the right to be here, since he's already made his presence known to me…twice."

She settled back against the arm of the sofa and yawned. "I'll call you when she shows up, okay?"

"Thank you." He began massaging both her feet and again, she groaned her appreciation. He worked his magic on her for five more minutes in complete silence before the sound of soft snoring reached him. He gazed at her softened features, saw the worry lines on her brow disappear, and her lips part in in her gentle state of slumber. He set her feet down and very gently, pulled himself up from the sofa. He covered her with a New Orleans Saints throw he found draped over the back of a chair, trying not to wake her. As soon as he tucked it in around her, her eyes opened.

"You going?' she said, sounding drowsy and a little drunk, though he knew she wasn't.

"Uh huh. You need to sleep now."

She yawned and sat up. "I need to lock the door behind you."

"I guess you do." He walked to the door and turned to face her. "You've got my number. Promise me you'll call if you need anything."

She nodded sleepily. "I will."

"And you'll let me know when that woman gets here?"

"I will."

He nodded, satisfied she was being truthful, and turned away from her. He reached for the door, stopped, and turned back. Without warning, he pulled her into his arms for a hug.

The two of them stood there for what seemed to him much longer than it actually was. Wordlessly, he held her, his hand rubbing gentle circles on her back, his chin resting on her head. At first she resisted, her arms hung limply at her sides. She lifted them, eventually, and locked them around his waist.

As badly as he wanted to kiss her, he held himself back, sensing she needed a friend more than a lover right now. Anything else meant to happen between them could happen later. When there was no more ghost throwing pictures across rooms, literally.

He pulled away from her and planted a soft kiss at her temple. "Good night Meg, and please be careful." He felt her nod under his lips.

"I will." She waited until he'd stepped onto the tiny front stoop. "Hey Mitch?"

He turned to face her again. "Yeah?"

"Feel free to come over and massage my feet anytime."

Her accompanying smile had him feeling good all over. Almost better than a kiss.

He turned and headed for his truck.

Almost.

CHAPTER 12
Empaths and Accidents

Unsure of what to expect, Meagan opened the door cautiously and peeked around the edge at eye level. Her gaze traveled up a good twelve inches to meet the other woman's gaze.

The six-foot-if-she-was-an-inch tall woman with skin the color of cocoa powder stood looking down at her.

"Sweet Pea, were you expecting Tangina Barrons?" She cracked a huge grin, revealing straight teeth so white they seemed to glow in her dark face…all except for her two gold front teeth.

Meagan stepped backed and straightened as she opened the door. "Excuse me, but who?"

The woman put her hand out about waist level. "Tangina...you know, the little psychic lady from the *Poltergeist* movies?"

"Oh! No—no—I've never seen them."

"Really? Ooh child, you ain't lived till you've seen Poltergeist. The sequels are mediocre at best, but number one is phenomenal!" She adjusted the brightly colored turban on her head that gave her the appearance of even more height, then offered her large-boned hand. "Elvinia LaBeau and it is a pleasure to make your acquaintance, honey."

Meagan gave the woman's hand a tentative shake. "Meagan Hutton. Nice to meet you, too."

After an uncomfortable moment, Elvinia cleared her throat. "Um, I'm not sure what you've been told about me but I'm not of much use at porch readings. Is there a possibility I could actually set foot inside the house?"

Meagan pulled the door open wide and waved at her guest to enter. "Oh...oh, God! I'm so sorry! Please come in, Ms. LaBeau. Honestly, I'm not normally this throwed-off but truth is, I just don't know how to act. I've never done this kind of thing before." She twisted the rings nervously on her fingers.

"Throwed-off?" Elvinia passed a skeptical eye over her. "You aren't from around here, are you girl?"

Meagan felt the blush creep up from her neck to her ears. "No ma'am. I'm from northeast Texas. I'm trying to lose my accent, but when I'm nervous, it rears its ugly head."

The larger woman patted her hand, reassuringly. "Don't you dare! There ain't nothing wrong with flying your own flag, just as long as it's right next to the stars and stripes. We're all Americans, aren't we?"

Meagan lifted her chin, deciding the woman was right. "You've got a point, Ms. LaBeau, and thank you for that."

"Please, child, call me Elvinia…and before you ask, my father's name is Elvin and my mother was Virginia. I never could get them to admit to anything, but I strongly suspect they were high the day they named me."

Meagan sent a smile in her direction. "I think it's a lovely name, and quite unique."

"Well, you're a sweet one for saying so. I don't know about lovely, but I'll give you unique." She looked around the tiny room and shook her head. "I don't get any readings at all in this room. Take me to the room where you've had the occurrences."

Meagan took a step and faltered. "What exactly has Niki told you about all this?"

"She said your little boy is seeing someone. That's it, and to tell you the truth, it's not all that unusual. Children don't have preconceived perceptions of the spiritual world. They don't show fear so they are approached more often." She leaned in closer to Meagan. "Sometimes those *imaginary* friends aren't imaginary at all."

Meagan wiped at the chill bumps on her arms and nodded toward the hallway. "Down there."

Head held high and straight-backed, Elvinia turned on her tall platform heels and headed down the hallway. She stopped two feet from the first door on the left and raised both hands in the air. She faced Meagan, as her right brow lifted curiously. "Oh my, my…" she whispered, pointing at Buck's open doorway. "Bingo in the Anchor Room!"

Meagan shook her head. "I'm sorry, is that supposed to mean something to me?"

Elvinia's deep chuckle resonated in the narrow space. "Not unless you spent your teenage years sneaking into the Lake Shore Club dances in Lake Erin, Louisiana as a teenager."

"Oh…No ma'am," she drawled in her all too prominent twang. "I haven't been here long enough for that."

Elvinia put back her head and laughed. "You don't say!" Her laughter seemed to lodge in her throat as she stepped into the room's portal. "Oh…Hello there."

Meagan let her gaze take in every corner of the room. "Do you see something?"

"Nothing but residue, just yet, but its resilience leads me to believe what you've all been feeling is a strong presence. Major shifts in temperature, for instance. And…" she turned to face Meagan. "It's not just the boy who feels him. You sense him too…the man…the soldier." Her eyelids drifted heavily closed. "Such a profound sadness about this one. And anger…he's angry at all he missed out on."

"Is it my fiancé?"

"Was he in the military?"

Meagan didn't know how long she stood there, shaking her head. "Marines."

"He died overseas?"

"Yes, in Afghanistan."

Elvinia walked over to the picture frame, lying face down on the dresser and picked it up to study it. "Did you place it face down?"

Meagan erupted in laughter, hinting at her state of near hysteria. "I don't touch it anymore. Sometimes it's face down, sometimes on its back, and sometimes the darn thing is throwing itself across the room."

"Seriously?"

Meagan nodded, surprised the woman's eyes could possibly look any larger than they already did. "It throws itself right up against that wall, right there." She pointed at a spot on the opposite wall marked by scuffs and scratches.

Elvinia stared at the spot indicated then reached out for the photo. Before she could touch it, however, it scooted to the far end of the dresser. In seconds, the room temperature dropped from comfortable to downright chilly.

Meagan held her breath, waiting for her guest to run screaming from the room.

Instead, Elvinia spoke in a voice that suggested admiration, even a reverence, rather than fright. "Oh, he's a sensitive one, isn't he?"

Meagan's jaw dropped. "You're not scared?"

"Pfft...of what? A spoiled child?" She rolled her eyes. "He's the one who's scared and confused. But he's not dangerous, although he may be a little annoying."

"Is it Christopher?" Meagan was almost afraid to hear the answer.

"Is that your fiance's name?"

"Yes, Christopher Buckley Martin."

Elvinia reached slowly for the picture. "Christopher," she whispered. "I mean you no harm. I'm only here to help Meagan understand what's going on. We just want to help you." She lifted the frame, still missing its glass, and flipped it to stare at the picture. She placed her hand over his face and closed her eyes. After several moments, her eyes flew open.

"What's wrong, Elvinia?"

The black Amazonian-like woman stared down at Meagan, one single, fat tear trailing down her smooth, brown cheek. "He...he's...it almost breaks my heart."

Meagan gave her a slow nod. "Welcome to my world."

~◡~

Mitch had already knocked several times before Meagan finally pulled the door open, looking slightly flustered and wide eyed.

"Is she here? Is that her car?" He pointed to the minivan parked in the drive.

"Yes, and I just want to warn you, she's a little..."

"Unconventional?" he finished for her.

"She's that too, but I was going to say tall. She's a real tall lady and her skin's the same color of my maw maw's homemade brownies." She opened the door wider. "She's real nice. Come on in and meet her."

Mitch followed her into Buck's room and halted at the door, glad that Meagan had taken the time for a quick description. Even knowing what to expect didn't quite remove the shock of coming face to face with the woman. "Hello," he said. "I'm Mitchell Hebert."

The instant he spoke his name, Christopher's picture took a nosedive to the floor, as the temperature dropped another several degrees.

The three adults stood there staring at it, until Mitch reached down for the portrait of the man in his dress blues. He straightened, arranging it carefully on the surface of Buck's dresser in an upright position.

The woman placed a hand on his shoulder and turned him slightly toward the door. "Let's go out there and talk, shall we?"

Mitch placed a hand at Meagan's lower back as he followed her into the living room. "How are you, Meagan?"

She ran her hands up and down her arms and nodded. "I'm fine, thanks."

"Mitchell?"

He turned to face the other woman. "Yes, ma'am?"

"I'm Elvinia LaBeau, and it's a pleasure to meet you."

He shook the gentle hand she offered and smiled into chocolate eyes at the same height as his own. "You also, ma'am."

She placed her left hand over the one she held and closed her eyes. "Mm...mm...another one filled with regrets...determined not to let someone he loves down." She gave his hand a pat and winked at him. "Don't you worry, man. Your sister's gonna be just fine. She's right where she's supposed to be with a man who cherishes her."

He stared at her, a little surprised that she possessed knowledge of his sister. Not that long ago, he would have balked at something like that, insisting it was some kind of trickery. However, his recent experiences with the unknown had opened his mind as nothing else ever had. Finally, he gave her a nod. "Thank you, that's good to know."

"Anyone else want coffee?" Meagan headed for the kitchen.

The psychic gave her another toothy grin. "Yes ma'am, I surely would. Just a little cream, I'm sweet enough."

"I'll take some also," Mitch said, turning to see Elvinia's gaze locked on him. He gave her a self-conscious smile. "So, is it her ex haunting the place?"

A sudden roll of thunder accompanied her reply. "I believe it is, but he's not dangerous."

He nodded, staring out the window as fat droplets of rain began to pelt the room's large plate glass windowpane. He turned back to find her gaze still pinned on him. "Is there something wrong?"

She shook her head slowly. "No...nothing wrong. But I want you to know that you won't let her down."

"I'm not worried about my sister. She'll be okay from here on out."

Elvinia's deep chuckle echoed in the room. "I know she will, but she's not the one I'm talking about." She reached out to place her large hand on his chest, right over his thudding heart. After several seconds, she leaned in close to whisper. "You're in love and you don't even know it yet."

Mitch couldn't manage more than a wide-eyed stare as she threw her head back in jubilant laughter.

Meagan entered, carrying a tray with three cups and set it on the ottoman. "Did I miss out on a joke?" She handed out two of the cups and took the third one for herself as she waved her hand at the sofa and chair. "Sit, please."

Elvinia sat with a flourish. "You didn't miss out on any joke. It's only that the truth is hard to swallow for some people."

Meagan glared at Mitchell. "You weren't making fun of her abilities or anything, were you?"

Mitch opened his mouth to protest. Before he could say anything, Elvinia jumped in.

"Not at all. I was only teasing him, and he was being a good sport about it." She gave him a wink before raising her cup to her mouth.

The three of them sipped their coffee in silence for a moment before Meagan cleared her throat. "Elvinia, is there anything you want to know about what's happened before? How Christopher died or anything?"

The psychic blinked twice, her heavily mascara coated lashes fluttering like two large, velvety butterflies with perfectly synchronized wings. "No."

Mitch stared at Meagan, waiting to see if she had some kind of comeback. Realizing she didn't, he turned his attention to Elvinia.

"What are you going to do?" he asked, more than a little curious.

"Well," she said, before sipping her coffee and settling back on the overstuffed chair. "I'm going to enjoy this delicious coffee…and wait."

"For what?"

"For *him* to approach *me*," she whispered.

"But he won't in here," Meagan insisted. "You have to go in there."

"Oh no, he'll come out here. He just didn't realize he could until now."

Meagan shook her head. "I don't understand."

"That's part of why he's so frustrated. He feels trapped and doesn't know what to do. Look how long it's taken him to get this far."

Mitch didn't even attempt to hide his confusion. "I still don't understand."

Elvinia sighed and sat forward on the chair. "Was Christopher a real talkative person when he was alive, Meagan? I mean, did the two of you sit together and have long talks about life and things?"

Meagan frowned and shook her head. "Not really. Chris was always on the quiet side. But we knew each other so well, it was as though we didn't have to speak to communicate. I could look at him and know what he was think…ing…oh…ooohh." Her eyes widened as she set her coffee cup down with a clatter and covered her mouth with one hand. She stood and paced the length of the living room several times then stopped to stare at Elvinia. "Are you serious?"

"Yes ma'am. He doesn't know how to communicate with you in any way other than face to face. And in case you hadn't noticed, he doesn't have a face anymore."

"But Buck sees him, so how is that possible?" Mitchell demanded.

"Only because Buck doesn't realize he's not supposed to. Children don't know that most people don't believe in ghosts. Heck, he doesn't even know he's a spirit. He just thinks he's—"

"The sad man," Mitch finished for her.

Elvinia's head tilted forward. "Yes, the sad man."

Meagan dropped to the couch and leaned forward. "What does he see, Elvinia? What do you see? *Can* you see Chris?"

"I don't see him with my eyes. I sense him, but in my mind, he doesn't look anything like that picture you have of him in that room. He's in his fatigues, and he's covered in..." She paused, flexing her fingers as she struggled to explain.

"Filth," Mitchell finished for her. "He's covered in layers of grime, sometimes weeks of sand and dust and dirt buildup with no water or way to take a shower. It's like I told you the other day, Meagan. He's lost and alone in Afghanistan."

Meagan dropped her head into her hands and sobbed quietly while Mitch looked on, helpless to do anything but let her cry. After a short round of tears, she wiped her eyes and lifted her chin.

"What I can I do, Elvinia? I don't want him reliving the worst time of his life...or death...or anything that has to do with that hell hole. I want him to be at peace, here in his own country."

The psychic seated herself alongside Meagan and placed a reassuring hand on her shoulder. "I know that, and he'll find his way back, eventually."

Meagan pulled a tissue from the box on the cocktail table and wiped her eyes. "I still don't understand. He's here already. His presence is here, not in the middle-east. Why can't he see where he is?"

"It doesn't work like that. He doesn't exist on the same plane as you or I. He's in the spirit world and he's confused. It's almost as if he's being haunted by his own memories. He doesn't realize he's not among the living anymore. We have to find a way to communicate with him, to let him know that you're okay."

"How? Should I use a Ouija board?"

"Heavens, no! Those things will bring in the kind of spirits you surely don't want to see around here. The way you communicate is to open your heart and your mind up to him. First of all, you have to accept what's happening for what it is. Clear your mind of all doubt. Then concentrate on the message you want to send him." She leaned in close. "There is no magic in this, Meagan, simply the act of controlling your emotions enough to get your message through to him. And no one can do it but you."

Meagan stood and began to pace, waving her arms animatedly as her voice rose in a hysterical rant. "I don't know how to do that! Isn't there some book…some website I can go to that will show me how it's done?"

Elvinia blinked several times before her low chuckle filled the room. "I guess you could always try Googling it…but good luck with that. No telling what kind of crazies you'd get in response." She gathered her purse and stopped on her way toward the door to widen her big black eyes at her. "You probably think I'm nuttier than a fruitcake, but honestly? I'm pretty tame compared to what's out there."

∽

Meagan stood at the door waving as Mitchell's truck pulled out of her drive. When she could no longer see the red of his tail-lights, she turned to study her surroundings.

Alone…She was alone in the place that suddenly seemed much larger than its actual square footage. She walked through the tiny den, wishing Niki and Buck would suddenly appear. No chance of that, since her friend had taken him to a movie at the local mall and wouldn't be home for another hour.

She made herself go into her son's room and lowered carefully onto his bed. With eyes closed, she took a deep breath and held it a few seconds before releasing it slowly into the room. Her heart pounded in her chest as she tried to conjure up some form of communication with the father of her child.

"I'm still so pissed at you, Chris," she whispered into the silence of her son's room. "You promised me you'd come back alive and healthy." Her head lowered, her chin rested on her chest as she remembered the first sight of a flag-draped metal casket holding her fiancé's remains.

She'd waited for hours in a hangar at the tiny airport of a suburb south of Lafayette, Louisiana, determined she'd be there when he arrived. The small plane taxied up to the terminal, stopping within clear view of the hangar's large window. She'd held her breath until the red and white stripes appeared, pushed slowly and carefully through the opening of the plane's cargo hold. Remembered how the breath had rushed out of her, how all air in the room seemed to empty suddenly, becoming a vacuum. A cold, dead vacuum, just as dead as her Marine was, inside that casket.

Until that moment, she'd been able to hold out for some form of hope. Even after the visit from the three men dressed in crisp uniforms. It was as if she'd been holding back for something…some military error…some miracle of mistaken identity…some reason for a phone call saying her Marine was in a stateside hospital, injured and weak, or even comatose.

Any other scenario would have been preferable to having what was left of his body processed in the massive port mortuary of Dover Air Force Base in Delaware.

His death hadn't seemed real until the moment she'd seen physical evidence. She'd made her way slowly through the door of the hangar to approach the casket. After researching the entire process, she'd known the stars of the flag would be placed strategically over his heart. She knew exactly where to lay her hand, and then her head, over the spot. In that moment, he wasn't a Marine being returned to her…but Christopher…her Chris. The only other person in her life who'd mattered until she'd seen that pregnancy test plus sign informing her of the other life she carried.

She'd waited a day before deciding to email him, somehow knowing it was important not to wait for the scheduled Skype call the next week. She wanted him to think twice about taking unnecessary risks while out on patrol.

A single tear made a barely audible *plop* onto her clasped hands.

She'd been too late. And she'd never forgive herself for that. Strange that at the very moment she'd hit the send button, she'd gotten a sick feeling in her stomach, like she knew he'd never see it. Once she'd received word and got the exact time of Christopher's death, she'd done the math to calculate the time difference and discovered it was within minutes of her sending the email.

Fate was a son of a bitch in combat boots.

Meagan looked up at the sound of his picture falling. She stood and approached Buck's dresser, lifted the fallen portrait of his father and brought it close to her chest. Violent flights through the air and into the room's wall had bent and weakened the frame's stand, causing its fall. No mystery there.

"You lied to me, baby." Her voice came out sounding tortured and hoarse. "You left me." She trailed her finger along the inside edge of the frame and winced as a tiny shard of glass caught at the tip of her finger. She pulled it out and squeezed her finger. A perfect dot of dark red blood pooled in its place. Meagan stared at it for a moment before grabbing a tissue from a box on the dresser to dab at it. She dropped it, along with the shard, in the small trash receptacle decorated with dinosaurs and walked to the doorway. Pivoting slowly, she addressed the emptiness of the room.

"If you can show yourself to our son, why the hell can't you show yourself to me?" Her heart pounded out its rhythmic beat as she waited, hoping for some sign, some hint that he knew she was there and wanted to communicate with her. Greeted with the room's silence, she turned away, feeling empty and alone.

The familiar ring tone of Train's "Hey Soul Sister" had her running for her phone. After a quick swipe of her thumb, she answered. "Hey, Nik, what's up? Is my son driving you crazy yet?" Her friend's sigh had her immediately on guard. "What's wrong?"

"First of all, he's all right, Meggie."

"Oh shit…"

CHAPTER 13
Broken Bones, Bald Tires,
and Blood Money

Meagan tore a check from the register and handed it across the desk to the woman seated opposite from her, noticing her nametag for the first time.

Shanna May's fingers flew across the keyboard and soon she was handing her a printed receipt. "We'll file this and if your deductible is all or partially paid you'll get a reimbursement check from us."

Meagan forced a smile from lips that hadn't lost their tightness since Niki's ominous phone call an hour earlier. "Yes ma'am…thank you, ma'am." *That's a hundred bucks I'll never see again.*

She turned, and went to meet Niki, who sat waiting with Buck, his left arm braced and in a sling.

"Hey Buckaroo…how you feeling?" She leaned over to kiss his forehead, smoothing his hair back out of habit.

He looked up at her, his eyes big and round. "M'okay Mom. Can we hab ice cream?"

"It's on me!" Niki insisted. "It's the least I can do for breaking your child's arm."

Meagan touched her finger to Buck's nose. "It's have…not hab, little man. And I don't see why not." She stood and hugged her friend tightly. "It was an accident, Nik. I don't want to hear any talk like that again."

"But he was in my care and I feel like the world's worst friend-slash-babysitter."

Buck grinned up from the wheel chair they'd seated him in. "Boys'll be boys, Aunt Nik. It's not your fault. I asked you to spin fast. I shoulda held on."

"Well, it won't happen again, Buckaroo." Niki wiped a residual tear from one eye. "Your pleas will fall on deaf ears from here on out."

"Huh?" He squinted up at her.

Her own burst of laughter took Meagan by surprise. "Never mind, son. Let's go get some ice cream."

They'd just left the Sonic when Meagan pushed the speaker button on her ringing phone. "We just left you and you're right behind me. What now, Nik?"

"God, I hate to be the bearer of more bad news, but you've got a low tire, Meg. Really low."

Meg released a frustrated groan. "Of course I do. I couldn't possibly expect something pleasant to counteract the first part of this day, could I?" She released a long slow breath to calm her nerves. "Pulling over now to check it."

She found a spot wide enough to get her off the road and pulled to a stop. "Hang on Buck, mama needs to check the tires." She stepped out and saw it immediately...the left front tire was noticeably low on air. Squatting to take a closer look, it didn't take long to find the culprit.

Niki pulled up behind her and approached her cautiously. "Can you tell what the problem is?"

Meagan grunted as she stood up and faced her friend. "I picked up a nail somewhere. It's okay. I've got a spare."

"You need me to call someone to change it for you?"

"Nah, I can change a flat. Just take Buck home for me and I'll meet you soon."

Within a few minutes, they transferred Buck to Niki's car and Meagan stood waving them off. She popped her trunk and pulled back the heavy liner to reveal her spare. Closer examination had her groaning in disappointment at the significant signs of wear.

Exhausted and anxious to be back with her son, she talked herself out of calling someone to help her. Instead, she got busy loosening lug nuts then jacked up the car to change the tire. When she was nearly done, a state police car pulled up in front of her. The female officer got out of the car and approached, asking if she needed help.

She waved off the officer. "Thanks, but I'm almost finished."

The officer, a Lt. Kerrie Pearce, walked over to inspect the scene. "That spare looks pretty bad, ma'am."

"Yes ma'am, I just noticed that."

Lt. Pearce alked around the car and met up with her again. "It looks like you need to spring for a whole new set."

Meagan tightened the last lug nut the way Chris had taught her to and jacked down the car. "I'll have to buy them two at a time. I just dropped a small fortune at the ER for my son's broken arm. Had my friend take him on home so I could change this one."

The officer sucked in her breath. "Ew, how'd that happen?"

"He fell off the merry-go-round."

The officer's eyes widened. "At City Park? One of my co-workers witnessed it. He said the baby-sitter freaked out but the kid barely cried at all."

Meagan smiled grimly. "Yep, she'd taken him to the movies, and said he was so good when he asked to go to the park she couldn't turn him down. Niki was still pretty freaked out at the ER, but Buck never made a peep. Just like his daddy," she added in a low whisper.

"His dad around much?" At Meagan's curious gaze, Officer Pearce shook her head apologetically. "Sorry, I'm a cop...I'm used to asking questions."

"Buck's dad was killed in Afghanistan before he was born. My friend watches my son for me when I'm at work and studying. Poor thing feels so guilty even though I told her it wasn't her fault."

The cop nodded and gave a grunt. "Always something with kids. You got insurance?"

"Yep. Got deductibles too."

"Deductibles suck, don't they?" The officer growled, picking up the flat and placing it in Meagan's trunk.

"Yes ma'am, they surely do. Thanks for the help, Officer Pearce."

The tall, thin woman gave her a nod. "Anytime, and, uh, try to get those tires as soon as you can. I'd sure hate to work an accident scene and discover it's you and your son. You're lucky that tire just went flat instead of blowing out. I've seen some horrific accidents because of blow outs, so I always check people's tires."

"Yes ma'am, I'll have to beg for extra hours at work to afford it now."

"Have you ever thought of donating plasma?" the officer said.

Meagan shook her head slowly. "No, but I donate blood every three months."

"Plasma is different. It takes longer because they have to separate it from the blood before pumping it back into you, but they pay you for it. I think my daughter made $100 her first week of donating and $60 or $70 every week after that. She and her roommate keep the rent paid with it."

"Really?" Meagan heard a distinct 'cha-ching' at the thought of making a quick hundred bucks. "I may have to check it out."

"You should. Years of police work have taught me what to look for and you look like someone who could donate. Trust me, those places are desperate for plasma they can actually use."

The officer took a card and a pen out of her pocket and scribbled something on the back of it before handing it to her. "Here's the address of the place here in Lake Coburn and that's my daughter's name. If you say she referred you, she'll get an extra bit of money on her next donation. If you refer someone else, you'll get extra money."

"Thanks, and I absolutely will." Meagan accepted the card and stared at the address. "I bet I pass this place all the time and never realized it was there. Do you know what they do with the plasma they collect?"

The officer smiled down at her and nodded. "Yes ma'am. They save lives with it."

~

After researching the process, Meagan contacted the plasma center. She found herself there at mid-morning on a Tuesday, tired of waiting and bored after a drawn-out screening process. She sighed in relief when they finally called her name.

"Is it always going to take two hours to get in to donate?" Meagan followed the technician to the back room where four rows of chaise lounge looking beds were set up to accommodate 24 donors at a time.

"Oh no. Your first time we have to give you the complete blood work up and physical. From now on, it's a much quicker process. We'll do a quick screening that takes maybe five or ten minutes then send you back out. Within a few minutes of that, we'll call you back. Go ahead and lay down right here. Don't use your cell phone to make calls, please. It can interfere with the machines."

Within ten minutes, she was hooked-up, and watching one of two flat screens mounted on the wall, each playing the same re-run of *Law and Order*.

"Is this your first time donating, honey?"

Meagan turned toward the voice to her right, seeing a pretty, well-dressed woman who looked to be in her mid-fifties. Blondish hair in a short and stylish cut, nails neatly manicured and clothed in an outfit that more than likely came from a higher end department store like Dillard's. Diamond studs sparkled in her ears and the single ring on her left hand could easily have totaled more than a couple of carats.

"Yes, ma'am, it is. Yours too?"

"Oh no, I started coming here about four years ago, after my husband died."

"Oh, I'm so sorry to hear that."

"Thank you, but we had thirty wonderful years together. The last five we wouldn't have been able to enjoy if it weren't for places like this."

"Really? Was he ill?"

"He had something called Hyperviscosity Syndrome and it made him miserable. Spontaneous bleeding, loss of hearing, dizziness, horrible headaches…the symptoms varied but always made it impossible to enjoy life. Then he began plasmapheresis treatment. In a nutshell, they hooked him up to machines like these, took out the infected plasma and replaced it with healthy plasma."

"And it worked?"

"He got his quality of life back for five years. Then I lost him in a car accident, but I was thankful for the years he got to enjoy life because of donors such as yourself. So, I became one." The woman held out her free left arm. "My name is Marilyn…Marilyn Istre."

"Meagan Hutton…it's so nice to meet you. You know, I lost my fiancé around the same time you lost your husband." The fact that they'd both loved and lost gave them common ground, and soon the two were deep in conversation. Not only did they have their grief in common, but also their home state of Texas. Meagan found herself discussing Buck, broken arms, insurance deductibles and bald tires with the woman who proved to be very likeable, as well as remarkably easy to talk to.

The next forty-five minutes flew by for Meagan and before she knew it, a technician named Shonda Thibodeaux had wrapped her arm with an ace bandage. Within two minutes, she'd punched in a pin number into an ATM and collected a nice little payment of $45.00.

She met up with Marilyn at the appointment book and smiled. "Which days are the best to come in?"

"Tuesdays and Thursdays are good for me. What about you? I'd love it if we were always here at the same time. You're so sweet and easy to talk to."

Meagan searched Thursday's page and filled in the open slot right under her new friend's name. "I guess I'll see you in a couple of days."

They walked out, laughing over the fact that they'd parked next to each other.

"You see? It's fate that we meet!" Marilyn patted her arm. "I know you need to get home to that beautiful son of yours now, but you be sure and get something to eat right away and hydrate honey, hydrate! I'll see you on Thursday."

Megan drove home, feeling somewhat uplifted despite being a quart low. She'd stopped off for a bite from the dollar menu at a drive thru and chugged down a bottle of water.

Once home, she tucked away the bills in an envelope and wrote **TIRE MONEY- $45.00** in neat block letters on the outside before stuffing it far back into the top drawer of her nightstand.

Meagan crawled under the covers and pulled the sheet up around her, tired, but smiling. By Thursday afternoon of the next week, she'd have money for two brand new tires. By the end of the month, she'd be able to pay for three more, including a new spare.

She closed her eyes, thinking of the Officer's warning. It amazed her how one seemingly bad stroke of luck had turned into a possible way to earn a little extra cash. It would be nice not to be such a struggle to put money aside. She drifted off to sleep, feeling a little more capable of providing for her child.

CHAPTER 14
Hovering Marine and a Message

Meagan wiped down the bar with a cleanser and tried to stifle a huge yawn. Of course, her action elicited a comment from Mitch, who'd kept his eagle eye on her ever since she'd given him the reason for the band aid in the crook of her left arm. He hadn't approved of her donating plasma and had offered to buy her tires.

"Rough night?" He sidled easily up beside her.

"No rougher than usual." She clipped her answer, unwilling to give him any more ammunition against her twice-weekly visits to the center. Maybe she did feel a little run down, but the extra money sure was coming in handy. She'd already replaced the two front tires, and felt much better about driving her son around. God knew she felt constant guilt for not being able to provide

Buck with the best of everything. She could only do what she could do.

"You keeping hydrated?" Mitch nodded in approval at the gallon jug of water she pulled from under the counter. "How about food? Are you getting plenty of proteins and carbs?"

"Yes, daddy." She laughed at his furrowed brow. "I didn't realize you were such a worrier."

"I'm not usually, Megs, but you're already neck deep in drama and problems that are beyond your control."

"That's right, but this one thing I can control. It's a way to keep my entire head out of the water, instead of just my nose."

"Well, yeah, but you, weak and washed out from giving plasma, hell, that's just one more reason to worry about you, piled on top of everything else."

"Who asked you to worry about me? I sure as hell don't remember appointing you as my body guard *or* my guardian angel."

He leaned over, his heated, brown eyed gaze boring into hers. "Nobody. But if you did, I'd jump at the chance."

She took a step back, not feeling threatened, so much as tempted by his nearness. The lack of a man in her life had begun to tell on her. The first several months after Chris died, she'd grieved so hard she couldn't possibly think of another man. Once Buck had arrived, she'd been too busy and exhausted to think about sex, or the lack of it. So where did that leave her? With a son nearly four years old who'd never known his own father, cohabitating with the ghost of a dead Marine…and horny as hell. The very least Chris could do is appear in some form of physical manifestation and…and…take *care* of her. The thought parched her and she lifted the gallon jug of water to her lips, hoping to quench her thirst.

"I can't help myself, Meg. I see you with Buck, and…and I just…want to take care of you."

Meagan sucked in water, choked, coughed as water spewed from her nose and mouth. She covered her mouth with a napkin as she coughed and choked even more.

"You all right?" He slapped her on the back then seemed to think better of it. "Raise your arms," he said, reaching for her forearms as she shoved his hands aside.

"Stop! I'm all right. I'm all *right!*" She gave one last cough and took a step away. Away from the headiness of him…his smell, his searching eyes, his brick shit house of a body that made her want to run her hands up and down the length of him and…touch him…touch him all over.

She stared him down, wishing just once he'd back off a little. "You know what, Mitch?"

"I know lots of things, Megs."

She frowned at the nickname he'd only recently insisted on calling her. She refused to tell him that she'd never let anyone get away with calling her that. Her dad used to call her that and it drove her crazy.

"You know far too much about my life."

He shrugged. "We're friends, and now we're co-workers. That's not unusual."

"The things you know about my life are extremely unusual. And the only reason you know so darn much about it is because you're relentlessly nosey." She rinsed out the rag and threw it in the laundry pile with the others before leaning over to grab her purse from under the counter. "I'm outta here."

"I am too, what a coincidence."

She turned at the back door to stare him down.

"What? I was off an hour ago. I hung around to make sure you didn't pass out on the job from the lack of plasma in your body."

She rolled her eyes and pushed the door wide to step out. "I should never have told you."

He followed her out and grunted his disapproval. "I'm sure as hell glad you did. I think it's wise to keep others informed in case something goes wrong, don't you?" His quick stride got him to her car first and he opened her door for her.

"I'm beginning to think it's wiser to keep my mouth shut around you. You're beginning to hover."

"Like a helo?" He extended his arms and imitated the sound of a helicopter.

She gave an adamant shake of her head. "I was thinking more along the lines of a mother hen."

He laughed. "That ain't gonna do. Hell, the least you could have done was compared me to a rooster."

Meagan settled into her car and buckled her seatbelt. "God, I hate roosters."

"I don't know why. Roosters are the alarm clocks of the barnyard."

"Exactly…all that cockiness and 4 a.m. crowing, and they never even produce a darn egg. They're useless animals, unless you butcher them young."

"Without roosters, you wouldn't have chicks."

"True, but they're kind of like bulls. You only need one and then, only when you need new chicks. You're better off being compared to a hen. Much more practical—"

"So you're saying you *need* a hen in your life." He lifted his arms triumphantly. "Thank you for proving my point so eloquently for me."

Meagan started her car and reached over to grab the door handle. "Quit hovering." She pulled the door closed and drove off, leaving him behind.

Several seconds after easing her car out onto the street, she watched in her rear view mirror for the headlights that she knew would appear and follow her all the way home. *Still hovering.* She wondered if he even realized she knew. She caught her own gaze in the mirror and smiled, somehow knowing it wouldn't make a difference to Mitch, one way or the other.

∾

Meagan tiptoed into Buck's room and stood still at the side of his bed for a moment. Other than a slight nip in the air due to a cool front that had passed through, everything seemed normal. She reached over to pass a hand lovingly through her son's thick hair. She kissed his forehead, filling her lungs with the smell of baby shampoo and soaped up little boy. God, she loved this kid. She sat on his bed and rubbed his back through the covers, allowing the warmth of his nearness to comfort her soul and reassure her of his safety.

Now who's hovering? The thought came to her suddenly, and she had to smile.

Light poured in from the hallway, illuminating the area over his bed where his first baby portrait hung on the wall. He was one month old in the portrait and already a beautiful child. But then, Buck had been one of those rare infants, born full-faced and handsome at birth, causing all the delivery room nurses to comment and gush over him. One nurse had called him "Angel Face" insisting it was rare to see a child born into such beauty. All Meagan knew was that she'd adored that child since the moment she'd laid eyes on him. He'd been her sole motivation for getting on with the business of living from the second she'd lost his father.

She stood, arching her aching back and walked to the window to check the seal and lock. Of course, no double paned window could keep a paranormal drop in temperature from chilling the room, but *this*, she could control. After pushing the curtain aside, she stood there staring at the moon, full and bright—bright enough to transform the night sky from the usual pitch black to a hazy gray. "Bright enough out there to play a game of baseball," she muttered lowly, recalling one of Christopher's sayings.

The chill came suddenly and without warning, altering her son's room from cozy comfortable to uncharacteristically icy in a matter of seconds. Hugging her arms and oddly disturbed at her lack of shock at the occurrence, she released a long, slow breath. Within seconds, it turned the window into a foggy blank canvas. She reached up with a closed fist to make an infant's footprint with the side of her hand, just as she'd done when she was a kid. She'd just added the last tiny fingerprint for a little toe, when the lines appeared on the icy pane. Lines that turned into capital letters, then into a single word. N-A-M-E.

The back of her neck prickled as the fine hairs stood up and she gasped, spinning around to make sure she was alone. Buck remained tucked in his bed, still deep in sleep.

"Chris?" The word came out in a hoarse whisper and she cleared her throat. "Chris, are you here?"

She waited, heard her own breath coming out in short puffs in the silent room. "His name is Christopher Buckley…I named him after you, baby. He's our son."

She jumped as his Marine portrait landed face-down on the dresser beside her. Was he angry she'd named their child after him? She stared out into the emptiness of the room. "He's yours, Chris. I swear he is. I emailed you to let you know, but you were on patrol. Your last patrol."

In an instant, the chill dissipated, leaving her shaken and alone in the room, other than her sleeping child. She crumpled to the floor and buried her face in her knees to cry silent tears of deep-boned misery. Surely, this couldn't be the cause of his appearance? Anger…because she'd given Buck his name? He'd always said when they had a son, he wanted to call him Buck.

Meagan allowed herself a few more minutes of tears before wiping her eyes and getting her emotions under control. She pulled herself up and left the room, wishing there was some way to communicate with Chris that didn't leave her feeling so desolate and drained.

She showered quickly and crawled into bed, but deep, restful sleep eluded her. When she did manage to fall asleep, it was fitfully and restless, dreaming of an angry, morose Chris…a complete stranger to her. Waking in a cold sweat, she felt an immediate sense of relief at ridding herself of the dark presence in that dream. Only to be replaced by a deep-seated guilt over feeling that way about a man who had given her nothing but happiness in previous years.

Moving mechanically, she gathered her things and prepared to leave the house, assured that Niki would watch Buck for Meagan's trip to the plasma center. Draping her purse strap over her shoulder, she grabbed her keys and yanked the door open.

Mitch stood before her, looking totally tantalizing in faded jeans and a plain white T-shirt and wearing a Saints cap.

"I was just leaving."

~~

One look at Meagan's face told an entire story of a long, sleepless night. "I see that…where to?" Her tight-lipped response, along with the electronic e-reader sticking out of her purse gave him the answer. "You look too run down to be going to the plasma center. Maybe you should skip today."

"I can't…I need the money."

He stepped aside as she pushed passed him. "I told you, I can loan you any money you need." He grimaced at her irritable reply.

"I'm not your charity case, Mitchell."

"I didn't say you were. But if you need help—"

Niki appeared at the door. "Hold off on the bickering you two. We have a problem. I need to get to work, Meagan. Amanda Lapoint went into labor two weeks early and screwed up everyone's schedules."

Meagan placed her hands on her hips and made a face. "Oh my God, the nerve of that baby messing up our plans!"

A grin appeared on Niki's face. "I know, right?"

Meagan laughed then quickly sobered. "There goes my last chance for a second donation this week. That means I'm out forty-five bucks from this month's promotion."

Niki slapped Mitch on the back. "Maybe Sergeant Major Oorah, here—"

"—That's Master Sergeant Oorah to you, ma'am," he said, touching the brim of his cap.

"Whatever!" Niki waved off his correction. "Maybe Mitch can help us out by watching Buck until you get back from your appointment."

Meagan gave one violent shake of her head. "Absolutely not."

Mitch stepped in front of her, insulted by her dejection. "Why the hell not?"

"Because he's my son and I don't leave him with just anyone." She glared at him, her mouth set and unapologetic.

"Just anyone? You saw how good he and I got along at the park. He's crazy about me."

"You ever babysat before?" she asked. "That's you, the child, and no one else around."

He crossed his arms, amazed at her ability to insult him so easily. "Yes, actually. Sarah trusted me to watch both of her daughters at the same time. And one of 'em even dumped on me." An involuntary shiver passed over him as he fought back a gag at the memory. "God, that was surprisingly awful."

Meagan waved her hand, dramatically. "I rest my case. One poopy diaper and he's scarred for life."

Mitch raised a defiant finger. "That was no ordinary poop. It was *nasty*. I'm talking poop all up her back and down both legs." He shivered, still revolted at the memory. "It was all over...*everything*. But, I managed."

"Put her straight in the tub?" Niki asked, snorting with laughter.

"Nope, took her outside and blasted her with the water hose." He balked at Meagan's look of horror. "What? It was a warm day and she loved it. Besides, by the time I got her out there, I needed a little hosing down myself. I was covered in crap...literally."

Mitch leveled his gaze on Meagan. "I'm assuming I won't run into that situation with Buck."

"No, he's been potty trained for two years." She seemed to consider his offer before giving him a brief nod. "All right, if you're sure you can handle it, you can watch him. Hopefully, I won't be gone over a couple of hours."

～

Meagan hung her keys on the pegboard and draped her purse over the nearest chair back before heading to the fridge for water. After several thirst quenching gulps, Buck's excited shouts and Mitchell's deep laughter, both coming from the back yard, caught her attention. She leaned over the sink just in time to catch a flash of red and yellow jet in front of the kitchen window. She refilled her glass and brought it along as she made her way to the smallish, fenced-in back yard.

"What's going on out here?"

Buck gave his mother a jubilant grin. "Mom! We're flying a aiwo-plane! Mitch bought it and he says I'm a good pilot."

"Are you?" She clapped her hands and leaned over to give him a kiss on his cheek. "I don't doubt it for a second, Buckaroo. Your great grandpa became an airplane pilot when he was a young man."

Buck cocked his head curiously. "I have a gweat gwanpa?"

She nodded. "He passed away a long time ago, but he used to tell me stories when I was little. He was in a war we called World War II."

Buck's mouth dropped open in awe as he stared at her with huge round eyes. "My gweat gwanpa flew aiwo-planes?"

She slipped her hands in her back pockets and stared down at the one thing she'd done right in this world. "He sure did. I've seen pictures of him in his plane. He painted my grandma's name on it—Diana Rose—with a yellow rose beside it. My Paw Paw said it brought him good luck because he flew the same plane for a whole two years and never got shot down."

Buck's face lit up as he contemplated her words. "I'm gonna fly a plane, too," he said, his tone seriously even and calm before running off, hands out and 'flying' around the yard.

She stared after him, still somewhat dazed at the frankness of her son's statement. "I bet you will, Buckaroo." It took a couple of repetitions before she realized Mitch had spoken to her. She turned to see him staring down at her. "What did you say?"

"I asked how long he'd flown…your grandfather, that is."

"Oh, he flew well into his seventies, so over fifty years. He became a crop duster once he made it home. He did that for about thirty years until he finally retired from flying full-time and just ran the business. But he still flew for the enjoyment of it."

"Did your dad follow in his footsteps? Or was he your maternal grandfather?"

"He was my mom's father, and no, there weren't too many women pilots back then. Of the two of my parents, mom probably could have flown. My dad was always terrified of heights. I've always wondered," she said, somewhat wistfully.

"Wondered what?"

"How she'd have turned out if she hadn't been held back by the standards of the day. My mom is a very intelligent woman. I believe she could have done anything she wanted to do, if only she'd been allowed...*encouraged* to spread her wings and..."

"Fly?" Mitch finished for her.

She chuckled. "Yeah, I guess so."

"What's she like, Megs? You never talk about her, or either of your parents." He sat on the long wooden bench at one side of the tiny patio and patted the seat next to him.

She settled in beside him and shrugged. "She's mom—always very sober and serious. Or she was when I was there. I care barely picture her with a smile on her face, much less laughing. She saved that for rare occasions, like when they had some of their church friends over."

"How about your dad?"

Meagan snorted with disgust. "God, he was even worse. Stern, unyielding, unforgiving…and oh, so full of holier-than-thou-self-righteousness. I'm sure he believes he'll be seated at the right hand of God when he goes."

Laughter rumbled from deep in Mitchell's chest. "Um…I think that seat's already taken."

She shot him a humorous look and winked. "But won't dad be surprised when *he* figures it out? It almost makes me wish I could be there to see that. But, according to him, we won't be in the same place."

Mitch placed a comforting hand on her shoulder. "I'm sure he's right about that, but not for the same reasons. He's one of those people who *thinks* he's on the right track, but won't find out until it's too late that there is only one judge…and he ain't it."

"Judge not, lest thee be judged," she whispered.

"You got that right."

She watched Buck. "You know, for years I had this weird feeling about the two of them. To me, Mom acted as though my father held something over her head. Like he used it to keep her in line."

Mitchell cocked his head to one side. "You think you'll ever find out?"

"I can't be certain of course, but I'm doubtful." She looked at her watch, grimacing at the amount of her day already gone. "Buck and I have some shopping to do before I leave for work tonight, Mitch."

He stood, arching his long back with a low groan. "I can take a hint. I'm going." He headed toward Buck and offered his hand. "See you later Buck, my man. Mom's chasing me off for the rest of the day so you can go shopping."

Buck's face crumpled in disappointment. "Oh man, I don't want to go shopping! That's girl stuff."

Meagan lifted one brow at her son. "Really? Here I thought you were looking forward to picking out your own Halloween costume this year. At least that's what you told me yesterday, and every day for the past week. But if you don't want to go..." She laughed as Buck's entire face lit up. "That's what I thought. Now thank Mr. Mitch for watching you."

The boy turned a sheepish look toward Mitch. "Bye Mitch, and thanks for bwinging the aiwo-plane to play with me." He gave it one last adoring look before offering it back to Mitch.

"I'll tell you what, Buckaroo. If you promise not to fly this without your co-pilot…that's me…I'll leave it here with you. You have to take excellent care of it. Keep it safe in the hangar, okay?"

Buck's eyes grew large and quizzical. "I gotta put it on a hanger?"

Meagan smothered a laugh while Mitch came up with a suitable answer.

"Just keep it in the box, Buck. That'll be good enough."

The child gave him a jubilant nod before running inside with the plane.

Meagan stood up, adjusting the bandage on her arm. "Thanks for watching him for me."

"It's been my pleasure, Megs. I guess I'll see you tonight at the club?"

Just for a second his statement threw her off.

"I'm on schedule to work, too," he added.

"Oh! I guess I'm still trying to get used to that," she said, feeling somewhat flustered as heat infused her face. She glanced up into his laughing eyes, knowing he enjoyed every second of her discomfort. "Oh, just shut up for once, Marine…and goodbye!"

"Later, Megs."

"And quit calling me that!" she called out to his broad, straight back and tight, jean-covered ass.

He turned at the gate, his voice a low, sexy growl. "Quit staring at my ass and I'll think about it."

CHAPTER 15
Big Needles and Bigger Promises

Meagan finished her third glass of water for the night and dabbed discreetly at her mouth. She tried, unsuccessfully, to stifle yet another yawn, frowning as she caught Mitchell's scrutinizing gaze on her. She turned away to hand a customer two frosty bottles of beer. Before she could recover, Mitch was whispering in her ear, low and disapproving, but still managing to raise the hair on the back of her neck in anticipation.

"Every time you donate plasma, you can barely keep your eyes opened during work. I know your school work must be suffering also."

"I'm fine, and I have a 3.98 GPA, thank you very much."

"You're not fine. I've been watching, you know," he growled.

"No kidding? I had no idea!" She couldn't suppress the sarcasm in her comeback.

"It's not necessary, Megs. You have a responsibility to keep your strength up for Buck."

She rounded on him, cutting off his reply. "Don't you *dare* talk to me about responsibilities," she hissed. "I know full well what my responsibilities are. Like keeping my child clothed, fed properly, keeping a roof over his head and decent tires on the vehicle I have to drive him around in."

"All I'm saying is, I want to help."

"I don't *need* your help. I don't *want* your help. Why can't you understand that?"

∽

God, but the woman was stubborn! Usually he bordered somewhere between anger and admiration for her hard-headed tenacity. Tonight, seeing her fight off her exhaustion, his anger, fuelled by concern for her, had the definite advantage.

He got nose to nose with her, determined to make her see his point. "And why can't you understand that I don't want to see you collapsing from weakness or dehydration on top of everything else? No friend would want to see that. It's called concern, Meagan. I know you aren't a charity case, but everyone can use a helping hand now and then. Let me give you what you'd be making in plasma donations."

Her face grew pensive, as she seemed to consider his offer. Finally she spoke, her voice containing a hint of mischief.

"You really want to help me that bad?"

He nodded, praying he'd found a chink in her armor. "I certainly do."

"Meet me at my place Tuesday morning at 7:30 a.m." She lifted her hand to stop him from asking questions. "That's it, Marine. If you don't show up, I don't ever want to hear another word about this. I'm serious!"

He nodded. "I'll be there."

∽

Accustomed to early rising and little sleep, Mitch waited in his truck for fifteen minutes before giving her front door a few tentative raps on Tuesday morning.

She pulled it open quickly, greeting him with a severity he didn't know she possessed.

"I'll allow you to help me *financially* under one condition."

He reached out, palms up and breathed a sigh of relief. "Finally! What's the condition? I'm game, no matter what it is."

"That's good to know." Her mouth curled in a twisted grin. "I'll accept money from you only if you've earned it donating plasma."

His hands lifted in protest. "Hold it! I don't think I heard you correctly."

"I'm sure you did. You come with me, list me as a referral so I can get extra money, donate, and I'll accept whatever you're paid, if you still want me to."

He pondered her resolution, thinking he was surely creative enough to find a way out of it before it happened. No way would he actually allow strangers to shove large needles up his arms to drain the fluids out of him. "All right. You've got a deal."

She nodded and adjusted her purse strap. "Good, are you ready to go? I hope you ate a good sized breakfast."

Mitch swallowed the lump that suddenly formed in his throat. "You mean, right now?"

"Sure. You can ride over there with me. It'll take longer your first time but I'm willing to wait."

He paused, studying the look on her face. "You don't think I'll do it, do you?"

She shrugged lightly. "Not everybody can take needles, Mitch."

"I'm a Marine, Megs. I laugh in the face of adversity." *Son of a bitch, he hated MoFo needles.*

She chuckled. "All I'm saying is that I've seen bigger men than you brought to their knees."

Her condescending tone gave him a steel resolve. He gave his head a brief shake. "And I'm about to show you that there's a big difference between a man and a Marine, Megs. Let's go."

～

"Oh man." Mitchell gulped when he saw the size of the needle.

"Second thoughts?"

Meagan's voice, jovial and teasing, came to him from the cot on his immediate right. He turned to her, determined to banish the amusedly smug look from her face. "Hell, no. I've waited two hours and I'm not leaving here without seeing this thing through."

The technician, Shonda, grinned as she leaned over his arm with the larger than normal needle. "Small stick…"

Mitch tensed, hissing lowly through his clamped jaw.

"All right, it's over," she said.

He'd just forced himself to take a relaxing breath when Meagan's voice reached him again.

"You can open your eyes now, Mr. Big Bad Marine."

He cracked open one eye, and the other, only then realizing they'd both been squeezed shut.

"Piece of cake," he whispered, releasing a slow breath as Shonda got him taped up and flowing.

"When the blood pressure cuff is tight on your arm, pump your hand quickly. When it stops, quit pumping your hand and rest it. It usually takes forty-five minutes to an hour to complete the cycle."

Mitch stared hard at the clear plastic tubing, now tinted a dark red from his own blood beginning the first loop from his body. He turned his head away from the sight, swallowing the taste of fresh bile rising in his throat. "I can do this."

"What was that?"

He caught Meagan giving him a curious gaze. "Nothing. I'm fine."

"Are you sure? Because you have to let them know if you start to feel like you're going to—"

"I'm fine!" Before he could apologize for his sharp tone, he caught the twinkle of amusement in her eyes. A long, slow growl accompanied his release of breath. He settled back on his cot, forcing himself to relax and do this thing. He concentrated on the wall-hung flat screen playing a *Bones* rerun and he concentrated on getting into the storyline. It seemed to work, because before he knew it, he'd filled his plastic container with the yellowish liquid and the tech was wrapping his arm with a stretchy bandage.

"Drink lots of water to rehydrate…stay away from caffeine and take it easy for the next few hours. And here's your PIN to collect. The ATM is in that booth. If you have any problems at all, don't hesitate to call us. You have to wait forty-eight hours to donate again and you can't donate more than twice in seven days."

After collecting his $45 bucks from the ATM, he walked to the front where Meagan sat, patiently waiting for him. She popped up from her chair and approached.

"You're not feeling faint, are you, Marine?" The edges of her mouth turned up in a faint smirk.

"Of course not," he lied, making a mental note to eat a larger meal before making his next donation…like there'd *be* another donation. After all, she wouldn't know if he actually donated or not, would she?

"I normally try to get here early on Tuesdays and Thursdays because Niki's home those mornings to watch Buck. You can put your name right below mine."

"I don't think that's a great time for me, Megs. I'll just find another time slot." He began flipping through pages, looking for a section where her name was nowhere to be found, when her voice came to him, soft and lyrical, but filled with unmistakable challenge.

"However, I will only accept money from the donations scheduled the same time as mine." She retreated a few spaces as he leveled a hard gaze on her. "Just saying."

Mitch turned away, trying hard not to curse under his breath. He flipped through the book until he found her name in the 8:00 a.m. Thursday spot. He placed his sticker just under hers and turned to her. "Let's go eat. I'm buying." He stuck his finger in her face as she started to protest. "If you know what's good for you, you won't say another word!"

～

Mitchell washed down the last bite of his burger with a gulp of sweet tea. He stretched his back in the red padded booth across the table from Meagan. Leaning to one side, he pulled three folded bills, two twenties and a five, from the front pocket of his jeans and held them out to her. "Will this give you enough to buy the last two tires for your car?"

She pulled them from his fingertips and stuffed them into her wallet. "Oh, I had those put on yesterday."

"Uh…then why the hell are you still doing this?"

"Savings account," she said. "I told you a year's worth of donations comes out to almost $2500.00. That's a tidy little sum for emergency situations. For the sake of my son, I can't afford to turn my nose up at that that kind of money. Besides, I like the idea that I'm helping. I'd like to think that, even if I didn't need the money, I'd still give just for the sake of improving someone's life."

He nodded. "Very noble of you, but remember that amount of money will be doubled from my own donations." He strained to hear something she mumbled just under her breath. "Sorry, I didn't quite catch that."

"Nothing." She pursed her lips.

"Tell me."

"No."

"I'm not leaving until you do."

"I drove here so I can leave anytime I want to." She gathered her purse and got up to leave.

Mitch deposited their trash in the receptacle and pushed the door open for her, deciding it would be best to stick close. He slipped into the front seat beside her.

"If you don't tell me what you said under your breath I'm going to stay at your house all afternoon."

"Good. Buck will keep you busy enough so that I can get some studying done."

"I will never stop bothering you about it. I'll ask DJ Silver to announce the question tonight at the club and you'll never get a minute's peace because then everyone will be asking you."

She stared at him for a second before pulling her attention back to her driving. "You'd do that too, wouldn't you?"

"Damn straight I would."

She gave him a final nod. "Okay, Curious George, word for word, what I said was, 'You won't be around that long'." His silence must have made her think he needed help putting the words into the right context. "You know, you said something about your donation money being added to mi—"

"—I know what I said. And I know what you meant." He turned to stare at her profile. "But you're wrong."

"Pfft! I don't think so, Marine."

"Oh I know so. As a matter of fact, you have never been so wrong in your entire life." A benefit of being a passenger was that he could stare at her profile the entire drive home. He'd take that trade-off any day. Nothing wrong with having a beautiful lady chauffeur him around. He watched the slow rise of blush as it pinked her skin from the base of her collarbone all the way to the tops of cheekbones, and even farther than that. He grinned, wondering how he'd never noticed before how red her ears turned when she blushed. Maybe he hadn't made her blush before. His mind rolled into overdrive, thinking of all the ways he'd like to make it happen…over and over again.

Mitchell's chest rumbled with laughter as his silent meanderings succeeded in making her steal a single, quick, uncomfortable glance in his direction. "What's so darn funny?"

"You are, Megs. For thinking you'll ever be rid of me."

CHAPTER 16
The New Normal

Niki met them at the door, trying to console a still sniffling Buck. "We've had an *incident*."

Meagan's stiffened posture at her friend's comment had Mitch wondering if she'd used some kind of code for something serious.

She lifted her son carefully from Niki's arms. "Hey buddy. What happened?"

"My plane is bwoken, Mom." Buck wiped his tear-streaked cheeks, before burying his face in his mother's neck.

Mitch smiled, at once sad for the boy but happy that he thought so much of his gift. "Aw Buckaroo, don't cry. I'll get you another plane. Toys break when kids play with them. It's no big deal."

Meagan shot him an appreciative glance before heading inside with her son. "You see? Don't cry, little man," she crooned softly as she rubbed his back in slow comforting circles.

Buck's head popped up unexpectedly. "I didn't bwake it, Mitch. I put it in the hangah just like you said. But when I woke up, it was all messed up."

Mitch patted the boy's head comfortingly. "How about if I take a look at it for you, okay? I bet I can fix it." With the kid's hopeful gaze fixed on him, he was determined not to fail him. Several seconds later, he realized that no amount of glue or tape...not even man's most versatile friend, duct tape, could repair the damage to the toy plane.

"Can you fix it?"

Mitch smiled at the small face lined with worry, more determined than ever not to disappoint him.

"Sure I can. I'll have to take it home, but I can fix it right up for you."

Buck scooted down Meagan's torso to run over and throw his arms around Mitchell's legs. "Thanks Mitch! You're my best fwend!"

Mitch cradled the boy's head in one hand and met Meagan's wide-eyed gaze just as a blast of cold air hit him in the face. "Glad to do it, Buck. That's what buddies do. Now you go on with Niki while your mom and I have a talk." He practically pushed Buck out the door so he could close it behind him.

"He's here, isn't he?"

Meagan nodded and answered, her words accompanying a puff of icy vaporized air. "Yes."

Mitch walked to the center of the room to face off with the spirit of Meagan's dead fiancé. "Let's talk man to man, Chris…or if you prefer, Marine to Marine."

"Mitch, no—"

His hand shot out to stop Meagan's protest. "It's okay, Megs. I can see where he's coming from. He's lost everything in the world that's important to him and if he wasn't dead already, that in itself would be enough to kill a good man. Chris was a very good man, but let's face reality, Megs. Even good men get angry, especially when they feel helpless…right, Marine?"

Mitchell threw his arm protectively around Meagan as she gasped at the resounding crack of PFC Christopher Martin's portrait smashing into the opposite wall.

"Meagan, you need to leave the room. PFC Martin and I need to exchange some info." He opened the door and pushed her gently out, closing it on her hesitant protests. Turning his attention to the center of the room, he squared his shoulders and faced off with the frustrated spirit of Chris Martin.

"I know you're angry. I know you're frustrated. I know you're sad at what you missed out on. But please, Buck's a great kid and Meagan's doing a fantastic job raising him. Please don't take it out on him or his mother. He's *your* kid, and nothing will ever change that. Meagan loved you—still—loves you to this day. But she can't move on, Chris. Neither of them will ever be able to move on as long as you're here, angry and frustrated."

He paced the room trying to choose his words wisely. "You've seen Meagan in her best moments, her happiest days with you. Is that what you see in her now? Or do you see the tension, the fear you've single-handedly caused in her life?"

Mitch passed his hand through his thick hair and released a long, drawn out sigh, before turning his attention back to the icy center of the room. "It's time to Marine up, Private First Class Martin. It's time to prove you're more than just a man. You're a Marine. A Marine would never put the two people he loves through this kind of hell. It's time to let them, go, Chris. Just let them go."

He turned as the door flew open, accompanied by Meagan's anguished cry.

"Noooo!" She ran to Mitch and slapped him hard on the face. "You have no right to make that decision! You need to leave—now."

Mitch caught her hands as she tried to slap him again. He stared her down as he began to put all the pieces together. "It's you, Meagan. You're the one who won't let go. It's your conflicted emotions throwing off the balance here. The balance between life and death…peace and dissension…good feelings and bad!"

"You don't know what you're talking about." She turned her back on him. "And you have no right to be here, in the middle of this. You have no part in this!"

"Don't I?"

She spun around to face him. "No, you *don't*."

"If that were true, neither you nor Christopher's ghost or spirit or whatever the hell you want to call it, would be feeling so conflicted right now. It's not him that needs to Marine up…it's you, Meagan. *And* you need to do it before you cause permanent psychological damage to your son."

Her arm shot up, finger pointed to the open door. "Get out. Now."

Mitch took a step back, then another, before heading out the door, but then turned to face her once more.

"You need to let him go, Meagan, so you and Buck can have a normal life together. This…" He lifted his arms to encompass the room. "This isn't normal…under any circumstances, and you damn well know it."

Tight-jawed and filled with his own frustrated anger, he paused just long enough to address Niki. "Tell Buck I'll keep the plane at my place from now on, but I'll bring it by for him to play with it." She gave him a brief nod before he stormed angrily out the front door.

~

Meagan shut her eyes tightly against the sound of Mitchell's truck starting and peeling out of her driveway.

"Mom?"

She spun around to find her son standing in the doorway, Niki's hands resting lightly on his shoulders.

She wiped at the corner of her eyes with her fingertips. "Yeah, buddy?"

"Whewe's Mitch? Did he go home to fix my plane?"

She knelt in front of her son, ruffled her fingers through his dark hair. "Uh, yep. I'm pretty sure that's where he went."

"Is he coming back?"

Meagan shifted her gaze from her son to Niki, then back to Buck. "Mm, I think so, sweetie."

"'Cuz it sounded like you didn't want him to. But I like Mitch, Mom, and I want him to come back." He pulled away from her and stared at the spot on his dresser where the toy plane had been sitting in its box. "Why didn't he want me to have it?"

"Who? Mitch? He does want you to have the plane, that's why he's going to fix it for you."

Buck gave his dark head a shake. "No. The sad man didn't want me to have it, but I don't know why." He turned to face his mother again. "I don't think the sad man likes Mitch vewy much. And that makes *me* kinda sad." He headed out of his room, pausing just long enough to grab his pterodactyl kite.

"My grandmother had a saying: From a child's mouth, wisdom rings as clearly as a bell on a still winter's day." Niki cracked a huge grin at Meagan, obviously hoping to lighten the mood. "She did that...put her personal stamp on several bible readings. Guess she figured if she was going to plagiarize, she may as well plagiarize the best."

Meagan dropped exhaustedly onto Buck's bed and hid her face in her hands. "Niki, what have I done?" She felt her friend sit beside her and shifted over to make room for her.

"Well, from what I see you haven't done much of anything except to try to keep the love of your life alive in some fashion. But you're a big girl, Meg. You're smart enough to realize there is no possible future with a dead man." Niki's eyes glanced to the center of the room. "Sorry bro, I hate to be the one to point this out to you, but you're not much good to her dead. If you're sticking around to send some kind of important message, maybe you should just do it and be on your way—"

"Niki!"

"—before they put us all away for conversing with ghosts!" She gave a nervous laugh as she faced Meagan again. "It's true Meg. Just look at us trying to communicate with a dead man, like this is something people do every day. We've become so desensitized by everything that's been happening that we don't see how weird it is!"

"Nik, calm down."

"No, Meggie. We're too calm about this already. What's next, setting a place at the table for your dead fiancé? Won't the kids at pre-k have a field day with *that* when Buck starts up next year? Nothing says *outsider* quite like having your own resident ghost-dad. We may as well start giving him wedgies, and stuffing him in lockers right now, for chrissakes!"

The two women stood there staring each other down, in a veritable female face-off. They jumped, breaking eye contact at the sound of Chris's frame sliding flat on its back.

Meagan picked it up, examined it carefully. "I think the easel part has had it. I guess it's time for another frame."

Niki approached cautiously to stand beside her. "We may need to go online to find something super heavy duty—"

"—with some kind of safety glass—"

"—or Plexiglas—"

"—or *no* glass at all." Meagan caught Niki's gaze on her, couldn't keep from cracking a grin at her friend. The grin proved to be contagious and soon they'd both burst into hysterical laughter.

Niki dabbed impatiently at her tears as she struggled to catch her breath. "Oh God," she gasped. "We're 100% certifiable, Meg!" Two deep breaths and one long sigh later, she looked over at her friend. "I'm sorry I yelled at you."

Meagan lifted her hand. "Everything you said was the absolute truth, Nik. You were right to yell at me."

"I was, wasn't I?"

Meagan caught the hint of laughter in her friend's reply. "You're such a bitch."

"Hey, it takes one to know one, bitchette."

Meagan collapsed alongside Niki on top of Buck's bed, both overtaken by another fit of giggles.

Meagan's hand flew to her chest as she coughed, struggling to catch her breath. "Oh God, it feels good to laugh again."

"We used to laugh all the time. Buckaroo was always making us laugh at some thing or another. His adorable belly laughs used to crack me up."

"And that funny little butt-scoot thing he did before he could walk," Meagan added.

"His first steps, his first words—"

"—how he mispronounced breakfast..." Meagan glanced over at Niki before they both blurted out the same word.

"Bleck-fuck!"

They fell back on the bed, chortling gleefully again.

Buck entered the room carrying his kite. "Hey, what's goin' on in hewe? Y'all aw messin' up my bed!"

Meagan jumped up, followed by Niki. "Yes sir, you are correct, but we'll fix it, won't we Nik?"

"You betcha, Captain Buck," she said, helping Meagan to smooth the covers neatly back into place.

Buck placed his kite back in its designated spot on the toy shelf and left the room, casting a last warning look at the two women.

"Wow, is he bossy, or what?"

"Neat freak, just like his daddy," Meagan stated wistfully before catching her friend's gaze on her again. "Nik, can you call Elvinia back over here for me? The sooner the better."

Niki pulled her phone from the pocket of her jeans and punched in the contact name. Putting the phone on speaker, they waited through three rings before the woman answered. Niki placed a comforting hand on her friend's arm as Meagan spoke to the psychic.

"Elvinia, this is Meagan Hutton. Would it be possible for you to come over?"

Elvinia's rich voice chuckled through the speaker. *"I surely can, Miss Meagan. What time is good for you?"*

"Actually, as soon as you can would be good."

"Ahhh...you ready to choose then?" Elvinia crooned.

"Choose? Choose what?" Meagan didn't quite know what choice she referred to.

"To choose the living over the dead, girl—flesh and blood over the ghost of a memory."

"O-oh!" she stammered as Niki's right brow rose in amusement. "I-I-d-don't..." Her voice trailed off as she sighed. "Just come over as soon as you can, please." She felt the heat of her blush clear down to the roots of her hair follicles as Elvinia's chuckle reached her.

"I'm on my way, child."

CHAPTER 17
Disappointments and Decisions

"Mommy, somebody's at the door!"

Buck's call from the living room startled Meagan as she stole a quick glance at her watch. It had only been ten minutes since she'd spoken to Elvinia. She hurried to the front door, stepping over Buck as he lay sprawled out on the floor watching his *Puss in Boots* video for the hundredth time. "Back up, Buck, you're entirely too close to that screen. You'll ruin your eyes." She garnered a giggle from her son by pulling him back by the legs.

She smiled to herself, remembering how her mother had spoken those same words to her a countless number of times over the years. She'd been extremely close to her mother. How had they managed to grow so far apart? Awash in the memories, she opened the door to Elvinia, standing as tall and regal as ever. Before she could speak, Elvinia's voice reached her.

"Oh, Miss Meagan! She'll be a part of your life again. Don't worry."

Meagan stepped aside to let her enter but the woman stood there. "Who will?"

"Your mother, dear. You were just thinking about her, weren't you? And you were filled with such melancholy, but there's no need for that. She will come back into your life when you need her the most."

Meagan shook off her shock and snorted lowly. "It's a little late for that, isn't it? I've already experienced the two most devastating things to happen without my parents' support. Losing my fiancé and raising a child alone. Not to mention *this*." She raised her arms for emphasis.

Elvinia reached out to place her large, brown hands on Meagan's cheek and closed her eyes. When she opened them, they had taken on an aura of foreboding. "God finds ways to make us strong, Meagan. Sometimes we don't like his ways, but he always has good reason for it. Your strength has been tempered, tough as steel, for a difficult time in your near future. It *will* get you through this time."

Meagan's eyes narrowed. "You must have gotten your wires crossed somewhere along the line. My mother never wants to see me again."

Elvinia dropped her hand to give Meagan's arm a gentle pat. "Things aren't always as they seem." She straightened and lowered her gaze to where Buck had hidden himself behind his mother. "Who do we have here?" She squatted, her knees popping and creaking like an antique rocker as she lowered herself to his level.

"This is my son, Buck. Say hello to Ms. Elvinia, Buck."

He stepped out from behind his mom and lifted his hand in greeting. "Hi, I'm Buck." He held up four fingers on one hand. "I'm gonna be this many soon."

Elvinia grinned broadly, her two gold teeth practically glowing in her dazzling white smile. "Four years old, huh? That's an important age, young man. But then, every age is important, so don't waste any of them."

Meagan watched as her son reached out his hand to touch the smooth, cocoa brown skin of Elvinia's face. His gaze focused on her mouth.

"I like your magic teef, Ms. Evina."

Meagan groaned out an apology as the large woman straightened with a chuckle. "I'm sorry

Elvinia. I believe he's thinking of the golden eggs on the video he's watching."

"Golden eggs and gold teeth…Why, of course! That makes all the sense in the world to me, Buck!" She turned to Meagan with a question. "Would it be okay if I brought my little dog inside? I just picked him up from the vet and I hate to pile more separation anxiety on him. No fleas, I promise."

"Sure, bring him on in." She and Buck watched as Elvinia went to her van and returned, carrying the most adorable white puffball she'd ever seen.

"Oh, my goodness, he is beautiful!" Meagan breathed.

Buck's huge blue eyes sparkled with wonder at the puppy. "What's his name?"

"His name is Samurai Sam, but I call him Sammy, for short. He's a handsome little devil, isn't he?"

"He looks like a baby polar bear, Elvinia. What breed is he?"

"Sammy, like both his parents, is a miniature American Eskimo. I'm quite partial to them. They make wonderful companion dogs and pets for children. This is my second Eskie. My last one, a female named Sophie, lived for seventeen years." She placed him in Buck's arms. "You think you could watch Sammy for me while your mom and I take care of some business, little man?"

"Yeah! Oh, mom, he's so soft." Buck sat on the floor with the puppy, breaking into a fit of giggles as Sammy's tiny pink tongue darted non-stop to lick the boy's face.

Elvinia placed her hand on Meagan's shoulder and turned her toward the bedroom. "Now, let's get down to the business of the living and the dead, shall we?" She marched Meagan into Buck's room and closed the door behind them.

"I'm sensing a change in you, Meagan. Have you made your choice?"

Meagan stared at the portrait of the Marine who'd dominated her thoughts for nearly ten years of her life. She couldn't remember a single day of junior high or high school that she hadn't loved him. "He's gone, and he's not coming back, in any form. Th-this-thing, this situation, whatever it is, is not a viable option. I need to get down to the bottom of it so I can end it, for good. I don't want to live like this anymore, tethered to a past I can't change."

Elvinia nodded, obviously pleased with her comment. "Good, you've chosen the living over the dead. That's the state of mind you didn't possess during my previous visit. Now you're ready to ask him."

"Ask him what?"

"What message he has for you, but you need to be willing to listen. Just be still and really listen. You *will* hear it." She walked to the door. "I'll be right outside if you need me."

Meagan grabbed at her arm. "But, I thought you could do it for me!"

"I could, but what good would that do? I didn't know the boy nor the man he grew into. What could he possibly have to tell me? Don't worry, you'll figure it out." She stepped into the hallway and pulled the door shut behind her.

Meagan turned to stare into the room, feeling somewhat like a thirteen-year-old girl trying to break up with her first boyfriend. She smiled at the thought, realizing that she had done that before. Only once, and only when she realized she was crazy about Chris.

She walked over to his portrait, and picked it up, examining the battered frame. She flipped it over and spun the tabs holding the back in place, then removed the portrait. Returning to Buck's bed, she curled up on top of the spread and stared at the picture.

"Christopher." Her mouth quivered as she struggled to hold back threatening tears. "Do you have any idea how difficult it's going to be for me to let you go?" A tear traveled across the bridge of her nose to trail its way across the opposite cheek. Shrill puppy barks, accompanied by Buck's high-pitched squeals of laughter came to her from two rooms over, mingled with words spoken in Elvinia's low voice. "But I have to, for Buck's sake. You see that, don't you?"

She wiped frantically at the fresh onslaught of tears tracking down her face to fall freely upon the brightly patterned bedspread.

"He's such a good little man, Chris, and he's got so many of your qualities. He's going to be super organized and neat, just like you. I already see that."

She passed a hand lovingly over the face in the portrait. "When I close my eyes I used to see you, before the Marines, when it was just you and me in our little apartment. Remember? When we had so little, but loved each other so much? But now, all I can see is this picture of you. In your dress blues with your high and tight, the brim of your cover pulled low over your brow…no smile…looking so stern and serious." She choked back a soft sob.

"That's not the Chris I want to remember, baby. This isn't the real you, and as sad as that makes me, it's still better than the 'sad man'. If we don't stop this, that's the only way your son will see you."

With a new resolve, she wiped her eyes and sat up, determined to change things for Buck's sake. "It's not fair, Chris, not to him and not to you. It sucks that the two of you never met. It sucks that I didn't even get to tell you about him, to hear the joy in your voice, the pride as you told all your friends, 'Hey, guys! I'm gonna be a daddy!' I *know* you would have been thrilled...I know it."

She pushed herself off the bed and stood, holding the photo to her chest. "But what will suck the worst is if Buck has to grow up without a father. I mean, Niki and I do our best, but it's not the same." She bit her lip to keep it from quivering, knowing her time with him was ending. "He's such a good kid, Chris. He deserves so much more than two mothering women as role models. He deserves a dad in his life. One who can teach him how to hit a ball, catch a fly, or throw a decent spiral...God knows I can't do those things."

She wiped her eyes with the back of her hand. "But somewhere in this world, there's a man who might be willing to do that, and to love him like his own. I may not find one right away. I may have to kiss a few frogs first, but I need to start looking for one who's right for both of us. And I can't start until I tell you goodbye, Chris."

One sob managed to escape before she reined in her emotions once more. "Elvinia seems to think you had a reason for all these appearances. Some message you were trying to get across to me." Lifting her arms in a helpless gesture, she continued. "I'm listening, Chris. Please, tell me…show me…somehow…please find a way to let me know."

Meagan smoothed off Buck's bedspread, yet again, then pulled out the small desk chair and sat, waiting in silence for a full ten minutes. A soft knock preceded Elvinia's entrance into the room.

"Are you all right?" She walked over to lay a gentle touch on Meagan's shoulder.

Meagan gave the empath a nod. "I'm okay. I've been trying to listen Elvinia, but I don't hear anything. How's he going to get the message to me if I can't make myself hear him?"

"I think that time is over."

"What?" Meagan looked up into the woman's sad, dark eyes. "What do you mean?"

"He's gone, sweetie, about ten minutes ago…I felt this surging presence…such a feeling of goodness and love. I know he's where he belongs now."

"No! He couldn't have."

"I thought maybe you'd seen something and I was giving you some time to yourself."

"I didn't see anything. I didn't feel anything." She turned to the woman, her heart breaking all over again. "Are you telling me all of this was for nothing? No word, no sign from above, no message. *Nothing*?"

"He must have found some way, or he wouldn't have left when he did, as peacefully as he did."

Meagan gave her head a wild shake. "No! No, I don't think he did. He left me alone…again…with an even bigger mess than before. How many years will Buck remember the 'sad man'? Will his image haunt him? Will he have nightmares or terrors about it? Will this leave him damaged…broken psychologically in some way he'll never get over?"

Elvinia stared down at her. "I think Buck will be fine, but sugar, I'm just a tad worried about you."

Meagan turned on her, furious. "How do you know he'll be fine?"

"Well, I guess there are never any guarantees, but you're talking like it's a given he'll be hiding on a rooftop with a sniper rifle, taking out one person at a time."

"Well, he coul—"

"—Oh, don't be ridiculous!" Elvinia snapped. "What did you ask of Chris?"

"I asked him to leave us so we could get on with our lives."

Elvinia threw her hands up in the air. "Well, didn't he do just that? Why are you so angry?"

"Because he didn't leave a *message*!" she hissed. "Why would he put us through all of this if there was no purpose behind it?"

Elvinia stood with her head held high. "I don't know, Meagan. But God will show you when it's time, if that is what is meant to be."

Meagan took a deep breath and released it slowly, staring up at the woman…feeling an emptiness she had never remembered feeling, even in the days just after losing Chris. "Bullshit."

Elvinia took a step back. "Excuse me?"

She crossed her arms. "You heard me. I said bullshit, and I meant it. The only thing God has to show me is the back of his hand for daring to disobey my parents. My good, Christian, holier than thou parents, who couldn't find it in their hearts to forgive their own child or reach out to their only grandchild." She slapped her hands together as though brushing off crumbs from a cookie. "I'm done with them, and I'm done with *him*." She jabbed her finger up in the air to make a point.

"Oh, child, you can *not* mean that!"

"You bet your ass I do. This is twice he screws me over." She took a step closer and lowered her voice a notch. "Two simple words would have sufficed: *I know!* As in, I know about our son. That's all it would have taken to give meaning to this miserable experience. But God couldn't even give me that!" She crossed her arms again. Good and ready to take her hurt, her anger, out on someone or something.

"So, I'm calling bullshit on him. I'm not wasting another second of my life believing in him."

Elvinia stared down her long, straight nose at her, unable to hide the smile behind her eyes.

The telltale signs of humor only made Meagan angrier. "Are you laughing at me?"

"Just wondering how long it'll take you to discover that no matter what you choose to believe, you can't stop God from believing in you."

She walked out, leaving Meagan alone in the room with her own thoughts.

CHAPTER 18
Bachelorettes and Barfing

Mitch approached Meagan, hard pressed not to notice the sheen of perspiration on her forehead and neck. "Man, they're bustin' y'alls butts tonight, aren't they? Neither ends nor the middle of the bar are getting any down time. Is there another rodeo in town?"

Meagan handed three Coronas to a customer and started making the first of several pitchers of Margaritas for the massive group of women that just turned in their orders. She pointed to two of them, both wearing cheap veils and pins that flashed I'M THE BRIDE in red lights. "Double bachelorette party: Two sisters marrying two brothers in a double ceremony."

"Is that supposed to be good luck or something?"

Meagan gave a loud snort. "You've gotta be kidding me, Mitch. You're asking *me* about good luck?"

"You were lucky enough to meet me when you did, fresh from the Corp and still in shape." He made a show of flexing his considerably large bicep for her.

"Whatever." She pushed the blender button, drowning out the rest of his comeback.

He waited until the whine of the blender's powerful motor halted. "How are things at home?"

"Uneventful, thank Go…" She paused, then seemed to think better of it. "Uneventful."

"So, he's really gone?"

She shrugged as she filled several glasses with the icy drinks. "It seems so, and I'd really rather not talk about this here if you don't mind."

"Sure." Mitch pinched the bridge of his nose as a wave of women clamored around the bar for their drinks. The scent of several different perfumes, mixed with alcohol and body heat had him craving a breath of fresh air. "Damn!" he rubbed at the ache in his forehead. "I wish women would wear the same brand of smell-good when they travel in packs."

"It can get to be overpowering, can't it?"

"That's one word for it. Another is downright nauseating."

"Are you going to be sick?" she asked, looking concerned.

"Nah, but it ain't helping this headache. We got anything back here for that?"

She opened a drawer and pulled out a bottle of aspirin. Wordlessly, she handed him a couple, along with a bottle of water from the cooler.

He took them, thankfully, and downed them with half the water. "Thanks. If you don't need me to stick around up here, I think I'll go stand over by the door for a while."

"Sure. A little distance will do you some good."

He stared at her, hoping like hell she was talking about the too sweet mixture of perfumes, and not her. "Okay." He unclipped his radio and held it up. "Call if you need me."

She stopped pouring glasses of margaritas on the rocks long enough to send him a look, heavy with promise and hidden messages. "I'll do that."

Mitch swallowed, unable to tear his gaze from her until she turned away. He wound his way around the crowded dance floor, somehow knowing her eyes were still on him.

～

Meagan studied him—the broad shoulders that pulled the T-shirt taut across his back, tight on his arms, and tucked neatly into a pair of jeans that fit the man like a pair of leather driving gloves. Trim belted waist, narrow hips, a firm butt and muscular legs. Everything combined to assure that Mitchell looked just as good leaving as he did coming.

She groaned as an ache started deep inside her. She'd had no sex since Christopher, who'd been her first, as well as her only. But that had been *making love* with the man she wanted to marry. Maybe it was time to step out of her box. She'd even been fantasizing about down and dirty, no strings attached sex. A little something to feed the need, though something told her that particular Marine had more to offer than the average man.

She smiled to herself and turned back to mixing drinks, feeling more alive than she had in years. Freedom was the key, freedom to live her life. The headiness had her wishing, *wanting* to be a bad girl for a change. Maybe it was time to shed her careful, good girl image. She cast another look toward Mitch, deciding tonight was as good a night as any to set the wheels in motion. She could hardly wait.

~

Ten minutes after the DJ announced the last dance of the night, Mitch locked up the front doors of the club. He headed to the bar area where Meagan was stocking her coolers for the next night, wondering if he'd imagined her earlier silent signals. "You want some help with that?"

She shook her head. "Nope. Just finishing up."

He discarded the empty beer crates and watched her efficiently organizing her space for the next night. Three nights on and two nights off—she had the same schedule as he did, and they'd just completed night number two. Red McAllister didn't expect any more from his bartenders than just serving drinks…he hired a cleaning crew for the club's upkeep. But Mitch knew that Meagan liked setting up her work area ahead of time. By the time she finished, he'd decided he'd read too much into the look she'd given him earlier.

The DJ had long been gone, and Mitch told the other three bartenders good night as they left through the back door. "I guess I'll be heading out myself." He wasn't certain if her change in demeanor called for disappointment on his part, or relief, considering his massive headache.

"Uh Mitch, there is something you can do for me. If you're up to it, that is."

The teasing lift of her lips—the crook of her eyebrow, had him holding his breath as well as the answer. A subtle lift of her brow had him offering a far-from-subtle comeback. "Sure! Anything!" He cursed himself silently for sounding so much like an eager junior high kid. "What do you need?"

She turned to him suddenly, lifted up on her tiptoes and looped her arms around his neck. "I need you," she said, before planting her mouth onto his for a kiss. Not a timid, quick, filled with innocent yearning type of kiss—but hot and aggressive—tongue seeking, teeth nipping, hands pulling and threading roughly through his hair. An extremely hot kiss that had him totally hard in a few, short seconds.

He leaned forward to place his hands on her lower butt and lifted her easily onto the bar surface. She spread her thighs and pulled him close, her nails biting into his back through his shirt as she looped her shapely legs around his waist. With one arm around her waist and the other tangled in her hair, Mitch pulled her closer. He hadn't thought that kiss could deepen, but damned if it didn't, strengthening with an intensity that had him about to explode.

The feel of her hands, first pulling his shirt out of his jeans, her hands—Meagan's hands—on his bare skin—good God—he'd never felt anything so fine before. Her nails lightly scraped along his ribcage, and he sucked in his breath, only to release it a moment later as she dragged them roughly across his back. Her hands slipped around to the front, caressing his abs, his pecs. A feather light brush of her fingers had his nipples tightening so quickly it was almost painful.

Suddenly her hands were unbuttoning his jeans, then on his zipper, jolting him to his senses. He pulled away, holding her arms.

"Hold it, Megs. Don't get me wrong, I want this, and I want it tonight. Just not here."

She pulled him back for one final kiss before jumping down from the bar. "I agree. Let's go to your place. You drive and I'll follow."

"My place isn't much to look at right now. I mean, I don't need mu—"

"—You have a bed?" She slipped her hands under his shirt again, touching, exploring.

He groaned as she pushed up his shirt and her mouth found his bare skin.

"Do you, Mitch?"

She had to repeat the question twice before he could manage to answer. "Uh, yeah."

"What size is it?"

Her question threw him off. Considering all his blood supply was in his groin area at the moment, it was no wonder he was confused. He stepped back, looking down at the front of his jeans. "Uh…right now, I'd say it's pretty big." He gasped as she pressed close to him. Her throaty chuckle broke through the fog of his sex-obsessed brain.

"I'd have to agree with you, but I meant your bed."

"What?" He struggled to concentrate.

"What size is your bed? You're not sleeping on a military cot or anything are you?"

"No! It's a bed…regular size…I mean not king, but not one of those small bunk bed sizes, either."

"Good," she purred before grabbing his hand. "Let's go."

~~

Five minutes later, he pulled his truck into his driveway with Meagan hot on his tail. He'd been so consumed with thoughts of her, he didn't realize until he stepped into the cool October air how badly his head ached.

A second later she was on him again, all aggressive hands and tongue, teeth and nails. His hand shook as he struggled with the lock and key, finally succeeded in pushing it open. She hurried in, pulling him behind her as she homed in on his bedroom—easy enough since there was only one bed in the house.

She squealed at the sight of the bed. "A queen size…that'll do nicely," she purred, before attacking him in earnest. His shirt was off before he could form a thought, and she'd pushed him back on the bed to pull off his boots. One boot flew off, then another, and soon he was laying there in his boxer briefs watching, in amazement, as she peeled off her own clothes.

The sight of her reaching for the front closure on her bra spurred him to spring to a sitting position.

"Wait! I want to do that." He reached out and she came to him, settling her hands on each of his shoulders. "I've wanted to do that for so long."

He curved his hands around her waist and explored the smooth landscape of creamy skin, tracing her ribs and splaying his fingers across her belly. He reached around to her shapely butt, slid his fingers under the waistband of her bikini panties and pushed them down until they fell to the floor, exposing her lovely hips and pelvis to his hot, hungry gaze. But, as beautiful a sight as it was, that's not what he ached to see or touch.

He pulled her close, fitting her between his legs and cupped her breasts, rubbing his thumbs lightly over nipples covered by a sheath of delicate lace. Even as he felt her tremble, his head pounded, and pain sliced through him. But he was a Marine, dammit. He'd pushed through many a confrontation with the enemy, dealing with one kind of pain or another. Damned if he'd let a headache ruin this night for him.

Slowly, he unclasped the front closure of her bra, releasing the most beautiful breasts he'd ever seen in his life.

"Good God, Megs. You are so damn beautiful." He reached out to cup the twin globes—just the right weight in his palms. He passed his thumbs, oh so gently, over the areolas, enlarged from having carried a child. He traced a barely visible stretch mark that ran on the side of one breast. *I bet you breast-fed Buck.*

"Yes, I did."

He looked up, realizing he must have spoken the question aloud. "I would have liked to see that." He suddenly felt weak, as though he couldn't support his head a moment longer. Strange how his need for this girl somehow sapped him of every ounce of strength he possessed. Pulling her close, he kissed the bottom curve of each plump breast then laid one side of his face on the soft, cool expanse of her abdomen and closed his eyes.

∽

Meagan gasped at the heat radiating from Mitchell's face. She pulled back, and he nearly fell forward off the bed. Supporting him with one arm, she placed one hand over his forehead. "Oh shit, Mitch, you're burning up."

"Nah, I'm fine," he said, reaching for her but coming up short. He winced and brought his hand to his forehead. "But my head is killing me."

She pulled back the covers and pushed him flat against the mattress. "You need to get in bed and stay there."

"I don't have a problem with that, as long as you're here with me."

"I need to make a call first. Niki said something today about a bad-ass-virus that comes on suddenly." She threw her shirt back on to ward off the room's chill and grabbed her cell phone.

"Meagan?"

"Just hang on, Mitch." She punched in Niki's number.

Her friend answered, sounding sleepy and slightly perturbed. *"This better be important, girlfriend. I was dreaming that Liam Hemsworth and Chris Pine were fighting over who was going to take me to senior prom. Kate Middleton had leant me her wedding dress to wear and I looked damned good."*

"Sorry Nik, but Mitch is seriously sick. Didn't you say there was a bad virus going around?"

"Meagan?" Mitchell croaked from the bed.

"Hang on Mitch! Nik, I think it started with a bad headache, and now he's developed a high fever."

"Any hurling yet?" Niki asked.

"Nope, no sign of that." She jumped, as a low roar came from the area of the bed—turned to see Mitch puking into a small trash can he'd pulled onto the bed with him. "Oooh boy…scratch that. We are suddenly having a major hurl fest here." Carrying her phone with her, she ran to Mitchell's kitchen in search of something larger than the tiny trash can. She found a never been used plastic mop bucket and brought it to him. "Here, use this," she said, then ran to get a wet washcloth for his face and head.

"Yep, we had a guy do that right in the office today. Said his head hurt worse than his tequila and Jagermeister hangover. Thankfully, I couldn't relate to that, but it brought that big ole red-neck to his knees, I tell ya. The hospital is overflowing with people dehydrating from this thing. Mostly old people and little kids, though. Strong as Mitch is, I'm sure he'll be fine. The good news is that the symptoms—nausea, headache, fever—are usually over pretty quick, like in a couple of hours. He'll spend the next 24 hours feeling listless, but it's over after that."

"What's the bad news?"

"It's highly contagious, Meggie. How close did you get to GI Joe tonight?"

"Close enough. Shit!"

"Shit!"

Meagan released a sigh. "Okay, what do I do for him? Fluids and fever reducer?"

"Yep, that's about it, and Pepto as soon as he can hold it down. You realize, of course, that right around the time he starts to feel better, you'll probably be laid flat with this thing."

Meagan cursed under her breath as Mitch took another turn at what sounded like a dinosaur roaring into the mop bucket. "I know there's a possibility of that happening, but I can't leave him like this, Nik."

"Listen, the last thing you should do is bring that crap home to Buck. You stay there, I've got the next two days off and if you're not back by Monday I can get him to that Mother's Helper *sitter you use occasionally. Don't worry about Buck and me. We'll be fine."*

"Thanks Nik, you're a lifesaver." She disconnected and went to Mitch, wiping down his forehead with the cool, wet cloth.

He fell back on his pillow, holding his hand over hers as it held the cloth in place. "You need to get out of here so you don't get sick."

She gave him a grim smile. "Niki says it's highly doubtful I'll escape getting it at this point. My main objective is not to infect Buck with this, because it's hell on children and old people." She flushed the contents of the bucket and basket down the toilet before rinsing them out. She turned at a muffled curse to see Mitch struggling to walk from his bed to the bathroom.

"What the hell do you think you're doing?"

"I need the bathroom," he groaned. "You don't have to stay here, you know. I can take care of myself."

"I didn't say you couldn't. Here," she said, handing him the bucket. "You may need this while you're in there. Call me if you need me."

He answered with a grunt and shut the door.

Meagan used the time to survey the rest of Mitchell's house. True to his word, there wasn't much to see: A few pieces of furniture here and there, a shelf holding a set of speakers and docking station for his phone, and a few framed snapshots of Mitch in fatigues with what she assumed were some Marine brothers.

Her search brought her to the kitchen where more photos littered the fridge, mingled with business cards and held up by an assortment of magnets, probably left by previous renters. One photo, in particular, stood out from the rest. It was a shot of a much younger Mitch, and Tex Broussard, flanking a third man, a tall, lanky guy wearing a huge grin and a Santa hat. Indulging her curious nature, she lifted it off the fridge to check the back for some kind of label or description. *Afghanistan, Christmas Day, 2001—The Marines have landed and have the situation well in hand...Me, Tex & Bobby*

Bobby…the one whose funeral he hadn't been able to attend? A shiver ran through her as she placed the picture back in its spot. A loud thump from the bedroom had her rushing back to find Mitch on his knees and trying to crawl to his bed, dragging the bucket awkwardly in one hand.

"I told you to call me if you needed help," she scolded.

He pinned her with a feverish gaze. "I thought you left."

She helped him to the bed and heaped the covers over his shivering body. "I'm not leaving just yet." She'd consider her options later, once she'd helped him through the worst of this. She ran back to the kitchen and scrounged around until she found a bowl. She filled it with cold water and carried it carefully back to his room to place it on the small nightstand beside his bed. Seating herself beside him, she dipped the washcloth in the water and rung it out before she placed it on his head.

"God that feels good," he groaned.

"How's the headache?"

"Hurt's like a Mofo…"

"Still nauseated?"

He held up the bucket with one hand and let it drop weakly to the bed. "Uh huh…"

"Think you could hold down some water?"

"No, but I'll drink it anyway. I already puked everything in my stomach. Anything's better than the dry heaves."

As soon as she returned with a glass of water, he downed it. She sat and watched in silence as his face revealed several steps of severe nausea, culminating, finally, in him emptying his stomach into the bucket, yet again.

Within the next two hours, they repeated the process four times. When Mitch finally dozed off, Meagan took the opportunity to catch some sleep on the one new piece of furniture he owned—a high quality, extremely comfortable, leather recliner.

She awoke at the sound of a muffled shout from the bedroom. Using the light from the bathroom to guide her, she spotted Mitch easily, swinging his arms as though he was lashing out at some invisible enemy.

Meagan dipped the cloth in cold water and placed it carefully on his forehead. Only after he seemed to calm a little, did she seat herself beside him on the bed. She reached up to feel his forehead and face, knowing it would be clammy and fevered.

As soon as she made skin contact, she was flat on her back with Mitch looming above her, his hands wrapped dangerously tight around her throat. She tried to scream, with no more success than a guttural whimper.

CHAPTER 19
Feverish Not-so-Friendly Fire

Meagan flailed, slapped, and pushed at him, but she was no match for his strength, nor whatever it was he was experiencing in his feverish nightmare. She banged her hand on the nightstand, sending a sharp pain through her wrist, but also jogging her memory. She reached for the bowl of cold water and missed, panicking at the darkness licking at the edge of her vision. She kicked and hit with renewed vigor, managed to knock one of his steely hands loose for a second—just long enough to catch a breath and reach the bowl.

Cold water doused the both of them and he let go, his eyes wide, though still blind to what had happened. He fell back on the mattress, instantly subdued, as Meagan gasped for air, sputtered and choked on water that had gone up her nose.

Still coughing, she sat up, managed to pull herself out of the bed. She ran to the kitchen just to get some distance between them and finally caught her breath. His moans reached her from the bedroom, and she stood there, alone, and wondering what to do. Obviously, she'd need assistance if she was going to help him, but who? Instinctively, she knew he'd feel strange about having just anyone around him in this state. Remembering a particular card she'd seen on the refrigerator, she walked over and pulled one from the center of the menagerie.

Matthew 'Tex" Broussard
Retired USMC
Putting Smiles on the Faces
Of Women Everywhere
Come Ride a Real Cowboy...Yee Haw!

She flipped it over to see a phone number on the back and thumbed it into her cell phone.

~∽

Thirty minutes later, Meagan stepped aside to let Tex inside, exchanging a grim smile with the man.

"I've gotta admit, Meg, you were the last person I expected to get a call from tonight." Tex stepped through the doorway and gave Meagan a friendly hug.

"Thanks for coming so quickly, Tex. I'd have done it myself but I don't think I can handle him alone."

"You shouldn't have to. Where is he?"

She pointed down the hall. "His bedroom's that way." After following him to the room, she stood two steps back, still wary of getting too close to him. The feeling of his hands around her neck, and her, desperate for air and fighting not to black out...*that* was a memory likely to stick with her for years to come.

As soon as Tex placed a hand on his forehead, Mitchell's eyes flew open. He gripped Tex's arm with one hand and his neck with the other. Tex, however, blocked the moves with astounding ease.

"Whoa there, Master Sergeant, it's only me— Tex. No need to be so fu—*freaking*—inhospitable, asshole...even if you are fighting off a raging fever. Sonofabitch, he's burnin' up, Meg."

Meagan ran around him to grab the bowl that had fallen to the floor, filled it with fresh water, and grabbed a handful of washcloths. She dipped one in the cold water, wrung it out slightly, and placed it on Mitchell's forehead.

Tex turned Mitchell's head to the side. "A cloth on the back of his neck is effective, also."

She plastered one there at the base of his skull, and another on the front of his neck and chest. She used a fourth to wipe his face and soothe his eyes.

Mitch awoke at that point and stared at her, his gaze heated with fever, his voice dry and raspy.

"Thirsty."

Tex held him up as Meagan gave him a drink of cool water.

Mitch gulped down the water and sighed afterwards, licking his lips. Once his head was back on his pillow, he looked up at Tex. "Why are you here?"

"Meagan called me. She needed some help with you. How you feelin', man?"

"Like shit on a shingle." His gaze travelled to Meagan. "Did I hurt you?"

A gut reaction had her hand flying to her throat, even though her mind longed to protect him. "Of course not, Mitch. I'm fine."

He gave her a listless nod. "Good. You're the last person…in the world…I'd want to…"

She released the breath she'd been holding as he faded off to sleep. After dipping all the cloths in the cool water again and replacing them on his heated face, she sat back, exhaustion oozing from her pours. She jumped at the question from Tex.

"*Did* he hurt you? Is that why you called me?"

She tugged self-consciously at her collar, and turned away. It didn't stop Tex from stepping around to face her and pushing her hands aside to examine her neck.

"Aw damn, Meagan! He attacked you?"

"I—I was able to dump the bowl of water on him before I blacked out." She despised the quaver in her own voice.

"Shit! You've gotta know that was from the fever."

She gazed up at Tex. "I know that. Unless he—he did—that sort of thing on a regular basis."

He shook his head, leading her into the living room to talk. "Not to my knowledge. Some guys reacted violently if they got wakened suddenly. Mitch was usually the one waking everyone else up." Tex turned to stare at his Marine brother. "He took care of all his guys—took it personal as hell if somebody got hurt, or worse."

"What was it like for y'all over there, Tex?"

"Afghanistan? It's a shit hole, hon. Ain't no other way to describe it. And Mitch and I were good enough at our jobs to spend a hellacious chunk of our last ten years in the Corps there. Sometimes being the best at what you do comes at a high price. Experience counts in a war zone.

Experience that could save lives on the side you're fighting for."

"I'm sure the men under your command appreciated having leaders around with wisdom and experience."

"Even though sometimes it didn't make enough of a difference to bring 'em all home, like in the case of your boy's dad. It sucked losing a good man."

She sighed, slumping forward on the couch. Using her hands, she rubbed at her sore neck. "It surely did."

Tex walked into the kitchen and returned with a clean, wet dish-drying towel. This one he draped carefully around her neck. "I'm sure as hell sorry about that, Meg. It must have been difficult for you. What was his name?"

"Christopher Martin. His middle name was Buckley. It was his maternal grandfather's name, and I believe it had been *his* mother's maiden name. Chris was crazy about that old man."

"It's good you gave his son the name, then. I'm sure it would have meant the world to him." He adjusted the towel around Meagan's neck.

"Can you tell me a little of what happened over there, Tex? I never found out what it was like for

Chris, but I'd like to know what it was like for Mitch."

"Like I said, he took care of his men. It's commonly known that Jarheads don't have much use for officers, but they'll go to hell and back for a good Sergeant. Mitch was one of the best I've ever known, and the men respected him." He regaled her with tales of the years they'd worked together…in Afghanistan, everything from daily life and pranks they'd pulled on each other to drunken leave in Hawaii. He left out details about the fighting, telling her when she asked, that some things didn't need to be relived or repeated.

After an hour, he took the cloth from her neck, ran it under more cold water and replaced it. "You'll develop some ugly bruising, hon. Mitchell's gonna wish he could kick his own ass ten ways from Sunday for that. He might even ask me to do it for him."

"Which, of course you won't do." She gave him a look of warning before closing her eyes to breathe in the scent of his freshly laundered shirt and spicy masculine cologne.

His chest vibrated with a deep rumble of laughter. "Not if he asked me, but I might consider it if you did."

His attention grabbing tone had her eyeing him curiously, as he sent her a sexy as hell grin. "I wouldn't ask, and you damn well know it."

"I know that. I also know my old buddy has a thing for you, and I wouldn't dream of making a move on you for that reason."

She shrugged. "It wouldn't matter if you did. You're not my type. Now, my roommate, Niki...*she* likes her cowboys."

"Niki, huh? So, when are you going to introduce me to this cowboy lovin' roommate of yours?"

"We...ellll," she said, drawing out the single syllable as she approached Mitchell's fridge. "I'm not sure if I want to, considering how I found your number." She pulled the card from the fridge and spun on her heels to show it to him. At least Tex had the good grace to cringe as he pointed to the tacky card.

"I hope you realize that I would never have ordered those myself. Haley had 'em made as a joke and gave them to me for my coming home party. Ask her next time you see her."

Meagan jabbed the card in his face. "Don't you worry...I'll do that...*before* I introduce you to my roommate, who is also my soul-sister, as well as best friend in the world." She placed the card back in its spot and tiptoed into Mitchell's room to check on him. She re-entered the living room a few minutes later, feeling a tremendous relief. "He's sweating out his fever, Tex. Hopefully this will be the end of it. Nik says the symptoms don't last long."

"That's good to know."

"Looks like I wasted your ti—"

"—Don't even think that! Nobody in their right mind would have expected you to handle him after what you'd just gone through," he said, pointing to her neck. Tex waited until she'd reluctantly agreed before he leaned back in the recliner and stretched out his long legs. "Now…we've established the fact that Mitch has a thing for you. What I'm most curious about is whether or not you, Meagan, have got a thing for him."

Her mouth twisted in a grin. "Do you honestly think I'd be here—tonight—if I didn't?"

He aimed his long forefinger at her face. "Good answer, Pee Wee."

"Pee Wee! I'm 5'4"."

"I know; you're a tiny little thing."

She snorted. "It's not like I'm a midget. I can't help that you're freakishly tall."

"Hey, just 'cause you're willing to settle for ordinary, doesn't mean other women don't appreciate—" he paused to flex his arms and kiss both bulging biceps, "—*real* men like me, who come in Double XL."

She shook her head, and burst into laughter. "My Granny had a name for people like you. She called 'em 'Shine-ola'."

He cocked his head. "There's an old shoe polish called *Shinola*. I still have a container of it in a box of stuff from my great grandpa. That's not so bad."

She choked back her laughter long enough to answer him. "It came from her saying… 'He's so full of himself, it's hard to tell the difference between the shit caked on the bottom of the boot and the shine-ola on the top'. So of course, to those of us acquainted with the saying, when she called someone 'Shine-ola', it was just a polite way of calling them—"

"—Shit!" he finished for her. "I get it. Gee, thanks, Granny."

Meagan snorted with laughter. "On behalf of my beloved Granny, if the shit-caked, double XL boot fits—wear it!"

A call from Mitchell's bedroom cut through Tex's booming laughter. Meagan jumped up and ran to the room, surprised to find Mitch seated on the side of the bed, his feet flat on the floor.

"Hey! It looks like someone's feeling better," she said, pleased at his quick recovery.

"Not really, but it's hard to sleep with *someone* braying like a jack-ass out there."

Tex leaned up against the door-jamb, his muscular arms crossed against his massive chest, and casually bent one leg to cross a booted foot over the other. "Yeah, he's feeling better. Feeling a touch of the green-eyed monster, are ya, Master Sergeant?"

∼∽

Mitch fairly growled at his old pal. "Stand down, Marine. And what the fuc—*flip*—" he added with a quick glance toward Meagan, "—are you doing here, anyway?"

"Well, once this little lady realized she couldn't handle you alone, she called on the only other person in the world who'd know how to keep your ass under control."

"Bull shit." Mitch threw a grunt in for good measure then turned an irritated glare in Meagan's direction. "It couldn't have been that difficult."

Her eyes widened perceptibly as she took a deep breath, held it, and spun on her heels to leave the room without a word, or a backward glance.

A low chuckle from Tex had Mitch glaring up at the annoying mountain of a man. "What the fuck are you laughing at, you east Texas piece of trash?"

"Cajun Heat," he drawled, "You don't even know how bad you fucked up...but you're damned well about to find out."

He left for several seconds, and came back in, dragging a reluctant Meagan with him. He pushed her forward, settling her in front of Mitch. "Apologize to her...*now*."

The sight of Tex's big hands resting so familiarly on Meagan's shoulders infuriated him. He'd be ready to kick his ass if he didn't feel like he'd been run over by a Humvee and starved for a week. "Okay, I apologize, but what the hell for?"

Tex puffed up like a bullfrog. "Show him, Meg," he demanded.

"Show me what?" Mitch was just a little tired of this asshole's attitude, which is why he didn't want him here. No Marine wanted another human being to perceive him as weak. He tried hard to convince himself that was the only reason he was pissed.

"Show him," Tex insisted, as Meagan rolled her eyes and reached for her collar, pulling it back to reveal the bruising around her neck.

"What the..." Mitch reached up to inspect, jerked his hand back when she flinched, pulling away from him. She shuttered her gaze, but not until he saw the flicker of fear in her eyes. "Aw...fuck no! I couldn't have done that! Did I?"

The sight of her biting her lower lip was all the answer he needed. He sat back, all the air leaving his lungs like a deflated balloon. "Shit...shit...what happened?" He had to know.

"You - you didn't know what you were doing, Mit—"

He lifted one hand, stopping her. "—Don't defend me. Just tell me what happened." He listened, heart sick and humbled, as she told him how close he'd come to choking the life out of her.

Once she'd finished speaking, the three of them remained where they were, speechless; the steady drip...drip...*plop*...of the faucet in his bathroom, the only sound in the otherwise silent room.

He took a deep breath, released it, and forced himself to look up at her, still standing with arms crossed as though trying to protect herself from— God forgive him—him.

"There are no words to express how sorry I am." He hung his head. "I can't—can't even imagine why you stayed—why you're still here."

"I told you, it's highly contagious," she mumbled. "Dangerous for kids and I don't want to bring it home to Buck." She lifted one shoulder. "I really don't have any other place to go."

He nodded, full understanding hitting him squarely in the face. "You'll be safe here, Megs, you know that, right?"

"Um, I guess so," she said, sending a quick glance at Tex.

That one brief glance felt like a knife wound to Mitchell's gut. Gathering all his strength, he forced himself to stand and face her. He moved slowly, reaching out for her, held his arms there and waited for her to move on her own. She did, finally, stepping into his embrace. He kissed the top of her head and closed his eyes, holding her close. "I'm so sorry, Megs. I promise you will *never* have to be afraid of me again." He smiled at her muffled response.

"I'm gonna hold you to that, you dumb Jarhead."

Tex cleared his throat. "And I'm gonna make sure she does. Now, if you two think everything's okay here, I've got a few things I need to take care of back home."

Meagan pulled away suddenly. "You can't leave!" she objected. "You'll bring it home to your family."

"I live alone and I'll tell everyone to keep away." He backed away from the two of them.

"You shouldn't be alone, Tex!"

Mitch placed a comforting hand on her arm. "He'll be okay." He followed his Marine brother to the door. "Do me a favor, buddy. Make sure you have a bucket to hurl in, aspirin for the headache and water...plenty of water...because for a brief period, you're gonna feel like you're burning up from the inside out."

Tex flexed his guns again and shot them each a big grin. "This big old Texas boy's got it under control, don't you worry." With a flash of Wrangler jeans and Justin boots, he was out the door.

The engine of Tex's Ford F-350 truck came to life, cutting through the quiet stillness of the early October morning. He revved it up and drove away, the sound fading slowly until all was quiet again.

Meagan turned to him, her face a mask of worry. "I sure hope he listens and doesn't bring this stuff to his family. You think he'll be okay?"

Mitch nodded. "Tex will fare all right, and I'm pretty sure he'll go right home. He's not that stupid." He turned away from her, still muttering under his breath. "At least I don't think so, anyway."

"How are you feeling?" she asked, her voice tinged with a hint of shyness.

He flexed his shoulders, testing his muscles a little, and winced. "Everything hurts *except* for my head, but I'm not burning up or barfing into a bucket. All things considered, I guess I'm doing pretty damn well." He sent her a look of concern. "More importantly, how are you doing?"

"My, uh, my head is starting to hurt some."

"Seriously?"

She rubbed at her forehead and nodded. "Yeah. Niki was right. This thing is contagious as all hell."

"You realize, of course, we probably both got it from the club. I mean, I do a lot of hand shaking, and you handle people's drinks and money."

"I know," she said, nodding. "And if it's an airborne virus, we didn't have an icicle's chance in Hades of escaping this thing." She rubbed at her head again and at the back of her neck. "I'm not too worried about the nausea because I never throw up."

"Never?"

She shook her head. "Not since I was a little girl. Not even morning sickness."

He searched her face for clues, wondering if she was serious. "Well, for your sake, I hope like hell your luck holds up this time around, too." He cringed at the thought of his all too recent experience with that very thing.

∾

"Oh…oh…that hurts so freaking bad!" Meagan fell back on the pillow, her hand plastered to her forehead as the pain sliced through her temporal lobe. "This is so humiliating," she said, as Mitch sat on the side of the bed, wiping her face with a cool, wet washcloth. She would have laughed at the face he made, if she wasn't so afraid it would make her heave…yet again.

"Never say never, Meg's."

"I won't," she groaned. "Oh man, I hope Buck doesn't get this."

"What about Niki, working as a receptionist in the doctor's office?"

"She works behind a glass window, but wears gloves. They also spray this stuff in the air to keep the workers from getting sick. It seems to work for her."

"Good to know." He reached over to feel her forehead. "No fever yet. Think you could sleep now?"

She grasped his hand and pulled it close. "Could you stay with me? I hate to be alone when I'm feeling bad."

He cast a doubtful glance in her direction. "You sure you don't mind?" The look she gave him made him want to shield her from any pain the world had to offer. "God, you look pitiful, Megs."

He took the towel from her neck, dunked it in the bowl of fresh water and arranged it so it looped the most bruised areas, hating himself even more, for what he'd done in his fevered condition. "Sonofabitch…" he whispered to himself.

"Wasn't your fault," she said, her eyes cracking open just a slit. She laid her hand on the side of the bed. "Come here."

"Hang on…" Mitch emptied her bucket and rinsed it before placing it on the floor beside her. He crawled in bed, molding himself to her back as she lay on her side facing the edge of the bed. "Is this okay?" He heard a barely perceptible grunt of approval before she settled into a deep sleep. Still exhausted from his own bout of illness, he followed her lead.

～～

A soft groan broke through his consciousness, alerting him. He lay there, eyes closed, waiting for her to speak. "Megs? Did you say something?" No sound came from her, no movement other than a violent shivering, causing the entire bed to shake. He moved his hand resting on her hip, slid it under her shirt, and muttered a long, low string of curses at the heat radiating off her skin. He jumped out of bed and piled the blankets on her before getting fresh cloths dipped in water to cool her head and face.

She rolled over on her back, flailing her head from side to side, as though trying to escape the cool cloth.

"Hang on Meagan. Jesus, you're burning up!" He tried again to pass the cool cloth over her face, her eyes, her heated cheeks, with some measure of success. He reached for the cloth around her neck, no longer cool, but warm from her heated body temperature. He soaked it and rung it out loosely. As soon as he placed it around her neck, her eyes flew open. She cried out then gasped for breath, slapping and scratching at him, her long nails connecting with his face, her right fist connecting with his eye.

"Ah...shit! Meagan! Shhhh...it's okay, Megs. I'm not going to hurt you, babe. It's all right...that's right...calm down, Megs."

Finally she settled, calmed into letting him care for her. He bathed her face, all the while beginning to feel sickened by a new realization. In *his* fevered state, he'd been back in Afghanistan, fighting off members of Al Qaeda, the terrorists, the enemy. But clearly, she'd been fighting *him*. He knew by the way she'd gasped and struggled for breath. In place of the cool, wet cloth around her neck, she'd only felt his hands wrapping tightly around her, cutting off her supply of air.

A fresh batch of shame washed over him. Shame and horror at having done something like that to a woman he cared so deeply for, along with something else—a knowledge that it *could* happen again. Was it likely to happen again? The odds were, no. Was it possible it could happen again? Hell, anything was possible.

He bathed her face, praying for the fever to abate. Hoping she'd feel well enough to go home soon. The sooner he got her out of here, the better off she and Buck would be.

CHAPTER 20
Costumes and Camouflage

Mitch waited three days before accepting a dinner invitation to Sarah and Tanner's place, hoping to spare the family from catching whatever it was he had. Once his brother-in-law, the doctor, had assured him they'd be fine, he showed up with a nice bottle of wine for Sarah, a six-pack of Dos Equis for Tanner, and cute little ladybug shaped lollipops for his nieces.

Sarah hugged her brother and grabbed the lollipops from him before her twin girls could see them. "Oops! Not until after their supper, Uncle Mitch, your nieces have a fondness for sweets. Those girls will pass up a decent meal over sugar any day of the week."

Mitch placed the wine on the cabinet and the beer in the fridge then looked around the otherwise empty living area. "Where are the munchkins? Usually they're all over me by now."

"Tanner couldn't wait to see them in their Halloween costumes." They turned at the sound of a door opening and screeches of laughter from the two little girls.

Mitch couldn't help but laugh at the sight of Tanner Collins toting not one, but two adorable little insects in each arm. One twin...Mitch hadn't mastered the skill of telling them apart yet...was dressed as a bumble bee, all yellow and black striped with fuzzy antennae sticking up from her furry little bee head hood. The second twin was just as cute as a red ladybug, complete with black spots, multiple legs, also sporting a pair of antennae protruding from her equally furry hood.

"Oh man," Mitchell gushed. "Have you ever seen anything as cute as that?"

"Hmmm...Nope!" Tanner admitted, putting the twins down to shake Mitch's hand. "Though I'm thinking your sister will run a close second in the costume she just brought home."

"You're dressing up too?" Mitch asked, squatting to scoop up his nieces and cover their giggling, adorable faces with kisses.

"Not for trick or treat, but for a costume party with our Mardi Gras Krewe. You know, the one I invited you to a couple of weeks ago and suggested you bring a date?"

"Oh...I remember now. So what's your costume?"

"It's a surprise, and don't change the subject. Who'd you ask?" Sarah's tone indicated she was more than a little curious.

"Nobody."

Her brow furrowed severely. "Why not? What are you waiting for? Don't you know it takes time to plan for these things...to buy costumes and make-up and such?"

"Sarah—"

"—You can't pop this on a girl at the last minute, Mitch."

"I have a job now, sis. I'll have to work at Red's club that night. Incidentally, the club has its own costume party. I hear Red goes all out and gives big cash prizes and everything."

"Oh." Sarah seemed to contemplate his comeback. "Does Meagan have to work that night?"

"Yes, Sarah. She and I are on the same schedule." He shook his head. "You *should* be going as some kind of pushy Goddess of Matchmaking."

"Excuse me?" Sarah stood there, with her hands on her hips.

"Babe, come on. It's not like you're attempting any show of subtlety." Tanner gave his wife a kiss to smooth her ruffled feathers. "Give the guy a break. Two months ago he was in Afghanistan."

"Thanks bro." Mitch raised his right arm for a quick fist-bump with his brother-in-law.

Tanner gave him a nod. "I've got your back, man. I keep telling her you're entitled to plan out the rest of your life *without* any interference from your sister." He aimed a look at his wife, just before he smoothed it over with another quick kiss on her lips.

Sarah snorted and rolled her eyes. "Well, excuse the heck out of me for wanting to see you settled and happy."

Mitch set his squirming nieces down on the floor before looping an arm around his diminutive sister's shoulder. "I am happy. As for settled, I want that too, sis, but I have some things to work out first. You forcing the issue won't help matters, I can promise you that."

She stopped and faced him, studying…what…he didn't know. Whatever she saw there seemed to appease her curiosity. Thankfully, she changed the subject.

Unfortunately, it didn't come soon enough for Mitch. Mention of Meagan had opened the floodgates of thoughts about her.

After their shared illness, they had both, somewhat remarkably, recovered enough to show up for work that night. By the end of their shift, Meagan had been dragging so badly, she'd regretted not calling in sick. He'd been a mass of confusion, torn between wanting to hover around her to make sure she was okay, and wanting to get as far away from her as possible.

The entire incident had made him do the one thing he'd never done in his twenty years as a Marine. That was to doubt himself. He worried now, as never before, that he'd come back from his years serving his country, bearing scars from old wounds, both mental and physical.

He had to wonder. What if? What if, he had the type of scars that lay dormant for years? What if something forced them to the surface one day and he snapped?

He'd heard stories over the years. Some Jarhead made it home, only to go ballistic over fireworks during the neighborhood July 4th block party. After twenty years in the Corps, the last ten in the 'armpit of the Middle East' as Tex called Afghanistan; he'd seen some serious shit. Shit that no normal person should have to see, but that Marines see on a regular basis—men blown in half, their limbs severed, or torn off. Faces swam before him, faces burned beyond recognition to match the rest of their bodies. Faces of Marines, still breathing, still alive enough to feel the excruciating pain, until that blissful shot of morphine put them under for their final trip home. Pain…suffering…fighting…death. Or not. Some men made it out alive, but never really lived again.

No. He could not, *would not* subject Meagan, or any other woman to that. It was far too risky, too dangerous, as he well knew. He'd contacted someone at the VA hospital already, had set the wheels in motion for a thorough psyche evaluation. He had to know if he was a danger *before*, not after, he drug anyone else into his life of doubt and uncertainty.

∼∾

Three days. Three long days without talking, *really talking*, to Mitch. They'd finished out the last of their three-day hitch and by the end of the shift, all Meagan had wanted was to sleep off her exhaustion. She hadn't heard a peep from him during the two days off, and she couldn't even imagine what ideas were swimming around in that head of his.

She put the finishing touch to her make-up, heavy black eyeliner and several layers of mascara, and stood back to view the results in the full-length mirror. "Not bad, Meagan. Maybe this will flip the Jarhead's switch."

A trip to the local Goodwill store had rewarded her with the perfect costume for very little money. She'd lucked out and found a sexy GI costume—a one-piece spandex romper in a desert camouflage pattern that fit like a glove, along with a matching military style cap. Further searching had uncovered a couple of faux leather ammo belts complete with fake rounds. She looped one low on her hips. The second fit around one thigh like a garter. She completed the look with black diamond thigh highs and a pair of black lace-up knee boots borrowed from Niki.

"You look pwitty, Mama!" Buck spoke from behind her in breathless admiration. She stepped aside to see her son's reflection and grinned down at him. "You think so?"

His little head bobbed up and down happily. "Yep. You awe the pwittiest mama…evah!" He threw his arms out for emphasis. "Awe you gonna weah that when you bwing me twick or tweating?"

Niki's laughter cut through the child's innocent question. "Yeah, Meagan. Are you gonna wear that for trick or treating on Thursday night?" She leaned against the doorjamb, wearing a pair of Daisy Duke cutoffs, a long sleeved shirt, its tails tied high at the waist with the sleeves rolled up, and her favorite pair of heeled, brown suede, harness boots.

Meagan threw a smirk in Niki's direction before kneeling before her son. "I think I'll wear something a little more *regular* mommy when I take you trick or treating, sweetie. It's supposed to be cool and this may not be warm enough."

"Humph...I bet that get up will be plenty hot enough for a certain recently retired Master Sergeant; that is, unless the fool is too much of a blockhead to notice."

Meagan stood and shot her friend a meaningful look. "Oh he'll notice...I'll make darn sure of *that*." She looped her purse over her shoulder, grabbed Buck's hand and his backpack before heading toward the kitchen door. She called back to Niki at the door, "You want me to swing back by to pick you up after I drop him off at Mr. Daniel and Ms. Leah LeBlanc's house?"

"Sure, if you think you have time to. I figure that by the end of tonight, I'll need a designated driver. That is, unless you plan on catching a ride home with *someone else* after tonight."

Meagan turned and gave Niki a wink. "I'll let you know, but it's not a problem. Red will have plenty of sober drivers on hand for tonight. I'll be back," she intoned, a la Schwarzenegger.

∿

Red stuck his head out the front door and closed it with a low whistle. "Tonight is showing all the signs of a full house and a ball buster busy night, Mitch. Stay on your toes buddy, and please, if anyone tries to bring in anything that looks remotely like a weapon, please check it out. If it ain't flimsy and plastic, it stays outside."

"Sure thing, boss, and uh, that's a damn fine costume, by the way." He nodded at Red, dressed as a biker, covered in studded black leather riding gear.

Red lifted the edges of the vest, decked out in chains. "Nice, huh? Tiffany picked it out for me. I don't mind telling you, though. Once I saw *her* costume I had a few second thoughts about it."

Mitch laughed as the lady in question joined them, looking every inch the buxom biker babe in Harley Davidson attire.

"Hey, I gave you a choice, so I don't want to hear any complaints!" Tiffany passed a hand down her husband's leather covered back, ending with a pat on his leather-covered butt. "You could have been Han Solo."

Red nodded at Mitch. "I really wanted to be Han, but she said only if she could dress like Leia as a slave…you know…in that skimpy little outfit when she's chained to Jabba the Hutt?"

"Oh, yeah…I know *exactly* what you're talking about. That's what Leia was wearing during my first wet dre—"

"—Mine too!" Red interjected. "So you *know* why I had to say no to that one."

"Uh, yeah. I'd have turned that down too," Mitch agreed.

Tiffany shook her head. "It's just a costume."

Mitch gave his head an adamant shake. "I hate to disagree with you, but no, it's not."

"It's like…every guy's fantasy, babe. I mean… Princess Leia in that flimsy get up and chains is a universal turn on for guys."

"Oh, that can't be true," she said, turning to Mitch for help.

He sucked in his breath and nodded. "Yep. It's true."

She threw up her hands in disgust as she stormed off muttering something about all men being pigs.

A quick glance over at Red showed him shrugging in agreement with his wife.

Mitch checked his watch. A quarter until opening and Meagan wasn't here yet. Thoughts of her, along with the recent Princess Leia comments, had his overactive imagination in hyper-drive, developing mental snapshots of her in that costume, complete with chains. He groaned, and adjusted himself to accommodate the tightness in his groin area.

That would have to be the single hottest thing on earth.

The familiar click and thud of the back door opening had him turning toward the sound—and slammed him with a sudden change of opinion.

"Oh…shh…iiiit…" He hadn't meant to speak the words, but somehow, he had. More disturbing had been the sound of his voice—more like a territorial growl of warning than anything else. Nothing could have prepared him for the sight of Meagan wearing some kind of clingy, tight-fitting, curve-hugging, camouflage costume that somebody must have poured her into.

He stood there, frozen and torn between wanting to run from the place, throw up his hands in surrender and bow to her every whim, or throw a blanket over her. She was *hot*—and soon every guy in this place would see her looking that way. As usual, the blood rushing to his groin area overrode all trace of common sense when it came to this woman. Within seconds, he'd approached her, stopping to appreciate her accessories, gone unnoticed before now. Black thigh highs, laced knee boots with tall blocked heels, and a military styled cap over her lustrous dark locks.

"What the hell are you wearing?"

Meagan turned, looking as though she'd just noticed him standing there, but he knew that was a load of bullshit. She'd homed in on his location, targeted his ass from the second she'd stepped through that doorway.

"Oh, hey!" she said, sounding innocent, as she observed his version of real desert camies. "You're a Marine, and so am I. Imagine that!"

"Yeah, imagine that," he said, tense, tightlipped, and not the least bit amused.

"I don't guess you had to go scrounging for that get up like I did, though, huh?" Her chuckle sounded easy, unrehearsed.

"Just my foot-locker."

She tossed her backpack under the bar and adjusted her suit's zipper, lowering it a bit. He supposed it was in order to show even more of her cleavage than she already was. His breath caught in his throat as she leaned over, practically spilling out of the damn thing, in order to adjust a fake ammo belt she wore around her upper thigh…over those damn sexy, diamond-patterned stockings.

"Every time I visit one of those Goodwill stores, I find something that saves me a ton of money."

"Seems like you could have let a little of that blood money go to buy a decent costume, or at least one that fits properly."

She straightened, flinging her thick hair back and adjusting her hat. "That's my emergency fund. Costumes don't count as emergencies. And what do you mean, anyway? This fits perfectly, although, if I'd had time I could have taken it in a little around the hips. What do you think?" She turned around to show him her ass. "It should fit a little snugger around the butt, don't you think?"

He choked back a reply, did an immediate about face and headed out through the door for some cool air. The line to get in had already begun to form, reaching halfway down the city block. From what he'd heard, Red's costume party was the place to be the weekend before Halloween, and the length of the line attested to that fact.

After checking his watch once more, he got the okay from Red and began letting customers in, one or two at a time, but only after checking for weapons.

"Oh, Mr. Marine, you want to check me out?" a frisky kitty cat purred in his ear.

"You're good," he said, giving her a gentle shove through the door to where Janice Cuevas was waiting to take her money.

"How about me? You want to check me for concealed weapons, partner?"

He paused at the familiar voice, realizing he hadn't even been paying attention to anyone's face. "Hey, Niki. How you doing tonight?"

"I'm okay. How about you? Got any after-shocks from that bug y'all picked up?"

"I've got an after-shock all right, but it ain't from that," he grumbled.

"Have you seen Meg, yet?" she asked, standing off to the side, he supposed to check out his reaction to her roommate's costume.

"Yup." He had excellent peripheral vision…could see her grinning…*waiting* for him to reveal something she could run back to Meagan with. Well damin if he'd give her a thing.

"What'd you think? Cute, huh?" she goaded.

He checked the next mob couple's 'toy' weapons. "Sorry, you can't bring this one in," he apologized to the guy. "It's made of metal and looks too damn close to the real thing. Just go bring it to your car and I'll let you right back in. Nice job, by the way, and here, this one's okay."

He lifted one shoulder, hoping to make Niki believe he couldn't care less. "It's a costume."

He breathed a sigh of relief when she finally left, looking somewhat disappointed in his response. Hey, if Meagan wanted to dress like a 'soldier', albeit a hot, sexy as hell soldier who'd been dipped in a bucket of camo paint, she had every right to do so. He wiped his forehead. Shit, just thinking about her in that get up, had him sweating bullets. *Bullets.* He had to admit, that garter thing with the rounds had been a nice touch, even though there was no such thing in the real Marines. Never the less, it was a hell of a nice touch. He wiped at his forehead again.

"Hey man, how many times are you gonna look at that thing?"

The question brought him back to the present. He looked across at the couple in front of him, realizing he'd been daydreaming. "Sorry, man. Here you go." He handed the cowboy back his cheaply made plastic Colt 45.

Get your mind back on your business, Marine.

Ten minutes later, the queue to get in the club had finally minimized enough for Mitch to catch his breath, when another familiar voice caught his attention.

"Look! It's a Jarhead. You'd think after twenty years he'd be sick of wearing those desert camies."

He looked up at Tex, accompanied by the prettiest little zombie he'd ever seen. "Is that you, Haley?"

"Yep! Don't pay any attention to him, Mitch. I love seeing you like that. It kind of reminds me of Ben."

"Ben? Oh you mean Lance Corporal Bonin! You mean you're dating someone who's not around to cater to your every need?" The answer was obvious from the way her face lit up.

"We saw each other every day before he had to go back!" She used her hand to fan herself. "Oh, God, he's such a nice guy."

"Yeah?" Mitch laughed. "Nice guys aren't usually the ones that make girls like you fan themselves."

"Well, yeah, but," she leaned in closer so Tex wouldn't hear. "He's *hot*, too!"

"I don't know about all that, but he does seem like a nice guy. Don't you think, big brother?" He shook Tex's hand.

Tex gave a reluctant shrug. "I guess."

Mitch gave his buddy the once over. "And what about you? You'd think after thirty-eight years of being East Texas trash, you could think of something different to wear.

"Oh, this?" Tex waved his hands at his normal cowboy attire. He unfolded a black knee length jacket and slipped it on over his black shirt. After a slight adjustment to his collar, he waved his hand again.

"And just who are you supposed to be? Doc Holliday?" Mitch said.

"Really? You don't see it? Not even with the neatly trimmed beard, the dimples, the blue eyes, and the brilliantly handsome smile?" Tex smoothed his hand over his blondish brown mustache and goatee and looked down at his sister. "He doesn't see it, kid. How can that be?"

Haley grinned adoringly up at her big brother. "Put on the hat and turn around, Matty."

Tex set a large black Stetson, it's rim curled excessively, upon his head. He made a slight adjustment at the back of the hat and turned, flipping a long, blondish ponytail that reached the middle of his broad shoulders.

Mitchell's brow furrowed a moment before a wide grin covered his face. "I'll be damned. Semper Fi, Mr. Trace Adkins!"

"Genius! The man's a genius!" Tex hooted.

Haley jumped up and down excitedly, clapping her hands. "He looks just like him, doesn't he?"

"I guess so," Mitch nodded, then motioned to a group of three young women, all dressed as sexy Disney princesses. "What do y'all think, ladies?"

Cinderella nodded vigorously, pointing her glass slipper prop at Tex. "He sure does."

Snow White and her framed photo of the dwarves agreed, as did Belle and her stuffed Beast.

Tex/Trace tipped his hat at the women and extended both of his arms. "Ladies, allow me to accompany the three of you inside." They wasted no time in latching onto him as he escorted them through the entrance. He stopped and tossed a backward glance at Mitch. "Hey bro, what can I say? Other than…wait for it…*Ladies Love Country Boys!*"

"Get on in there, asshole," Mitchell growled. "You are holding up my line."

～

A low whistle cut through the air. "Man, if I knew any Marines that looked that good, I'd still be in the Corps!"

Meagan recognized the voice before she saw the face. She looked up at the huge man and beamed as she took in his attire. "Thanks…it's not every day a girl gets a compliment from Trace Adkins!"

Tex flashed his pearly whites and boyish grin at Meagan before lifting the fake tuft of hair at the back of his hat. "And you got it *without* seeing the ponytail!"

"Of course, I did. *Cowboy's Back in Town*, accompanied by his little zombie sister!" She reached out to hug the two of them. "You alone tonight?" she asked Haley, exchanging a knowing look with her.

"Yep. Ben left for seven months." The edges of her bottom lip curled down in a little pout.

"So, the two of you are…"

"We are communicating," Haley added. "We'll see where it goes from here." She clasped her hands together. "He sent me a rose last Monday!"

"Aw, that is so sweet! And promising."

Tex snorted. "One damn flower…big freaking whoop. When I send roses to a lady, I never send less than a dozen. Can I have a long-neck Corona, please? And get Haley whatever she wants," he said, slapping a five on the bar.

Meagan handed him an icy beer. "Ah…but sometimes a single rose makes an even bigger statement."

Haley lifted one hand and let it fall. "I tried to tell him that but he doesn't understand."

"Most guys don't. If Ben does, that's one mark for him in the pro column," she said, drawing an imaginary check in the air.

"He's got several in the pro column so far, but who's counting?" Haley giggled.

"Oh brother…"

Meagan laughed as Haley punched Tex in the shoulder and told him to shut up. "I always wanted a brother, but when I see the two of you together…" she paused and turned to face them, "I want one even more. What'll you have to drink, Haley?"

"Aw, I'll share Matty with you, Meagan. God knows there's enough of him to go around. Give me a Dos Equis, please."

"Well, thanks, but he's Mitchell's Marine brother, so there could be a conflict of interest." She handed her a beer and deposited the money in the register.

Tex grabbed a free barstool and rested his forearms on the surface. "What happened after I left the other night?"

"He got better, I got sick, he held my head when I puked in the bucket. We fell asleep, I developed chills and a high fever during the night. When I woke up the next day, Mitch was…different. Kind of reserved, you know?" She lifted one shoulder. "He hasn't called or gone out of his way to talk to me since then."

Tex's brow rose dramatically. "Has he seen you tonight? Dressed like that?"

"Just long enough to disapprove, apparently."

Tex's deep rumble of laughter rolled in the air. "Yeah! I can see that. Every guy in this place is gonna go home tonight and fantasize about you with a bar of soap."

Haley made a face. "Matty! Ew."

"Tex! That's disgusting."

"Well, I don't mean me!" he said, seeming completely unfazed by their snorts of disgust.

"What's so disgusting over here?" Niki said, joining their group. "And who the hell is this big guy looking almost yummy enough to be the real Trace Adkins?"

"Niki! I want you to meet some friends of mine. This is Haley Broussard and her *brother*, Matthew "Tex" Broussard. Haley and *Tex*, this is Niki Reeves, my *roommate* slash *soul-sister* slash *best* friend in the whole world." She lifted one brow, trying her best to convey the silent, though effective, *'hurt her and you die'* message.

"Ah, the aforementioned Niki..." Tex took her hand, and then to everyone's shock, lifted it slowly as he leaned over to place a gentle kiss upon it. He straightened, giving her the most charming, dimpled grin Meagan had ever seen on a man.

She turned to him, her eyes wide with wonder. "Holy moly, Tex. I had no idea you could turn it on like that."

"Well, you know," he drawled, "it's Niki's fault for throwing down the gauntlet, so to speak."

Niki pulled her hand back slowly and gulped. "I did…it is? I mean…I didn't realize I had…not that I'm complaining, mind you."

Tex gave her a slow nod. "Yes ma'am you certainly did—as soon as you uttered the words, '*almost* yummy enough to be Trace Adkins'. I don't like that word almost. With me it's gotta be all or nothin'."

Niki crossed one booted foot over another and hooked her thumbs in the pockets of her shorts. "Is that so?"

"Yep. So, the way I figure it, I've been challenged to turn your *almost* into *definitely*, or even *way better than*."

Meagan watched the sparks fly between the mountain of a man and her friend, who seemed to be weighing his words carefully. Finally, the tall, buxom blonde, with short spiked hair and big green eyes, gave him a nod. "Well, hell. Let the games begin, big boy."

He flashed another brilliant smile her direction. "By any chance, is Niki short for Nicolette?"

"It's short for Nicole...Amanda Nicole...but I prefer Niki."

He took a step closer and bent his elbow. "Nicole, could I please have this dance?"

Niki's mouth opened, perhaps to protest his use of her real name, but she seemed to think better of it. She snapped it closed, the lifted her chin as she reached out and took his arm. "I'd love to."

"Wow..." Meagan shot Haley a look before they both turned to stare after the couple already swinging into a Texas two-step.

"I know, right?" Haley's voice purred with admiration. "Did you feel that electricity crackling between those two?"

"Major vibes...major! Man, do they look good together, or what?" They stood watching the two dance in moves that totally complimented each other.

"Meagan?"

"Huh?"

"I have never seen my brother act like that with a woman. And let me tell you, he's brought some women to my parents' home, before. Always girls we knew he couldn't possibly be serious about. You know the kind, don't ya? Bleached blonde bimbos with tiny waists and big boobs...usually fake."

"Oh yeah, the kind of girls who wear lots of eye makeup, and short shorts with high heels?"

"Exactly. So, what's Niki like?"

"She's good people and so are her parents. Her mom treats me like her own daughter. Why?"

"No reason." She released a long sigh. "I've always wanted an older sister."

~~

Several hours later, Red closed and locked the front door, turning around to address his crew of employees. "Good job, gang; a full house and not a bit of trouble. Now, y'all go home and get some sleep. That's an order."

Mitch heard several shouts of thanks from various areas of the large space, but he only searched for a single face. He found Meagan exiting the storeroom with a case of beer.

"You heard the man," he said, grabbing the beer from her and placing it on the bar above her cooler. "Go on and get some rest. I'll fill up the cooler for you."

She nudged her way around him. "I like to do it myself. I have a method, and it makes it easier on me for the rest of the night."

The feel of her brushing by him in that clingy spandex had him hissing in discomfort.

She turned to him, surveyed the situation and gave him a cheeky smile. "You gonna live, Mitch?"

He grunted under his breath. "The jury's still out."

She started filling her cooler methodically, everything in its own designated spot for easy distribution. By the time she'd emptied several cases, he and Meagan were the only remaining people in the club. He'd been forced to pick a spot off to the side, far enough away to keep him from losing his mind. The sight of her, bending over the cooler in that second skin, desert camie suit, had just about done him in.

She approached, reaching for her backpack. "Thanks."

"You're welcome. We need to talk."

She pulled her keys from her pack. "We are, aren't we?"

"Seriously."

She dropped the backpack on the floor and sighed, whether from exhaustion, or irritation at the suspected subject matter, he couldn't tell.

She leaned back against the bar, her elbows resting on the marble surface. "So talk."

Mitch stifled the urge to gawk at her breasts, straining against the confines of her spandex suit. He swallowed hard, wishing for some other noise in the silence of the huge building. "We can't let what almost happened the other night—I can't let that happen again."

"So why are you here?"

"To tell you." He braced himself as she pushed herself away from the bar to approach him.

"Well, hell Marine, you could have called me to tell me that."

He looked off to the right. "I didn't want to call. I felt like I owed you an explanation face to face."

"The irony in that statement is that you can't even look at me."

He clenched his jaw to steel himself before he turned his gaze on her, and groaned aloud. At some point, she'd unzipped her suit to somewhere in the area of halfway down. He couldn't tell how far down, because he couldn't seem to pull his gaze any further than her breasts spilling out of the top of her push up bra.

"Look at me, Mitch."

"I thought I was."

"Not my face." She reached up to pull his chin upward until their gazes met. "It's kind of difficult to do that when my entire persona is sending a different message, isn't it?"

He swallowed again and managed to nod.

"You see, that's what you've been doing to me. Avoiding me, yet getting so upset because I wore this tonight. Why? I can tell you like it on me." She paused to run her hands slowly down the silky material along her sides. "Is it because you wanted me to wear it just for your eyes?" The edges of her lips curled in a seductive smile as she took a step closer. "That can be arranged."

"I don't want to hurt you."

"Rejection hurts."

"I don't want you to be afraid of me."

"I'm not."

"Ever. I don't ever want you to be afraid of me."

"I won't be."

"Even when I lose control?"

"You won't."

"Even when I wrap my hands around your neck and squeeze the life out of you?"

He saw it then…a flash…a millisecond of fear…of remembering those several moments. He reached out slowly for her, turned to the long mirror behind the bar and pulled her in front of him. He wrapped his right arm around her waist, holding her there as he used his left hand to pull her hair back then up, away from her neck. He lowered his mouth, so tempted to taste her, lost in the luscious smell of her, the feel of her in his arms, against his chest and the hardness of his arousal. She was ready for it, her eyes closed, head tilted just so…her pulse throbbing at the base of her neck.

"Open your eyes, Megs." He stared ahead, meeting her gaze in the mirror, then used his right hand to trace the still visible bruises on her neck.

"I can't let this happen again…ever. Do you understand?"

She reached up to hold his hand, kissed it tenderly. "You won't."

His heart nearly burst from wanting this woman in his life. His need to protect her prevented him from speaking those words. "I can't be sure of that, babe. And until I can, I can't be around you."

"Then do what you have to, Mitch, to be sure of that."

"I'll try, but it may be impossible to know for sure." A barely perceptible movement, a slight rise of her left eyebrow, caught his attention.

"Marines don't try, Mitch. They *do*."

CHAPTER 21
Accusations, Denials, and Restless Nights

Meagan tried to get comfortable—fluffed her pillow for the fifth time since she'd crawled into bed at 2:30 a.m.

At 3:30 she gave it up and made herself a cup of chamomile tea. In an unusual turn of events, she had the place to herself. There was no sign of Niki yet, and the LeBlanc's had insisted that Buck spend the night with them. She sat in the darkened living area, and sipped at her tea, lamenting the waste of such an opportunity.

The sound of light tapping caught her attention. She stood, goose bumps rising on her flesh as she waited for the sound to return. It did, and she panicked once she realized it was coming from her bedroom. "Oh...Go-d..." she whispered, stammering on the word once she remembered she didn't believe anymore. "What now?"

Meagan tip-toed into the dark of her bedroom and waited, holding her breath, until the tapping sounded again. This time she pinpointed it, coming from the southernmost window. Thankful for the black as pitch cover, she tiptoed to the window, hoping to find a squirrel or some other critter illuminated from the street light. She pulled the heavy curtain back, screeching at the sight of a human form hulking just outside the window. An instant later, a small light shined on the culprit's face.

"Open the door." Mitch spoke in a low monotone.

"What are you doing here?"

"Open the damn door before somebody turns my ass in for either breaking and entering, or a peeping tom."

She grabbed her robe on the way to the front door, and turned on a living room lamp. She pulled it open and he entered, looking panicked, as well as thoroughly confused.

She threw her arms around his waist, hugging him tightly. "I'm not sure I understand you, but I'm glad you're here."

"You sent me a text, so I came," he hissed, hugging her back hard before grabbing her arms and holding her away from him. "What's wrong?"

"Nothing's wrong, and what are you talking about? I didn't text you," she whispered.

His jaw set angrily, he pulled out his phone and showed her the screen. It showed a text from her.

SHE NEEDS YOU

She shook her head. "It wasn't me."

"Is anyone else here?" he asked.

She shook her head, remembering they didn't have to whisper. "No. Niki's not home yet," she said, her voice at a normal pitch.

"Good. Where's your phone?"

"In my backpack."

"Get it."

"Are you calling me a liar?" She didn't much like the tone of his voice.

"Please, just..." He raised one hand for emphasis. "Get the damn phone."

She released a huff of pure indignation as she looked around for the pack. It wasn't in the living room, or the bedroom. She checked the kitchen and the back bedrooms, even knowing she wouldn't have brought it in either of those rooms.

"Where'd you put it?"

She turned on him, angry and fed up with his attitude. "I don't know! I didn't call you dammit."

"It must be here somewhere."

She looked in a few more places then threw up her hands. "Call the damn thing."

He did, smirking at her. "How convenient that you couldn't find it."

"Shut up and listen for the ring tone, jerk!"

They stood stock-still and quiet. *Nothing.*

"What are we listening for?" he asked.

She glared at him. "Uh…a ringtone?"

"No shit? I meant is it an old fashioned ring, or a specific ring, or do you have a song programmed in?"

She turned away from him as though listening, but more to conceal her face from him. How could she have forgotten the song…his personal ringtone song? She closed her eyes and sucked in her breath, praying wherever it was, her battery was good and dead. In that instant, she pictured her backpack as she'd last handled it…car keys in one hand, bag in the other.

"I didn't bring it in. It must still be in my car."

He walked to the kitchen door and opened it. "Let's go get it."

"How many times do I have to tell you I didn't call you?"

"None, if you show me the fucking phone!"

"You watch your mouth in my home."

He hissed through his teeth. "I'm sorry! But, after everything that's gone on in this house, do you doubt how it made me feel to get your message?"

"It wasn't my message!"

"Prove it!"

She grabbed her keys from the counter and stormed to the door, mumbling about Jarheads being more trouble than they're worth. She checked the front and back seats, and found nothing. Mitch checked under the seats and even in the trunk, even though she insisted she hadn't opened the trunk since getting the new spare tire. She cringed a little less as he called her number again, this time absolutely certain he wouldn't hear it.

"I left it at the club."

"But you had your car keys," he argued.

"I removed my keys just after you handed me the backpack, remember? But I dropped the damn thing on the floor when—when I—when you rejected me. And *that's* where it is…in the club."

"Seriously?" He looked doubtful.

She ran her hands through her hair and tried to keep her tone from sounding hysterical. "You're trained to notice details. Did you see me walk out of the club with it?"

"No—I didn't."

"Well, there you go. And now that you've called me a liar to my face *several* times, I'd really like you to leave."

"Why were you so glad to see me when I got here?"

"Because I didn't know you were such a jerk, then." She pointed to the Chevy truck he'd parked in her drive. "Go. Now."

∾

Mitch was half-way back to his place before a thought came to him. He pulled his truck into the next turn lane and headed northeast of his current location. Within ten minutes, he was at the back door of the club and using his keys, the only other set besides the ones belonging to Red, to unlock it and let himself inside.

Before it even shut behind him, he'd spotted her backpack. He picked it up from the spot, exactly where she'd dropped it, and pulled the zipper. He dug around for a while before he gave up and dumped the contents on the bar. The phone fell out, slid across the slick marble to hit the concrete slab under the cooler.

"Son of a bitch!" He grabbed it, or rather the three separate pieces it broke into, meaning the back, the front, and the battery. He put everything back the way it was supposed to be and pushed the power button. *Nothing.* He popped the back off again…no easy feat when you *wanted* the son of a bitch to come off. He checked the battery, the card, every connection he could think of and snapped it back into place. Wondering how in hell he was going to explain a busted phone, he held his breath and hit the power button again. "Oorah!" He pumped his fist when the screen lit up. Hit the phone function and the call log button.

Calls received: None

Text messages received: None

Calls sent: None

Text messages sent: None

"No…no…no…Aarrrgghh...*dammit it to hell!"*

After he'd turned it off and on several times, and discovered varied new and unique ways to cuss like a Marine, with the same results, he finally gave up the fight. He threw everything back in her pack, and dropped it right back where she'd left it.

Totally disgusted with himself and his luck, he walked over to the men's restroom. He used the head and washed his hands afterwards, using lots of soap and hot water. As he lathered, he wondered about the percentage of men in the civilized world who actually washed their hands after taking a piss. If they'd spent as many years as he had in the dry, middle-east, sleeping in sand with nothing but your helmet, or an empty water jug as a pillow, they'd know. Afghanistan—where a man spent as much time fantasizing about showering for hours at a time, as he did about women with big tits. If they only knew what it was like to not be able to, they'd wash their fucking hands. He finally finished and toweled dry, then hit the back door to lock up and make the drive home.

His side door stuck, as usual, so he kicked the bottom to get it open and entered his drab-looking rent-house. It wasn't exactly a palace, according to middle class standards, but he figured it wasn't bad, considering the rent was cheap as shit and utilities were included. Anybody and everybody had informed him that was non-existent these days, but he'd lucked out. It just so happened the husband of the couple he rented from was retired USMC, circa Vietnam war, and didn't need the rent money to survive. The dude was slightly disfigured, but Mitch didn't want to ask if it happened in Nam. He figured if the man wanted to talk about it, he'd bring it up. If not, it sure as hell wasn't *his* place to ask.

An hour later, Mitch tossed his Lee Child novel onto the bed and got up. He'd read the same page several times and still didn't know what the damn thing said. Maybe getting a little two-legged distance between him and these four walls would help.

He changed into some sweats and eased his feet into a pair of expensive running shoes, a gift from his new brother-in-law. He stood, sighing with satisfaction at the better than average fit. One more thing civilians took for granted—running in anything other than combat boots. What a certifiable pain in the ass—as well as back, feet, and knees.

He warmed up by doing some stretches then hit the street running. He'd almost completed the first mile without incident, but nearly shit himself when an old piece-of-shit truck backfired. One more thing civilians didn't respect: the ability to walk, run, drive for days, weeks, months…anywhere in this entire country without having to worry about an IED blowing off various parts of your body or snipers taking pot shots at you.

Nope. They just didn't get how precious the gift of being here, living *here* in the USA was. With all its problems…crooked politics, ignorant voters from all parties, biased media coverage, congressional standoffs, and what not…it was still the best fucking place in the world to live. Anybody who didn't think so could kiss his ass and move the hell out.

The next two miles produced very little excitement for him. Someone blew a car horn unexpectedly and a guy loading some sheets of plywood in the back of a flatbed let one get away from him, causing a loud pop when it fell. He still hadn't rid himself completely of the basic instinct to duck for cover. So far, he'd managed to keep it to a mild flinch rather than a full-fledged 'hit the deck' type of move.

Mitch reached Lakefront Park, and ran the length of the boardwalk extending over the water before heading back home. By the time he turned onto his street, a red and orange glow was beginning to light up the eastern horizon. He'd just finished his stretches in the front yard when the husband half of his land lord couple pulled up in the drive. Roger Guidry's truck, an old Ford, battered and spotted with primer, might look like crap on the outside, but ran like a piece of well-maintained equipment.

"It's a great morning for a run, ain't it Mitch? It's nice and cool and not too humid. How far'd you go?"

"To the boardwalk, about six miles, I think."

"Yeah…yeah…sounds about right."

"I'm glad you came by, Mr. Roger. I've got your rent for next month. Let me go get it for you."

Roger gave him a slightly crooked smile. "That ain't why I'm here, but I do need your help to unload a few things, though." He opened his door with a little difficulty and stepped down, then walked to the back of his truck. "Some things are kind of difficult to manage with this thing." He waved one prosthetic arm with a type of grabber attached where the hand should have been.

"What'cha got here?"

"Things for the house. My old lady has been after me to fix this place up, put some money into it. Just didn't want to make it too nice for the trash that was living here the last few years. Every time I'd put something in, they'd tear it up. Now that I have a good renter, I'm glad to do it."

"Well, thank you, sir. I appreciate the compliment." He lowered the tailgate and slid a large box to the edge of the truck bed to examine it. "What do we have hear? A portable heater?"

"It's a portable fireplace. We got one for our family room this year. That old fireplace of ours wasn't cuttin' the chill for the wife and I anymore, and we used one of these as an insert. Son of a gun works like a charm and does it, using a lot less energy, too." He elbowed Mitch with his right arm. "The wife said this place could use a little romantic ambiance, and you can roll it wherever you need the heat. Living room or even…the bedroom," the old man said, with a wink. I also bought some paint for the inside. I got painters coming to give me an estimate in the next couple of days."

Between the two of them, they got the truck unloaded quickly. Mitch set the several gallons of paint in the utility room, and unboxed the new heater. To Mitch's surprise, it looked more like a fireplace than an electric heater. "No assembly required?" He rolled it out of the box in one piece and ran his hands over the solid wooden mantle and trim in a rich walnut stain. "This is a nice piece of furniture."

Roger nodded as he leaned over to plug it in to an outlet. "We've enjoyed ours so much and since this place is kind of small, the wife figured it would work nicely in here." He pulled the remote out of the box and put in the batteries. "Watch this." He pointed the remote at the heater and realistic flames lit up the logs in three different settings.

"Well kiss my ass!" Mitch nodded. "That's pretty cool, and that fan is blowing some hot air but you can barely hear it." He beamed down at Mr. Roger. "Just in time for that cold front we're expecting tomorrow night."

"Oh Lord, I know. I hope it doesn't come in earlier and ruin trick or treat. Bessie must have bought five hundred bucks worth of candy. If we don't give that crap away I'll go into sugar shock for damn sure." His deep chuckle rumbled in the air. "It's kind of difficult to hide that much candy from an old Marine scout with a sweet tooth, but every year, my wife sure as hell gives it her best shot."

He looked around to survey the place. "Somebody will be in tomorrow to get measurements for flooring for me. When the painting is done, I'm having new wood and vinyl flooring installed throughout the house. Hope it won't be too much of an inconvenience to you."

Mitch laughed and waved at the sparse furnishings. "What few things I have can be moved from room to room pretty easily."

He grabbed two mugs from the cabinet and turned. "How about some coffee, Mr. Roger?"

The older man nodded. "Sure, if you don't have some place to be."

"Nope. Normally I'd be sleeping right now, but that plan got shot to shit when I got a two a.m. message and had to go check on a friend." He poured the coffee he'd programmed to brew fifteen minutes earlier.

"I take mine black."

Mitch handed him a mug and poured a second for himself—also black. In the absence of a dining table, they sat in the living room with their coffee.

"Did I ever tell you how this happened?" Mr. Roger held up his stainless steel hook.

"No, and I didn't want to ask." Mitch sipped from his own mug.

"Damn grenade blew off the arm. While I was knocked out, I caught a bullet in the jaw when my buddy was dragging me to safety. Hell of a thing to wake up with no arm and only half of a jaw." He sipped his coffee and set down the mug on the makeshift coffee table.

Mitch stared down at Roger's arm and utilitarian claw. "Has it held you back? Did it keep you from doing what you needed to do?"

The older man lifted his mug from the makeshift table and smiled. "Wanted to do? I couldn't bring myself to pick up my guitar again. Need to do? Naw…I built a successful business, bought several pieces of real estate that have allowed me to provide for my wife. We never could have children and they wouldn't allow us to adopt because of our combined medical histories." He waved his right arm to indicate his jaw and prosthesis. "I had this and my wife has had insulin controlled diabetes all her life. I guess they thought we wouldn't be able to raise a child properly." He shook his head. "Sons-a-bitches! The worst thing is that they've deprived us of grandchildren. Man, we see all our friends with their grandbabies and it just twists my insides, you know? Poor Bessie became a kindergarten teacher so she could be a part-time mother to those kids."

After several moments of Mitch not knowing what the hell to say to that, Roger's gaze landed on Mitchell's own guitar.

"Please tell me you play. It'd be a big disappointment if a man with a vintage Gibson LG-2 sitting in his living room couldn't play it."

Mitch laughed at his coffee drinking guest and picked up the guitar to break into *Bottle of Wine*.

"Damn, that's a mighty fine sound coming out of there. That wood has got to be aged at least a good fifty years."

Mitch ran his hands lovingly along the stock. "Closer to seventy; it's a 1946 model and it was my dad's. It's about the only material thing I've given a damn about since I joined the Corps. Twenty five years of playing it has only increased my appreciation for its sound."

"Beautiful…nice full neck you can wrap your palm around. That's what I liked about that style. It was kind of like holding a full-bodied woman. I don't know why everybody goes crazy over those bony assed models on television and magazines. And whoever the hell that Victoria chick is, she can keep her damn secret as far as I'm concerned. Sheesh…those gals are nothing but skeletons with skin."

"And wings, Mr. Roger…don't forget the angel wings."

Roger threw back his head as he laughed. "They look worse than some of the guys we rescued from those 'non-existent' Vietnamese POW camps."

Mitch nodded. "I gotta agree with you. I like a woman with muscular thighs rather than toothpicks, and some meat on her. To me, there is nothing appealing about a woman whose butt is too damn bony to do anything but slip right out of your hands when you grab hold of it."

Roger's laughter rang out in the no frills interior of the room. "Kinda sounds like you got your eye—or your hands—on some particular girl. Give this nosey old man the scoop, son."

Mitchell's mood grew somber at the thought of the only woman he'd ever considered as more than casual entertainment. "I, uh…I've got some issues to deal with before I can even think about that." Keeping his gaze averted, he felt, rather than saw, the man's eyes on him.

"Do you have any other family members around, Master Sergeant?"

"Yeah, I've got a sister here." After filling him in on his twin nieces and new brother-in-law, he looked over at the man. "How about you? Do you and your wife have any other family around?"

The old man's eyes grew dim as he delved deeper into his family history. "I had two brothers. I lost both of 'em the same year I got injured. One, was a pilot in the Air Force. He got shot down before I was hit. Our younger brother got his head split open in a riot protesting the same war we were fighting. Called us both murderers to our faces the last time we saw him." He sent Mitch an amused look. "Didn't make for a very pleasant family gathering. Son of a bitch brought his supply of drugs into our parents' home, even lit up his bong in his old bedroom, yet still had the nerve to accuse Wayne and me of being irresponsible adults."

He sighed and shook his head. "Don't get me wrong, I loved my baby brother, but he was always spoiled ass rotten. The irony was that the dude who cracked him with the bat was also protesting the war. Assholes were on the same side. That guy was too high to know who the hell he was swinging at. Denny's *girlfriend* got the whole thing on her 8mm recorder. Screwed her up so bad she shot herself.

Left behind the roll of film, along with a letter saying she blamed herself because she'd been the one to introduce Denny to that whole 'scene' in the first place. Said she realized what a cop-out it was after the fact, but couldn't live with it."

"God, that's gotta suck, for everyone affected."

"I know. Little brother had brains, too. The kind that could have changed the world, made it a better place for everyone." The old man wiped at his eyes with the back of his hand. "What a waste."

After an entire pot of coffee and a two-hour visit that went by surprisingly quick, Mitch walked his landlord out to his truck. They'd made several agreements during their talk. For one, Mitch had offered to do the prepping and painting of the interior himself, as well as installing the new flooring afterwards. He also agreed to draw up a floor plan for the place with his laptop's drafting software and get it printed to scale. Roger was thrilled at the prospect of free labor, as long as Mitch agreed to put it toward six months with no rent.

"Oh hell, I almost forgot to give you this." Roger reached inside his truck and handed Mitch a plastic container full of tarts. "Here you go, son...fig pies and sweet potato pies, courtesy of the wife. You won't find any better."

Mitch opened the container and tried a fig pie, rolling his eyes in appreciation. "Oh man, is that good, or what? Tell the lovely Ms. Bessie I said *merci beaucoup*, and any old day of the week she feels like spoiling me, I'm available." He took another bite and nodded again. "Yup. I'm about to go all quart of milk ballistic on a few of these babies."

"She'll be glad to hear that. It makes her feel good to pamper people. Oh, by the way, in case you were thinking about going out to buy any pieces of furniture, you might want to check out our storage unit first. All of our rent houses started out as furnished years ago, but over the years, most of our renters have begun to bring their own furniture. So we just started keeping some stuff in a climate controlled storage building."

He pointed to the house. "I noticed you don't have a dining table, and I'm pretty sure there's one in storage, along with a set of chairs, some end tables, and night stands, too. It's a shame to have it all just sitting there when someone could be using it." He handed him a key. "Here you go, it's the storage facility behind the Market Basket on East 7th street, right across from the bakery. Use whatever you think you can fit in here."

Mitch took the key from him. "Thank you, sir. I'll take a look, if you're sure you don't mind. I don't have much because I don't need much…a bed and a recliner and a couch from my sister. But maybe I could save you the rent from having to store the furniture."

Roger chuckled as he started his old truck and threw it in reverse. "Oh, we don't have to pay to rent it—we own the place." He pulled out of the drive and waved as he drove off.

More than a little curious as to what he'd find in the storage unit, Mitch remembered he needed to do some grocery shopping, and the grocery store was near the storage facility. He went inside just long enough to grab his truck keys off the counter and yank the grocery list from the fridge.

CHAPTER 22
Storage Units and Chance Meetings

"Holy crap."

Mitch stared at the conglomeration of 'stuff' in the storage unit. He inched his way to what looked like a table, yanked off the blanket used as a dust cover and nodded in appreciation. It was one of those retro looking tables from the fifties, all chrome and covered with red and gray Formica. Judging by the spots worn smooth and pattern free, this was no reproduction. He pulled tarps from the three stacks surrounding it to find six chairs, all covered in red vinyl.

Turning in a slow circle, Mitch saw several items he could use, such as end tables, lamps, rocking chairs and various other forms of additional seating. Everything from antique *chifferobes* and dresser drawers to an old china hutch just like his and Sarah's old Maw Maw Dee used to have in her home. A good half of the items in the storage facility looked as though they could have held a place of honor in that old woman's house. The other half was a hodgepodge collection of pieces of furniture that didn't seem to match anything else in the room.

He left the storage unit, satisfied with his little foray, and promising to pay a return visit once he'd completed the minor house-remodeling project.

∿

Fifteen minutes later, he rounded the fruit section, nearly colliding with a small boy wearing a brace on his arm. He grabbed the child by the shoulders to keep him from falling. "Whoa, sorry little man!" The boy lifted his face, staring up with familiar blue eyes as Meagan's voice reached Mitchell.

"Don't run, sweetie. You already have one broken arm."

Mitch grinned down at the small boy. "Hey, Buckaroo!"

Buck stared at him until it clicked. "I know you. You gave me a pterodactyl." He turned to face the woman just rounding the corner. "Mama, look who's here!"

Meagan stopped, the smile for her son frozen on her face. "Oh. Hi."

"Try not to get too excited."

She gave a light snort. "Why should I? Experience is a wise teacher, and it's taught me it does no good where you're concerned."

He winced. "I guess I had that coming."

She nodded. "Yes, you did."

"I apologize, Meagan."

"For what? Scaring the crap out of me in the wee hours of the morning or calling me a liar?"

He grabbed his shopping cart to keep it from blocking the aisle. "Both, I guess. I don't know where the hell that text came from but I know you didn't send it."

She nodded before turning to examine a bin full of apples. "I accept."

He grabbed a bag of oranges from the shelf and dropped it in his basket. When he turned, she was facing him wearing a curious look.

"How can you be so sure?"

He assumed an at ease position, his shoulders relaxed. "I just know."

She crossed her arms, as though daring him to lie to her. "Yeah, right."

He glanced at her buggy, saw her backpack in the front section. "I see you found it."

"I left it at the club, just as I thought. But you knew that already, didn't you?"

"I sus—" The lift of her brow stopped him from going through with the lie of omission. "I went by the club after I left your place and saw it, right where you left it."

"You broke my phone." Her tone was dry and accusatory.

"I did not."

"Don't you lie to me."

"I didn't. I just—it fell." He huffed, annoyed that she knew. "The damn thing flew across the counter and fell on the floor. It broke into a few pieces but I put it back together." He shifted uncomfortably, rested his hand on his hip. "How'd you know?"

"I suspected."

Just when he thought her glare was equivalent to no further explanation, she spoke.

"We were the last two people to leave the club. I woke Red this morning to ask him to come unlock for me. He told me *you* were the only other person who has a key to this place. It didn't take a genius."

He looked down at his feet, adjusted his stance. "If I broke it, I'll get you a new one."

"It's not broken. But did you find what you were looking for?" Mitch didn't answer so she repeated the question. "Did you?"

"It erased the damn call history when it fell." The words rushed out of his mouth in a jumble. The rest was a low murmur. "Before I could check it."

Her face transformed from stern, school-teacher glare to an unexpected grin as she released a deep-throated chuckle. "I *know* I should be more pissed at you for snooping, but the thought of you panicked, with my phone in pieces, and wondering how the hell you're gonna explain it?" She giggled. "Well, that's just funny, right there. I don't care who you are."

Mitch would have been looking for a hole to crawl into if Buck hadn't come to the rescue. The boy started pulling on the bottom of his shirt.

"Hey Mitch, guess what I'm gonna be for twick aw tweat? Guess! Twy to guess!"

He looked down at the boy, admiring his energy and excitement, and always amused at his inability to make the 'r' sound. "Oh, I don't know…a pterodactyl?"

"No, not that! Guess again."

"Frankenstien?"

Buck's face twisted in confusion. "Who?"

Mitch waved off the choice. "Never mind. I guess you're a little too young for that. Uh, can you give me a hint?"

"He's gween and has *big* muscles!"

"Oh…and he goes like this?" Mitch bowed up with his two fists and attempted a somewhat quiet Hulk-like roar.

"Yeah! The Hulk!" Buck gave an identical roar only much, much louder.

"Okay, okay! Not here, please." Meagan hissed, trying to shush them. "You two are gonna get us thrown out of here."

Mitch laughed and ruffled the boy's hair. "Well, I bet you get a ton of candy tomorrow night."

Meagan groaned. "Yeah, just what he needs. *More* sugar in his system."

Buck nodded excitedly, his face lit up with a huge smile. "Aw you coming with us?"

"Um, I volunteered to pull the hay ride trailer full of parents and kids for trick or treating tomorrow evening. Red insists that a single trailer is less dangerous than everyone going in separate cars."

She nodded, keeping her arms crossed tightly at her chest. "We'll be on that hay ride, also."

Mitch squatted in front of Buck and gave him a big smile. "Well, then I guess I'll be seeing you tomorrow night, little man."

"Okay, see ya!" Buck took off down the aisle like a shot, followed by his mom, who grabbed his hand to stop him.

"Buck!" she hissed. "What did I say about running in the store?"

He stopped long enough to face her. "Um—it's not safe?"

She raised her finger to point at his nose. "That's right. You could hurt yourself or someone else, remember?"

He nodded once. "I wememba, Mom." He went to wipe his nose on his sleeve.

"Don't you dare!" She pulled a tissue from her pocket and wiped his nose. "Blow."

He did as his mom asked and grinned up at Mitch. "Bye!" He waved just before he headed off down the aisle.

Mitch laughed as he watched the boy bounce from one side of the aisle to the other. "Man, I wish I had that kind of enthusiasm for life."

Meagan stuffed the tissue in her pocket and pulled out a small bottle of hand sanitizer from her backpack. "I wish I had that kind of energy. Just for a week or two, anyway." She squirted some of the clear gel in her hands and rubbed them together. "I could make a serious dent in my to-do list."

"Yeah, I know what you mean. So, how long does he have to wear that brace on his arm?"

"It's been two weeks and the doctor said at least four. It's just a hairline fracture rather than a full break, but he didn't want to take any chances with it not healing as it should." She stared off after Buck.

"I guess I'll see you tomorrow night."

"Yeah, but don't worry," she said, stuffing the bottle into the zip compartment of her backpack. "You'll be too busy driving to see much of us."

"Meg—"

She raised her hand to cut off his reply. "Look, I get that you're not ready for a relationship, Mitch. It's cool. Forget it."

Mitch watched her push her buggy over to her son, just in time to thwart Buck's efforts to reach a bunch of bananas from the top of the heap.

He knew he'd hurt her…again. What he saw as pure and simple concern for her safety, she deemed as nothing less than rejection. Considering his words and actions in the past, he couldn't very well blame her.

Forget it, she'd said.

If only it were that simple.

CHAPTER 23
Hulks and Heroes

Mitch sat in an empty lot near the middle of the block, waiting for the trick or treaters and their parents to catch up to him. Red and Tiffany had decorated a trailer with lights and bales of hay for everyone to sit on. The method of dropping them off and waiting had kept the cumbersome vehicle out of the heavily trafficked areas for most of the evening.

Halloween night in Small town, USA had changed in one significant way. Judging by the number of cars on the streets, nobody walked anymore. Hell, when he and Sarah were kids, they'd set off on foot with their dad to visit the houses on their block.

Mitch watched nervously from the side view mirrors of his truck, cringing as the silhouettes of costumed children stood out in relief against the headlights of multiple vehicles. He prayed everyone was watching their children closely.

He raised the volume on the country station radio he'd been listening to just in time to hear Trace Adkins belting out *Swing*. He smiled to himself, picturing Tex on the bandstand at the club a couple of nights ago. To Mitchell's surprise, the big man had swung his hips and lip-synced his way through *Ladies Love Country Boys*. His looks and mannerisms had been close enough to the real Trace that he'd walked off with the club's "Look Alike" cash prize of $100. He shook his head, remembering how women were hanging off that son of a bitch by the end of his 'performance'.

Mitch hadn't discovered until the next day that he'd narrowed the swarm down to one woman. Tex had shown up at his place, wearing a remarkably sheepish, though somewhat satisfied grin. As it turned out, he'd spent the entire night acquainting himself with Niki, Meagan's roommate. Mitch assumed Tex had taken her to one of the two hotel rooms he and Haley had booked for the night.

Mitch had spent the better part of fifteen minutes chewing his friend's ass out. He'd tried to make Tex see that a one-night-stand with Niki could only mean trouble between Meg and himself.

"How?" Tex had asked. "You have nothing to do with this. I barely even saw you all night. Besides," he'd thrown in, "Nicole is thirty years old. Plenty old enough to know what she wants."

"That doesn't matter, and you damned well know it! If you hurt her, I'll be guilty by association—plain and simple."

Haley had shrugged and eventually agreed with him, telling her brother that the bonds of friendship between women didn't always have to make sense…they just were.

Something had been off with Tex since then. Some strange look on his old bud's face had signified a change, a shift, in the paradigm of Tex's former attitude toward women. Yep. He definitely sensed a shift—major or minor—it still wasn't clear to him.

Mitch popped a butterscotch candy in his mouth and frowned at his reflection in the rearview mirror. Change, good or bad, was always cause to be on the alert.

"Don't run, Buck!"

Meagan's voice cut through his contemplations like a hot knife to butter. He stepped out of the truck in time to see her make it back to the trailer first.

Buck held up his glow in the dark trick or treat bucket like it was a prizefighter's gold belt. "I got candy, Mitch."

Mitch lifted him onto a bale of hay circling the edge of the trailer. "Hey, let me take a look at that haul." He made a show of checking out Buck's container full of goodies. "Yep, you got enough there to keep your dentist happy for a good while."

Meagan pulled her son's foot closer so she could retie his sneaker. "And his mother broke and exhausted. *Every* overly energetic almost-four-year-old boy needs more sugar in his diet."

"Aw hell, Meg, we did it and our folks survived. Besides, if it weren't for Halloween, you may never have discovered how good your son looks in hulky green muscles."

"I gotta admit he's a handsome little devil."

"I'm not a devil. I'm the Hulk."

Mitch laughed. "That's right, and whatever you do, Mom, *don't* make him angry—"

"—because you won't like me when I'm angwy," Buck finished. He faced Mitch and roared, bowing his bulked up plastic green arms. Mitch roared back at him, bowing his arms as well. The two of them joined forces and roared in unison.

By the time Mitch turned his watchful eye on Meagan, she was trying hard not to laugh at their antics, but losing the battle. She broke finally, ruffling her son's hair above his green painted face and grinning at him. "You're such an adorable little mutant!" She stifled a yawn and rested one booted foot on the trailer. "I don't know about you Mr. Hulk, but I'm ready to call it a night. I've still got some studying to do."

"But you haven't made it to the haunted house yet. I think that's our next stop."

"Yeah, I want to go to the haunted house!" Buck started jumping up and down on the bed of the trailer.

"Okay. We'll go, but that's the last one. You already have enough candy there to last you until next Halloween." That seemed to satisfy the miniature Hulk enough to sit still for a minute.

"Jeez-Louise! You'd think he'd had enough of haunted houses, wouldn't you? Being that...well... you know," she finished weakly, before biting her lower lip.

Mitch tried, he really tried, to stop the spontaneous snort from erupting. He failed miserably. Before he knew it, he and Meagan had both doubled over in hysterical laughter, while Buck watched on, looking thoroughly confused.

Meagan wiped the tears of laughter from her eyes. "I can't breathe," she said, gasping for air as she straightened and held her sides.

"Oh God…that timing couldn't have been more perfect if you'd planned it!" Mitch wiped his eyes on the cuff of his long sleeved shirt.

"I didn't," she insisted.

"I know you didn't. That's what made it so damn funny." Without thinking, he pulled her into his arms and gave her a long, lingering kiss on the lips. Her guttural groan made him pull back suddenly. Clueless as how to explain himself or justify his actions, he simply set her away from him. He took two steps back and turned to go sit in the truck.

After instructing her son to stay right where he was, Meagan met Mitch in the front of the truck. She pulled him around, her face a perfect composite of anger and hurt. "What the hell, Mitch?" she hissed.

"I know…I didn't mean…I'm sorry." His words sounded lame to his own ears. He could only imagine how they sounded to her.

"You know, I'm a little tired of your mixed signals. One minute you act as though you want me, then you push me away. I have had about all the rejection I can take from one man. I don't think this 'friendship' of ours is healthy for me, Mitch. Maybe you'd better keep your distance from both me and my son from now on."

"Meagan, wait…" He grabbed her arm to stop her from walking away. The crunch of tires meeting pavement caught his attention as a small sports car turned down the street, its rpms revving at an entirely too high rate of speed for a street crowded with trick or treating children.

"Buck?"

The single word had his head whipping around to where the child should have been seated, but wasn't.

"Buck, noooo!"

The screech of tires and a sickening, bone-breaking thud preceded Meagan's horror-filled scream.

CHAPTER 24
Halloween Hell

The lights of Lake Coburn winked and sparkled in the night sky. Meagan stood there, her head pressed against the large plate glass window, just outside the 3rd floor surgery waiting room. The room itself was full—too full—of people, and she couldn't take it, had to get out. She knew they meant well. They were all concerned about her son.

The fact remained, that if Buck didn't pull through this surgery, it wouldn't be their loss. It would be her loss. Her loss and her fault—hers— and hers alone.

Her eyes drifted closed, shutting out the steady ribbon of car headlights travelling over the I-10 bridge.

"Megs."

She didn't need to see him to know the voice. Mitch stood behind her, torn up, blaming himself, wanting to make things better for her. He couldn't. Not this time. And if Buck didn't come out of this surgery perfectly fine, he never would, but she didn't blame him in any way, whatsoever.

"It's not your fault, Mitch. It's mine. He's my son, and I should never have taken my eyes off of him—not even for a second."

"Can you turn around? Please?"

"I don't want to see anyone right now, Mitch. I can't have anyone trying to console me or tell me everything is going to be fine. And if things go south, I absolutely do not want to hear the words 'It's God's will' from anyone. So, if you want to help me, you can go in that room and tell them all not to say that to me...ever. Because if they do, I will surely..." She clamped her jaw and spoke through clenched teeth. "I *will*...lose...my...shit."

"I-I can't keep you from losing your shit right now, Megs. I'm too damn close to losing my own."

His voice reminded her of silk running over broken glass, jagged and catching. She opened her eyes, letting the lights from outside come into focus, and then turned slowly to face him.

If anyone had told her another human being could look that miserable over someone else's child being hit by a car, she'd never have believed it. The man was hurting every bit as much as she was.

She supposed it shocked her so badly because the contrast was greater. He'd had a much longer distance to fall than she before hitting rock bottom. Whatever the reason, she couldn't help but go to him.

Without saying a word, she looped her arms around his waist, and laid her face against his heaving chest. Silently, she willed his breathing to even out, the rapid beating of his heart to slow, and his tears to stop.

Meagan hadn't realized until that moment of seeing Mitch so near broken, how being needed by another adult could be so empowering. She practically felt her strength seeping into him, melding with his own, and multiplying, increasing to all-time highs for them both. Buoyed by a sudden realization that things *would be* fine, she began to relax in the knowledge, letting that sense of inner peace seep into every pore and nerve ending in her body. The two of them stood in silence, holding each other, united in their concern for Buck.

You're stronger together.

Meagan started at the voice, then smiled as she hugged him tighter. "I think so too, Mitch."

He put her at arm's length, stared down at her, his gaze curious. "Did you hear that?"

Her own gaze narrowed. "That wasn't you?" She frowned as he shook his head. "What did *you* hear?"

"You're stronger together." He blinked twice. "At first I thought it was Red, but he's still in the waiting room with everyone else. We were totally alone."

Meagan's eyes were already on the two scrub clad figures approaching them. Tiffany McAllister reached Meagan first, as Tanner Collins brought up the rear, looking as though he wished he had better news to report.

"I set his leg, Meagan. It was a bad break but since he's still growing, that bone should stitch together properly with time. You can be sure I'll keep an eye on it for you. The brace on his forearm from the merry go round incident took the brunt of the punishment to his arm. I put a cast on it, encompassing the elbow to stabilize it more thoroughly." She stepped aside, as though to give Tanner the floor.

"He's got a concussion, and some brain swelling…"

Meagan felt Mitchell's hand tighten around hers, giving her the strength to quiet the screaming in her own head, enough to comprehend Tanner's words.

"It's not nearly as serious as it could be considering what happened. I've induced a coma until the swelling goes down, giving the brain time to heal itself." He shook his head, running one hand through his hair. "Honestly, the fact that the vehicle hit him just hard enough to throw him smack dab in the middle of the yard of the month…that was kind of incredible. I mean that lawn was some kind of thick. If he'd landed on the pavement we would be looking at a much more serious head injury."

"And the fact that both of you were there when it happened, jumping into action as quickly as you did," Mitch added. "It all works for him."

Meagan nodded. "So how long will he be in this coma you've induced?"

"That depends on Buck and how his brain reacts. It could be as little as two days, or as long as a week." Tanner placed a comforting hand on her shoulder. "I wish I could give you a definitive answer, Meagan, but I can't. I *can* tell you this. Buck is a strong, healthy little man, and he comes from a loving home. He's got everything he needs to give him the will to fight his way back to you."

Mitch nodded. "He's right, Megs." He shook his brother-in-law's hand then pulled him in for a man hug and pat on the back. "Thanks man."

Tiffany and Tanner continued on to the waiting room to talk to their own concerned spouses and friends, leaving Meagan staring up at Mitch again. He smiled down at her, linking the fingers of both hands through hers.

"I guess we are stronger together," he whispered, lowering his forehead to hers.

CHAPTER 25
The Sad Man (Part 2)

"Hello?"

"Don't be afraid."

"I'm not."

"That's because you're such a brave little man."

"Who awe you?"

"Don't you recognize me?"

Buck stared hard at the man in front of him, watching as his clothes changed from regular pants and a shirt to something his mama called 'dress blues'. The man reached up, took off his hat and held it in his hands.

"Awe you my daddy?"

The man knelt in front of him, and smiled as he nodded. "Yes, Buck. My name is Christopher Buckley Martin, and I am your daddy. Could I get a hug from you?"

Buck walked slowly into the man's arms and gave him a big hug.

"Mmm...it feels so good to hold you, after all this time, son. Thank you."

Buck stepped back and smiled at the man. "You aw welcome."

The man who said he was his daddy laughed. "You know, I couldn't say my R's when I was little, either."

"You couldn't?"

"Nope. So don't worry about that. You'll get the hang of it one day."

"Okay." Buck looked around. "Whewe awe we?"

His dad looked around the small room they were in. "I'm not too sure, but I'm glad he gave us this time together. I guess he has his reason for doing it."

"Who does?"

His dad used his thumb to point above them. "Him. The Big Guy... God."

"Oh, I don't know *him*."

"Yes you do."

"Well, I used to pway to him evwy night. But I nevuh did see him."

"You don't pray anymore?"

"No." Buck raised his hands and dropped them. "I dunno know why."

"Well, that's okay, because he sees you. He watches over you all the time. That's why I know you're going to be fine."

"Okay."

"Listen, Buck. I wanted to tell you how sorry I am, that I can't be a part of your life. I really wanted to be. That's why I was so sad before."

Buck frowned as he stared even harder at his daddy. "Awe you the sad man?"

His daddy nodded. "Yeah, I hope I didn't scare you. I was lost for a long time. I had to wait until things fell into place."

"You didn't. Mommy and Aunt Nik, but not me."

"That's because you're brave like your mom."

Buck cocked his head as he considered that. "She said *you* was bwave."

"Nah. You don't have to be brave in order to die. But you have to be very brave to keep on living. Especially when you're raising a child without a dad."

"But I have one now."

"You mean me?"

Buck nodded. "Yes. Awe you gonna be a weal daddy now?"

"Well, I'll always be your father, Buck, but I can't really be your daddy. A daddy should be there to throw a ball to you, teach you to bat and catch, and how to ride a two-wheeler. Things like that."

"And fly a kite?"

His dad smiled and nodded. "Yes and fly a *pterodactyl* kite."

"That's a dinosawr that looks like a bewd!"

"I know, buddy. It was always my favorite, and you got that from me, too."

The room started to grow fuzzy, like smoke but Buck didn't smell smoke. "What's happening?"

His daddy frowned, and Buck could suddenly see a little of the sad man in his face. "I think I'm about to leave. But before I go, I wanted to meet you. And...I want you to give your mom a message for me. Can you do that, Buck?"

Buck nodded. "Yeah, but I don't want you to go."

"I have to, son."

Buck got an idea that made him happy. "I can go with you."

"No, not this time. Your mom still needs you with her. We *will* see each other again, but it won't be for a long, long time."

"Okay then."

"I'm not worried about you, though. Because I know you're going to have another daddy. A good daddy who can be there for you to teach you all the things I couldn't."

"Is it gonna be Mitch?"

His daddy smiled at him. "I can't tell you that." Then he winked at him. "Tell your mom…"

Before Buck's eyes, his dad faded completely from sight. "Daddy?" He turned in a circle, searching the room, now filled with a white smoke that didn't smell like smoke. "Daddy?" Buck stood in the room, knowing he was alone, but then he heard it. It was like he whispered the words in his ear, but he'd heard them loud and clear. He *knew* it was the message for his mom, from his very own daddy.

CHAPTER 26
Houston Texans and #8

Meagan lay on her side, facing her son in his hospital bed. Very softly, she hummed a tune to an older song, one that had been a favorite of hers and Christopher's. She passed her fingers through her son's hair repeatedly, combing it back and away from his eyes—waiting, wishing, willing them to open…to see her, and to know her.

A possibility of brain trauma…some loss of memory…cognitive powers…no way of telling how severe at this point…possibility he wouldn't wake up once he stopped the coma inducing meds.

Tanner's words of warning looped in her mind like a message running on one of those highway signs.

"Don't you *dare* take him from me."

She spoke in a quiet but firm voice, the words echoing in the otherwise silence of the hospital room. She'd asked the nurse to mute the steady beep of the heart monitor.

But to whom did she speak the words? Whom could she blame if her child didn't wake up totally aware of his surroundings, or worse, didn't wake at all? Mitch? Definitely not. That left only herself, since she no longer believed in God. If that were the case, her dare wouldn't make any sense, would it?

She thought how empty her life would be without Buck. It suddenly hit her like a kick in the gut that if he didn't wake up, he'd be alone out there, wherever he'd be. He wouldn't know a soul that he'd met in his previous life. No grandparents or great-grandparents, or cousins, or *anyone* there to greet him in…where? In heaven? But, if there was no God, then there would be no Heaven, and that…that…for the sake of her son…was an inconceivable image.

"Okay." She tried it on for size. "Okay, God. You win. I believe in you. I do. I guess I always have, even when I tried not to, but…I'm totally serious, here…" her breath hitched as she held back a sob. "You already have his father. Don't you dare take Buck from me, too."

She lifted her son's hand to her mouth, kissed it, held it, until her tears tracked a path from her face down to his small fingers. She held them close to dry the dampness from his hands, then held her breath as she felt him twitch.

Meagan stared at her son's face and waited. There. His eyelid moved.

"Buck? Can you hear me?"

Mitch pushed open the door and spoke, his voice vibrating with anxiousness. "Is he talking?"

Meagan's gaze never left her son. "No, but I think the drugs are wearing off. God, I hope he isn't in any pain. Can you tell the nurses, please?"

Mitch left for a minute, then poked his head back inside. "Can I stay, Meagan? Or do you want to be alone? Or you want me to call Niki in?"

Meagan gasped as Buck's head jerked toward Mitchell's voice. "No! Yes! I mean stay! And talk to him, Mitch. I think he hears you! Buck, can you open your eyes, baby?"

Mitch wet a paper towel and sat on the opposite side of Buck's bed. "Hey buddy, how you doing?" Very gently, he wiped at Buck's eyes with the towel, trying to wipe away any build-up. "Your mom sure misses you, Buck, and so did Nik…and me too." His voice cracked, and he had to clear his throat to go on. "If you can hear our voices, try to wake up and talk to us, okay Buck?"

Meagan bent closer. "Hey, my brave little man, can you open your eyes for mama?"

They sat, taking turns talking and cajoling, letting him hear their voices, working together, until his lids finally fluttered opened.

Mitch stood aside, so that Meagan's face would be the first one he saw.

"Hey little man," she cooed. "Can you say something?"

"Ptewodactyl."

Meagan beamed into her son's eyes as Mitch burst into laughter from the opposite side of the bed. "Hi baby boy."

"Hi mama," he said, before yawning suddenly.

Mitch leaned over the opposite side of the bed. "You've been sleeping for a while, buddy. How do you feel?"

"Sleepy." He turned his head slowly in Mitchell's direction. "Hi Mitch."

"Hey buddy."

Mitch crossed one arm over his chest and slapped the opposite hand over his mouth. Meagan supposed it was to keep from blubbering like a big ole baby. There was nothing quite like a kid coming out of a coma, to turn a big, bad Marine to a blubbering mass of emotions.

Buck faced her again, tried to lift his hand. "Whaew am I?"

"You're in a hospital, baby. Do you know why?"

"No."

Buck turned toward the door as Dr's. Tanner Collins and Tiffany McAllister entered the room.

"Hey, look who's awake!" Tanner said, obviously pleased at what he saw. He took a penlight from his pocket and checked Buck's pupils and reflexes while Tiffany called out his vitals from the monitor readings. "How many fingers am I holding up, Buck?"

"Thwee."

"That's right. Do you know who these people are?"

"Mommy and Mitch," Buck said, before pointing to Tiffany. "And you aw Bwianna's mommy, and you…" he pointed to Tanner. "Aw Dani and Sami's daddy."

"Look at you showing off!" Tanner said, beaming down at his patient.

"Do you remember what happened Buck?"

A tremendous relief washed over Meagan when he said he didn't. Maybe it would save him from a little mental anguish.

"You don't remember trick or treating?" Tiffany asked.

His face lit up in a smile. "I was the Hulk! And we had a hay wide, and Mitch dwove the twuck."

"You are exactly right. And *that,* little man, is all you need to remember about that night. Besides a couple of broken bones, and a bump on the head, you are just about perfect!"

He turned to Meagan. "We'll get him down for a CT scan later today, but I want all those drugs out of his system first."

He stepped aside to let Tiffany sit next to him on the bed. "Hey Buck, how are you feeling?"

"Good. I'm hungwy. Can I have some pizza?"

Tiffany grinned, having to talk over the laughter in the room. "Well, how about some chicken noodle soup and jello for starters? We'll work our way up to that pizza, okay?"

"Okay."

"Now Buck, you had an accident, so your leg is in a brace. And you remember when you hurt your arm on the merry go round?" She continued at his nod. "Well you hurt it again so I had to put this cast on you so it heals better. The cool thing about a cast is that people can draw on it! Like this…" She pulled a red pen from her pocket and drew a stick man on his cast. "Pretty cool, huh?"

"Yeah!"

"So, are you hurting anywhere? Your leg or your arm?" She nodded when he said he wasn't. "Good, because we don't want you to hurt. So if either your leg or your arm starts to hurt, you let somebody know, okay?"

The doctors walked out, asking Meagan to join them. Reluctantly, she left Mitch with Buck so she could go talk to them, immediately worried they were holding back.

"He's good, right?"

"He's excellent from what I can see," Tiffany admitted.

"The CT scan will tell the entire story, but from what I've seen and heard, I don't think it will show any abnormalities." He sent Tiffany a cautious glance. "We did want to talk to you about what some patients have experienced while under induced comas of this type."

Meagan felt her hackles rise. "What is it?"

"Nightmares. He hasn't mentioned anything yet, has he?" Tiffany asked.

"No, and I've been with him since he woke up."

Tiffany nodded. "Good, let's hope he bypassed that little curve in the road. Some patients have said they were extremely disturbing. We just wanted you to be aware that it was a possibility."

Meagan gave her a slow nod. "I'll be sure and let you know if he says anything." She re-entered the room quietly, watching Mitch interact with her son.

The attentive Marine had pulled a chair close to the bed and sat up with his hand touching Buck's head, as though afraid to let go of him. "Hey Buck, can you tell me why the first word out of your mouth was 'pterodactyl'?"

Buck's next words, spoken in a reverent whisper, had her immediate attention.

"Because my daddy said his favwite dinosauw was the ptewodactyl, too."

Mitch looked up, letting his gaze land on Meagan as she approached the bed slowly.

"Your daddy?" she asked, as a cold sweat swept over her body. "Buck, did you have a bad dream about your daddy?"

"Nu-uh. But I saw him and he said the ptewodactyl was his favowite one…just like me. And mama, you know what else he said?" He turned to her, his eyes wide and wondrous.

"What's that Buckaroo?"

"He said when he was little he couldn't say his 'aw's either."

"Really? Well, I sure didn't know either of those things." Her heart pounded as she sat on the bed next to her son. "It's nice that you had a good dream about your daddy while you slept."

"I didn't dweam it, mama. I saw him, but I didn't know who he was at fiwst."

"Why not?" Meagan was imagining all kinds of horrific circumstances in her mind. Did the sad man's face appear first on the body of a monster?

"He didn't look like he did in the pictuw in my woom. He was dwessed," he looked at Mitch and pointed. "He was dwessed just like Mitch...in blue jeans and one like that." He pointed to the black and gold number 9 New Orleans Saints jersey Mitch wore. "Assept daddy's was blue and it had a big cow on it."

Meagan covered her mouth suddenly.

Mitch chuckled. "A cow?"

Meagan wasn't laughing. "Buck, did it have a number on it?"

"Uh huh...it was a number 8. It did this." With his good arm, he drew two circles in the air, one below the other. "He had one heah and heah." He pointed to both his arms.

Meagan swallowed. "A number 8, are you sure?"

"Yeah. One, two, three, four, five, six, seven and *eight!*"

"Oh my God." She stared at Mitch, then her son, then Mitch again.

Mitch walked around to meet her. "What's wrong?"

"It's his Texans jersey. Navy blue with the bull mascot on the front and number 8 for Schaub, he liked Schaub. Said 8 was his lucky number. I sent it to him his very last Christmas. Never even got to see him wear it in person, accept for once during our Skype calls. I...hang on..." She slipped her wallet from her backpack and thumbed through a stack of cards and photos until she found something. "He emailed this image to me and I cropped him out and printed it. It's kind of low resolution so it didn't enlarge very well." She held out the image of Chris in a pair of jeans wearing his jersey proudly. "It was a group shot of several of the guys all wearing their different team jerseys."

She turned slowly, held the photo up so that Buck could see it. "Sweetie, is this the shirt you saw?"

Buck's brows drew together as he concentrated on the picture. "Hey, that's my daddy." He reached out to touch the picture, its laminated surface a little scuffed and cloudy. "That's what he was wawing, mama. You see the cow?" He gave Meagan a toothy grin. "And he was smiling, just like that. He was vewy happy to see me. I gave him a hug and evwything."

The breath left Mitchell's lungs in a rush. He stared at Meagan and whispered, "Oh, man."

"Mama?"

Meagan turned to him, attempting to wipe the tears from her face. "Uh huh?" she managed before biting back the onslaught of fresh ones waiting to overwhelm her.

"I hafta tell you somethin'…fwom daddy."

Meagan choked back a sob as Mitch slipped his hand into hers. She latched onto it, lacing her fingers through his, using his strength to pick herself up. "What is it, Buck?"

"He said to tell you…he knows, and he's glad you gave me his name…and that he's home now."

CHAPTER 27
Returns and Revelations

The door of the house swung open before Mitch even shifted the car into park. Niki came running out, with Tex bringing up the rear.

She jerked the car door open and gushed at the little boy in the back seat. "My little Buckaroo! I'm so glad you're home, little man. Did you miss Aunt Niki?"

Buck nodded. "I missed youw pancakes, Aunt Nik."

"Ah, the boy's using me for food already!" Niki's tone was overly dramatic, as she gave him an awkward hug, trying to work her way around his arm cast and leg brace. "But guess what, Buck? I baked for you."

Buck's face lit up. "Is it bwownies, aw cupcakes?"

Mitch laughed as he came around to lift Buck gently from the back seat. "Not even through the door yet, mom, and he's already thinking of junk food."

"That's because his Aunt Niki has brown-nosed her way into his heart, via chocolate, since before he's even had teeth."

Niki shrugged at her friend. "Hey, when you're good, you're good."

"You're such a sugar pusher." She reached out to give her friend a one armed hug. "But you're allowed, this one day. Hey, Tex. Glad you could be here for this." She kissed him on the cheek before following Mitch, carrying her son, into the house.

∾

Niki covered her mouth, and held back tears at the thought of what could have happened. She leaned against Tex, happy that he'd turned up for Buck's homecoming. "Lord, this could have been so much worse, Tex."

"But it wasn't." He pulled her to him for a hug. "They make a good couple, don't they?"

"They sure do." She looked around to make certain the two of them were alone. "I don't think either of them suspects it was us who sent that text. Has Mitch mentioned it to you?"

"Only that Meagan thinks it somehow *could* have been Buck's dad." Tex shivered. "That's some freaky shit, there."

"But convenient, don't you think? After the crap he'd been putting us through in that house, I figure I earned the right to use his presence, just this once, to get those two together."

"Uh huh." Tex leaned in to give her a quick kiss. "*Almost* as convenient as getting locked in the club after hours with no way of getting out."

"At least not without setting off the burglar alarm, anyway, which we never would have lived down," she added. "Thank God, Mitch went to the club to look for Meggie's phone."

Tex laughed. "And his bladder that he had to go to the head, so we could sneak out of there without him seeing us." He turned her in the direction of the house. "You think they'll ever figure it out?"

She let him lead her inside. "I won't tell, if you won't."

∼∽

A little before 10:00 p.m., Mitch looped Meagan's waist with one arm and planted a soft kiss on the side of her neck. "Come sit with me for a while, before I go home, Megs. We've done all the cleaning we can do in this kitchen for one night."

She folded her dishcloth in half and draped it over the edge of the sink. "I guess you're right." A long, low roll of thunder echoed in the distance as rain pelted the windows. The lights had flickered and gone out about a half-hour earlier, necessitating the lighting of candles in some rooms. A couple of said candles were scented. As a result, the soft scents of warmed cinnamon, combined with a light orange and vanilla candle to fill the air with deliciousness.

Meagan leaned over the jar candle sitting on the kitchen counter, and used its own lid to smother the flame.

She let Mitch lead her into the living room, feeling just a little shy. Her stomach churned with butterflies as he pulled her to the couch. Since Buck's accident, they hadn't really 'talked' about much more than that. Mitch had hinted a few times that they would, once her son made it home from the hospital. Here it was, November 6th, already, six long days after the accident, three days after Buck had woken up with no loss of brain function.

Part of her looked forward to what Mitchell had to say, suspecting he'd given up the idea that she and Buck weren't safe with him. The other part of her was too accustomed to disappointment, and terrified to hope for a life with this man. Her run of luck had been so bad for so long. Why should now be any different?

Mitch settled on one end of the couch, his back up against the arm, and pulled her down with him, holding her close. "I think we need to talk."

Candlelight flickered from the end table while a hurricane lamp on a stool at the opposite end of the hallway cast an ethereal glow from the opening.

Oh God, here it comes. She swallowed the bile building in the back of her throat. When had she begun to rely so heavily on Mitchell's presence for strength? When had she fallen in love with him? She could almost hear the words forming in his mind. *"You and Buck are entirely too much trouble to risk a relationsh—"*

"I love you, Meagan."

What? "You do?" Her mind couldn't seem to grasp and accept his words. There *had* to be a catch.

"And I'm crazy about Buck."

Someone started a drum cadence in her chest with a pair of sledgehammers. She finally got the courage to face him, biting on her lower lip to keep the quivering to a minimum.

He reached out to brush a stray lock of hair from her forehead. "Well?"

She swallowed. "I'm waiting for the but…"

He frowned. "You're waiting for the butt…it's not a joke. There's no joke and no butt. I love you and your son."

She shook her head. "Not like the butt of a joke, the B-U-T…like 'I love you, *but* we still can't be together,' or something to that effect."

He pursed his lips, almost as if he was trying to hold back a laugh. *What in hell did he find so funny about this situation?*

"Are you trying not to laugh at me?" *Her heart was about to pound out of her chest from anxiety and this son of a bitch was trying not to laugh?*

He coughed and seemed to sober. "Ooo-kay…" he drawled. "You're absolutely correct in assuming there is a *B-U-T,* and here it is." He cleared his throat loudly. "I love you, and I love Buck, and I want you both in my life permanently…but…" He held up a finger and touched the center of her forehead. "I can't have that unless you and Buck both want me in your lives also."

She blinked several times, trying to keep the tears from blocking out the sight of him.

He looked at his watch. "I guess it's kind of late to ask Buck tonight, so I guess his answer will have to wait until tomorrow. *But…*it sure as hell would be nice to get an answer from you right now." He slid to his knees on the floor in front of her, fitting himself between her legs. "So, are you gonna keep me in suspense all night? Because I'm not leaving here without an answer. No—scratch that! I'm not leaving here without the *right* answer."

She slipped her arms around his neck and smiled. "You don't have to wait until tomorrow Mitch. I'm making an executive decision for both Buck and me."

"You are?"

"Uh huh. I know how I feel about you and I know Buck's crazy about you...so yeah. Yeah, you can be a part of our lives." She kissed him then, a long, lingering kiss that left both of them wanting for more. He didn't have to say a word for her to know that...every square inch of his body revealed how much he wanted her. She shivered at the nearness of him, breathed in his masculine scent. Then she ran her hands down the front of his shirt to his belt.

He stopped her hand from travelling any further. "Uh uh uh...not so fast. You don't think I'm going to let you use me without getting a commitment from you first, do you?"

"But, I already said you could be a part of our lives..."

"That's only part of the right answer and I'm a total package kinda guy."

She wrapped her legs around his hips and pulled him closer. "Oh, God…You sure are."

"So?"

"So…I love you. But you knew that already…Didn't you, Marine?"

Mitch kissed her, then nibbled and traced a sensual path from her mouth to her ear. She shivered, her entire body anticipating his next move as he growled low in his throat.

"Mm…I suspected."

Excerpt of
RAINY SEASON
(title subject to change)
(Haley Broussard & Ben Bonin's story)
Introducing a new character, Bo McAllister, into the
Niki and Tex story, as well as a continuation of
Meagan and Mitch's storyline.

CHAPTER 1
Thanksgiving and Thanks for Nothing

Tex glanced up from reading the paper. Haley entered the room, looking about as cheery as a Golden Retriever with a dead duck tied around its neck. "What's going on, sis?"

She flopped down on the couch, her laptop tucked under one arm and holding a family size bag of skittles in the other. She dug around in the bag and came up with a handful of red ones, but still didn't answer.

"Why the hell don't you go to the mall and buy bags of just red ones?"

Eventually, Haley graced him with an irritable glare. She picked up the remote and began flipping through the stations, finally landing on the Thanksgiving Day Parade.

"You know, little sister, your boyfriend may be dealing with something that requires a higher priority than keeping a phone date with his girlfriend."

Haley turned to him, her eyes wide and filled with threatening tears. "No! Really? *That* thought *never* crossed my mind…jerk."

"Hold on, now. I doubt there's a hell of a lot going on where he is right now. He's in the North Helmand Province, isn't he? He's probably spending most of his time on the base, being bored out of his mind."

"If he was on base, I'd have heard from him by now." She pulled her phone from her pocket and waved it at him. "He said he'd call, or email, or message me first thing this morning to wish me a Happy Thanksgiving." She dropped her phone on the couch beside her and popped a couple of Skittles in her mouth. "He always calls when he says he will. Wherever Ben is, he's sure as hell not sitting around being bored."

Tex folded the Beaumont Enterprise and rolled it up as he'd found it on the doorstep of his parents' front porch this morning. He swatted his knee a couple of times, then stood suddenly. "You need a change of scenery, Haley girl. Go get dressed, because you and me are takin' a little road trip."

"Where to?" She let him pull her up by the hand.

"We're going to Louisiana. Just 'cause mom and dad decided to go skiing in Colorado for the holidays, doesn't mean you and I can't have a decent Thanksgiving."

"We'll be back by tonight, won't we? I've got to be here to take care of my horses."

"Nope. Pack a bag for the night. Give 'em a little extra hay, they'll be fine until tomorrow evening."

"But I hate leaving Dakota."

Tex stared down at his petite sister. "For Christ sake, she's a twelve hundred pound horse, not a child. I think she can handle one night away from you without succumbing to separation anxiety. Besides, she has three other horses out there to keep her company. She'll be fine." He grumbled under his breath. "God knows their stalls are all nicer than my own house."

"That's only because you live like a slob. Bachelor pads are supposed to be welcoming to women, but yours is disgusting." She shivered. "You can't set foot in that place without having to step over takeout cartons, empty beer cans, or dirty laundry." She tucked her computer under her arm and scooped up her phone. "You really should hire somebody to clean once a week. God, I thought Marines were supposed to be neat and organized."

"Hey, I had to be neat and organized for twenty years. Now I can be as sloppy as I want to be. Besides—" he slapped one of his biceps. "Once the ladies get a hold of this, they're too mesmerized to see anything else."

Haley walked away from her brother, snorting with laughter. "Yeah, Stud…you just keep tellin' yourself that."

Tex watched his sister slip her boots on and head outside, thankful he'd been able to pull her out of her temporary depression. There were a few good reasons for a Marine not to contact his favorite girl on Thanksgiving Day. Worse-case-scenario? Him, lying dead from some sniper, rocket, or IED, which was a possibility, though less so at this point in the war. Other reasons were injuries, which were also a possibility, a lack of signal, or wanting to dump one girl for another. From the sickly-sweet phone conversations he had witnessed on occasion between Haley and Ben Bonin, he figured that was *highly* unlikely. Chances are he was busy with supply runs or on patrol and lacked the equipment to phone home. Both included an element of danger. She'd just have to wait it out. In their parents' absence, he figured the least he could do was to make the waiting less painful for her.

He pulled out his phone and found the contact he was looking for. He punched in the number and waited through three rings before Mitch Hebert picked it up with a jovial *"Happy Thanksgiving shit brick!"*

"You also, jerk wad! You up to a visit from your two favorite Texans?"

∿

"Mom!"

"Hang on, Buck, I'm coming." Meagan topped the green bean casserole with the last of the French fried onions and slipped it back in the oven for the last 10 minutes of baking time.

She wiped her hands on her jeans and went into Buck's room. He sat on his bed trying to dress himself, but without much success. She laughed at his half-dressed predicament, one leg in and one leg out of a pair of oversized sweat pants, and one arm and his head through a #8 Texans football jersey.

After a struggle, she finally got his braced leg through the second leg of the sweats. She sat back and groaned at his choice of shirts. "Son, you have other shirts, you know. Two weeks straight of the same football jersey is getting old."

"But it was my daddy's favwite team, and Mitch gave it to me." He looked up at her with pleading eyes as he kicked his good leg against the side of his bed. "Please mom?"

"Okay, but after this cast comes off, I don't want to see you in jerseys for a while. And you will be dressed up in an adorable little suit for Christmas if it kills me!" She finagled until she finally got the cast through the arm of the jersey. "You want me to carry you in the living room?"

"No, I want to go in the kitchen with you and Nik." He got his crutch and hopped to the kitchen as if he was born using the darn thing.

Niki passed him in the hallway and groaned. "God, I can't wait until he gets off of that crutch. It's like having our own little Tiny Tim from that Dickens novel."

Meagan laughed as she placed the buttermilk pies on the snack bar next to the pumpkin pie. "I know, but it's so much better than the alternative, right?"

"Definitely! Hey did you remember to pick up whipped topping for the pumpkin pie?"

"I'd forgotten, but Mitch is bringing it."

"Are you sure? Because, I only have pumpkin pie once a year and it's not the same without it."

Meagan looked up at the sound of knocking at the front door. "There he is, go ask him yourself."

~~

Niki jerked on the door and held it open wide as Mitch entered, carrying a large roasting pan. "Good Lord, that smells awesome!" Her gaze followed the roaster as she pushed on the door. "But where's the whipped topping?" Something large stopped the door from closing. She turned to see Tex Broussard in the doorway, wearing a shit-eating grin.

He pushed his way inside brandishing two cans of whipped topping and a twelve-pack of domestic beer. "Ask and ye shall receive, madam." He bowed gallantly at the waist before holding the cans out to her.

His younger sister, Haley, pushed her way around him. "Yeah, yeah! Mitch already bought it, you just carried it in. Hey Niki, how are you?" Haley reached out to give Niki a hug. "I hope y'all don't mind that Mitch asked us to come along. Our folks went to Colorado and it sucks being alone on a holiday with only *him* for company."

"Not at all, and I'm good, Haley. More importantly, how's it going with Lance Corporal Bonin?"

Niki watched enviously as Haley's soft brown eyes lit up with barely concealed excitement. "God, I miss Ben so much! He sends me a rose every single Monday, Niki. Isn't that the most romantic thing? He wants me to fly out with his mom to Hawaii when he gets back from this deployment in six months."

Tex groaned and made a show of rolling his eyes. "Jesus Christ, that's all I hear lately. 'Ben said this!' and 'Ben did that!'" He shook his head. "Give me a break, would you?"

Haley surprised her brother with an effective punch to his gut. "Shut up, you jerk! You know, it's not a sin for a guy to be romantic. From what I hear, you could take a few lessons from him in the consideration department." She winked at Niki before heading to the kitchen and leaving the two of them alone at the doorway.

Niki stood with her hands fisted on her rounded hips. "Well, I sure as hell didn't expect to see *you* here."

"Disappointed?" he said, stepping in close for a kiss. What he got was a barely-there brush on her cheek as she turned her face.

"Well no, but I am surprised."

He stood to his full height, looking somewhat shocked at her reaction to him. "After those fabulous couple of nights we spent together, I figured you'd be glad to see me, Nicole."

She smiled at him, showing her dimples. "I was *disappointed* two weeks ago, when you didn't call after *said* nights. I've moved on since then. Now, I'm simply surprised that you're here." She batted her eyelashes at him. "Thanks for carrying in the topping though. That was surprisingly… considerate…of you."

She made a show of checking her watch as another knock sounded at the door. "Oh, hang on, Tex. That must be *my* dinner guest." She swung it open, greeting the newest arrival with squeals of delight at the gorgeous basket of fall flowers in one hand and two bottles of wine in the other. "Hey, sweetie, come on in!" The tall, good-looking man leaned over and she threw her arms around his neck to kiss him soundly on the lips.

"Happy Thanksgiving, Niki. And thanks again for inviting me to this dinner." He held out the bottles of wine. "This is for the two lovely hostesses, but the flowers are all yours. And uh, there's a little surprise inside for you, but you'll have to look for it."

"Oh, I love surprises!" She took the wine from him and placed it in the fridge to chill, then set the flowers down on the table to start her search. "Oh,

Bo McAllister, this is Tex. Tex, this is Bo," Niki threw in, while continuing her search for the surprise. She pretended not to pay much attention, as the giant of a man from Texas seemed to size up his equally large competition. She smiled to herself, doubting seriously if Tex ever came face to face with someone as big as he was.

Tex was the first to step forward and offer his hand. "Matthew Broussard, but everyone calls me Tex."

"Bo McAllister. It's nice to meet you man, and Happy Thanksgiving."

"You t—"

Niki cut off his reply with an ear-splitting screech as she jumped up and down. "The ballet! You got tickets to the ballet? I adore The Nutcracker! Oh thank you, thank you Bo!"

Bo caught her easily as she jumped in his arms. The room resonated with his deep laughter as he spun her in a circle. "You know I aim to please."

~~

Tex stood by, watching the display with a growing sense of alarm burning in the pit of his belly. Mitch approached his side.

"What's going on in here?"

Tex looked at his friend and cocked one eyebrow. "He scored some tickets...to the *ballet*…something about cracking somebody's nuts. Looks like it could be his. Who is this kid, anyway?"

Mitch gave him a friendly shove into the kitchen once Meagan joined the noisy melee in the living room. "He's Red McAllister's first cousin, and he's a hell of a nice guy, so don't even think about giving him a hard time, or I'll have to pull Nik *and* Meagan off of your ass."

"Thanks bro…semper fi to you too," Tex snorted at his friend.

Mitch gave him a casual shrug. "Hey, I told you to call her, but you had more important things to do. You remember, like that blonde pole dancer in Beaumont?"

Tex hooked his thumbs in his belt loops and cocked his head. "Dude, do you have any idea what kind of muscles those girls *use* to hang upside down from those poles? That is some serious stuff, man, I shit you not!"

Mitch raised one hand to shut him up. "Whatever, man, but you screwed up. Meagan warned you. She well told you Nik has a low tolerance for jerks and assholes. She told me she even *called* you to let you know Nik was getting tired of waiting for you to call. You blew it."

"Well hell, I guess I did." Tex leaned his shoulder against the door and crossed one booted foot over the other as he watched the adoration fest in the other room.

Within seconds, Bo freed himself from the women and came over to meet the men in the kitchen. "Damn, something smells good in here! Did you deep fry that turkey?"

"Sure did," Mitch said, shaking Bo's hand. "How you doing, man? You two been introduced?"

"Yeah, just before he brought out the big guns...the ballet tickets," Tex snorted.

Bo grinned at him, his McAllister blue eyes sparkling with mischief. "Oh that?" he said, jerking his head toward the women, who were already making plans. "That's a diversionary tactic. I told them I'd watch Buck if I could get them tickets for that ballet. I also knew the ballet was scheduled for the same night as the heavyweight prize-fight in Vegas. I figured while they're at the ballet, we can be at my place watching the pay per view fight on my 70" flat screen. I ordered the fight today."

Mitch slapped him on the shoulder. "Good plan, buddy. Excellent plan!"

Tex nodded, hating to agree, but unable to think of one damn reason not to.

ABOUT THE AUTHOR

Photo of Ms. Leger provided by Joan Granger
Simple Memories Photography in Welsh, LA

Lori Leger resides in south central Louisiana with her husband. Between the two of them, they have five amazing, adult children. Though they love having the house to themselves, they adore getting frequent visits from their children and grandchildren, who range in age from one to eighteen years old.

In March of 2012, she resigned her eighteen plus year career as an Engineer Technician to pursue her dream of writing full-time.

She has five books published in her **La Fleur de Love** series, and this is the third book in her spin-off **Halos & Horns** series.

She also contributes to, as well as publishes, a series of seasonal anthologies called **Seasons of Love.** The fourth book in the series will be out by November, 2013.

Lori is the sole proprietor of Cajunflair Publishing.

www.CajunflairPublishing.com
www.lorilegerauthor.com
cajunflair@lorilegerauthor.com
lleger641@yahoo.com
Join me on Facebook, Twitter, Goodreads and
Pinterest

LORI LEGER

3 Series - 3 Ways to *Feel* the Love

La Fleur de Love

HALOS & HORNS

Seasons of *Love*

SAM
Carrie

ISBN-10:
1466454210

JACKSON
Giselle

ISBN-10:
1466454334

GREG
Melinda

ISBN-10:
0985719230

"RED"
Tiffany

ISBN-10:
147011366X

DRAKE
Annie

ISBN-10:
0985719214

*Enter Lori Leger's World
of La Fleur de Love*

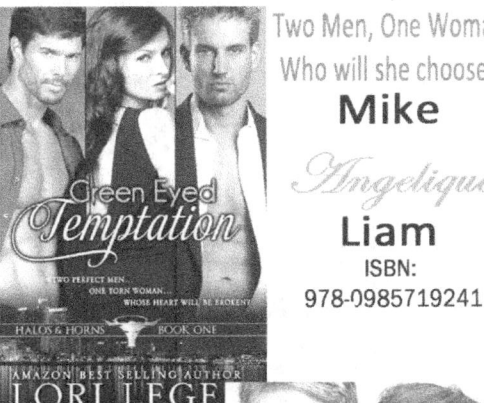

Seasons of Love Anthologies

Seasons of Love: Book Two

Spring Promise

Karen Sue Burns
Trish F. Leger
Alicia Dean
Lori Leger

Seasons of Love: Hearts, Hearths & Holidays

Karen Sue Burns ✚ Jessica Ferguson
Kellie Kamryn ✚ Jennifer Jakes
Alicia Dean ✚ Lori Leger
Trish F. Leger

Seasons of Love: Book Three

Sweet Summertime Love

Lori Leger   Kim Hornsby
Karen Sue Burns   Carmine Valentine

Cajunflair@LoriLegerAuthor.com
WWW.LoriLegerAuthor.com

CAJUNFLAIR
PUBLISHING
www.CajunflairPublishing@gmail.com

www.ingramcontent.com/pod-product-compliance
Lightning Source LLC
Chambersburg PA
CBHW061924170626
46813CB00006B/2289